OUT OF THE COLD

Out of the Cold

Erin Reed

Contents

For Meredith

1

Chapter One

The preacher's gleaming face was a white blot in the darkness of the lone hill in the Old Saint Andrew's Parish Cemetery. It was a minor plot of dead grass, the sort where fathers buried family pets while their children were away at school. A small lantern sat on the damp earth between them, its flimsy light catching the fog that curled about their feet. Cicadas whirred in the hunched oaks, whose mossy beards tickled the grass. They grew louder as he stuttered, blinked, and glanced to the other member of the party.

"That's all, I think," he said.

Detective Cassandra Wake lifted her gaze from the freshly covered grave. His graveside service had taken all of three minutes. He had commented on the loss of someone so young and declared that the woman's suffering was finally over. His stomach had growled the entire time, urging a quick end to the tragic affair. Cassandra figured three minutes had nearly been too long. The girl who now lay beneath their feet had neither name nor personality. It was a loss that no one felt. She bent and picked up the lantern.

"Thank you for this, Father. Her original funeral date was postponed, and this was the earliest we could get."

He wore a pair of black trousers and a black dress shirt, its sleeves rolled up to reveal thin, tanned wrists. His face seemed to hover above the shadowy mass of his body; his eyes, sharp and dark, observed the surrounding gravestones in the early-morning silence. A cramped row of crosses jutted up to their right. A thin mist, oozing unceasingly from the ground, swallowed up the crosses and then Cassandra. She felt a chill in her bones despite the heavy humidity that clung to her skin.

"Would anyone else have shown up? Even if the funeral was at noon?" he asked.

Cassandra noted the illumed high beams of a rusted Chevy Impala glaring out from behind the cemetery's frail wooden fence. She handed the lantern to the minister and watched as the shadows on his face grew long and distorted.

"No. But I didn't know funerals needed an audience," she said.

"You're right," he said. "They don't even need a body."

She left him and crossed over a final patch of dewy grass. The car door slammed as she slipped into the passenger seat. The Impala's driver, a long, lanky man, bolted up, releasing a muted shout.

"I didn't know you could watch for suspicious persons and sleep at the same time. It would've been a very helpful skill during college––"

"Sorry, I'm sorry–– I didn't mean to, well, sleep. But I was awake a minute ago. It's only been a few seconds."

"You're not in trouble, Mills. Let's get out of here."

She leaned forward and adjusted the vents pointed her way. Gravel crunched beneath the car's tires as they turned out of the cemetery and sped onto a thin, poorly lit road. To their left arose a dense belt of slender pine trees, through which she could see the distant lights of a few scattered, somber houses. The whirring of cicadas dissolved beneath a burst of static that sprang abruptly from the radio. Mills fiddled with the volume knob and cleared his throat.

"No one else showed up, then?"

"It's four-fifty-two in the morning. Not a soul around except us and the minister."

"Nothing happened? Lieutenant Crawford thought for sure the guy would come down to see her for himself."

At the younger officer's question, she gave a dismissive noise and turned to look out the window. She crossed her legs and swiped at her forehead with her sleeve. Trees sped in damp splashes of color past the glass.

"It's kind of sad," he said.

"What?"

"No one bothered to show up. Even if we don't know her name, we know she was someone. And the person who did this. He didn't even come."

She watched the wan profile of his face and the shifting of his eyes on the road.

"It's not kind of sad, Mills," she said. "It's horrible. It should keep you up at night. But if it makes you feel better, no one was ever going to show up."

"What do you mean? I don't—"

Her phone vibrated in her pocket. She lowered the radio even more but waited to pick up the call.

"Why does a murderer go to a victim's funeral? Why do you think?"

"Remorse?" Mills said, his eyes flicking to the side.

"Pleasure. He takes pleasure in watching the destruction he has caused. Takes pleasure in watching the misery he has inflicted on the victim's loved ones."

"That doesn't explain why he didn't come here," Mills said under his breath. His hands were white on the steering wheel. She turned in her seat, studying him for a moment.

"She had no loved ones, Mills. There was no one else to prey on. No other Troy to burn. Something like that."

"We were here," he said. "We showed up." His voice was fierce but hushed, as though he were desperate to prove something before the phone stopped ringing.

"We're here because we were ordered to be here. Don't fool yourself into thinking otherwise."

With that, she lifted the phone to her ear. When she answered, she was met with a flurry of harsh and frantic words. The caller's voice was thick and weary, tinged with the remnants of a struggling professionalism.

"We've got a body all the way out at Drayton Hall Swamp. Norton wanted you there five minutes ago."

Michael Heyward was a senior patrol officer in the Charleston Police Department, and he always seemed to receive news of Cassandra's cases long before she did. She slipped the phone between her shoulder and cheek as she fumbled in the backseat for her bag.

"Any details?" she asked.

"Just that it's a homicide that's being handled with extreme caution." He paused, and she could hear the shuffle of papers. "Be careful, Wake," he said, hanging up.

A quiet command sent Mills swerving the car around with a spray of mud and speeding down the empty highway. She glanced once more out the window, but the stars had long ago been strangled by pollution, and the cicadas had succumbed to silence.

Drayton Swamp was a slim stretch of wetlands along the Ashley River, located on the outskirts of Drayton Hall Plantation. A persistent drizzle splattered against the windshield of the Chevy Impala as the George McDaniel Education Center, as well as a legion of patrol cars, came into view. Streaks of rain flashed blue and red as the car lights flickered and steamed.

Cassandra pulled her navy CPD raincoat tight around her as she stepped out of the car into the squelching mud. Noiselessly, Mills followed behind her. The Education Center loomed in the corner of her periphery as she walked to the throng of officers. It was a majestic two-story house with a broad white portico and a deep red roof. Its brown bricks often appeared orange in the sunlight but were currently dimmed by the early morning shower. The house sat like an old monarch behind a neatly trimmed grass field. Having visited the tourist sight a few months prior, she remembered the entire property being about 175 acres.

A loud, frantic voice cut through the morning as she rounded the cars and glimpsed Chief Norton. The chief was a tall, dark-faced veteran who taught summer courses at the local technical college. He always seemed to have a sore throat or a dry cough. Today it seemed the latter plagued him, as he held a finger up to his conversation partner and put a damp handkerchief to his mouth, anticipating a rather long coughing fit.

"The property has been preserved so carefully because of our stringent rules. We are currently in the one and only parking lot. Parking anywhere else on the property is strictly prohibited—"

"I understand, but you said the body was right next to the Ashley River, and that's a long way to walk back and forth with this equipment." The chief's voice was hoarse but insistent. He held his palms up as though to sympathize with the park employee but received only a polite look of scorn. He stuffed the handkerchief into his pocket and turned to Cassandra, who had previously remained unacknowledged.

"We're walking. Forensics is already up there. We didn't want to risk any more contamination by rain or animals. Let's go."

The plantation worker, presumably the property caretaker, issued curt orders to another uniformed man near him and set off with the pair. The pale gravel beneath their feet softened to slick mud as they stepped onto a walking trail. Fishing in his pocket, the worker retrieved a pack of reflective red stickers and began reluctantly applying them to trees along the path.

Ancient oaks rose around them, their limbs bristly with damp moss. Turning back, she saw that Mills had followed her.

"Go and aid officers in collecting testimonies from the property employees. Ask around for any camera footage of the parking lot. Good luck."

His heavy footsteps squelched and slid through the mud behind them, growing softer as he retreated toward the distant gathering of park employees. After a moment, she gestured at a random tree and slowed her pace, putting a short distance between herself and the worker.

"Who found the body?" she asked quietly.

Chief Norton didn't look up as he answered.

"This guy. He's the assistant property caretaker. Name's Connor Veal. Property caretaker is at a destination wedding in Thailand, so there's no reaching her. He was on his way back to check if any trees had fallen from the rain. Came across a woman shoved between the roots of a cypress tree."

The sparse grass was soggy and uprooted from the rain. Thick, salty air rushed into her lungs as she crept down a muddy bank and came upon the forensic team. A single figure clad in a white

Kleenguard suit aimed at the surrounding underbrush with a Lumix camera. Two identical figures knelt beneath a distant tree, sheltered by a skimpy, lopsided blue tent. The figure with the camera pulled her hood back and gestured for the chief to come over.

Cassandra recognized the woman as an experienced forensic photographer who had worked in the department longer than Chief Norton. Her eyes were dull, but she smiled weakly, as though attempting to diffuse the oppressive atmosphere. She tucked the camera under her left elbow and headed for the tent.

"She's been partially submerged in water for no more than twelve hours. No skin is sloughed away, and a worker walks through here at least once a day. Her nails are cut short, so no skin samples found just yet. Notable traces of a white, grainy powder on her fingers. Samples were collected earlier."

As they drew closer, one kneeling forensic officer stood and put his hands on his hips. He began to speak as Cassandra knelt, taking his place. A dark, knobby cypress tree hunched over the group like an old, hobbling man. Sharp, knotted knees jutted through the damp dirt around them. Lying on her side, half of her face submerged in a brackish puddle, was the dead woman. She was completely naked. Her skin was grotesquely white, as though she had remained her entire life in the dark. Cassandra recalled the videos she had seen of beached whales.

The woman's size or color did not incite this abrupt thought, but rather her hard, broad belly. She had been eight to nine months pregnant at time of death.

"Can you tell if she's given birth?" Cassandra asked, interrupting the forensic officer.

"We can't be sure until an autopsy. Abdominal swelling suggests she carried the baby to full term. From what we've seen, there's neither vaginal tearing nor bleeding. She's--" the forensic officer grimaced, giving a short shrug, as though searching and failing to find better words. "She's remarkably clean. It's very unlikely."

"She was cleaned manually." Cassandra slid a latex glove on her hand and gently gripped the woman's right knee. Bearing the woman's inner thigh to the chief, she pointed at visible streaks of water which gleamed in the morning's soft glow. She noted ligature marks on the woman's left wrist and right ankle. Leaning over, she glimpsed identical bruises on the other limbs.

"Ligature markings have signs of old scarring. They were left alone long enough to heal. No recent bondage. The scars would have opened again," she said, fingers cradling the woman's wrist.

"Cause of death can't be confirmed without an autopsy," the forensic officer added from behind her. "There are no external injuries besides the bruises on her wrists and ankles. No signs of internal bleeding or a head injury. You'll have to wait for a forensic pathologist to come down and confirm any theories."

"It could have been pregnancy complications. She was obviously in a stressful situation when she died," the photographer suggested. "High blood pressure triggers a placental abruption. Mother dies from hemorrhaging."

"It did rain," Chief Norton agreed. "Any blood is probably ten miles down the Ashley River." He leaned over Cassandra and ran his eyes over the woman's face. "Do we know what the white powder is?"

His voice faded into the tense silence that consumed Cassandra's mind. The scene's details coiled like a labyrinthine knot before her eyes, nearly impossible to comprehend and untangle. She drew a deep breath. There came the thick, dewy scent of rainfall. Then the heavy stink of death. She turned the woman's knee again and gazed at the wet streaks marking her inner thigh.

There was no afterbirth, no immediately apparent cause of death. Either the perpetrator had cleaned the afterbirth, explaining the woman's unstained appearance, or the afterbirth had never been there. Caught in her musings, she hardly registered the shrill sirens going off in her mind. Leaning forward, she lifted the woman's leg and opened her to the surrounding group. Chief Norton choked on a cough that was halfway out his throat, and the photographer raised a hand as though to stop Cassandra. Waving off the photographer's gesture, she pointed to the jagged stitches crisscrossing the woman's labia.

"Genital mutilation," she said. She waited as the forensic officer knelt beside her and replaced her hand with his. Salty air clung to her skin as she stood and removed the latex glove from her hand. White stripes of sunlight filtered through knobby tree limbs and coarse gray nets of Spanish moss.

"Why in the world would that happen here?" the photographer wondered aloud.

"Female genital mutilation," Cassandra clarified. "A practice that has thankfully diminished in the past decade. Prominent in some African countries like Kenya and Senegal. This appears to be Type Three-- infibulation. The vaginal opening is manually narrowed with a seal. Said seal being the surgical repositioning of the labia."

"We shouldn't claim anything like that without a medical examiner experienced with those procedures," Chief Norton noted, reaching for the handkerchief in his back pocket. "But you're right that it's not typical genital mutilation committed during an assault. This is surgical. And the stitches don't look recent."

"They look professional," Cassandra said. She puffed out her cheeks in a long breath. After a moment, she retrieved a yellow notepad from the inside pocket of her raincoat and began to take notes. She lifted a hand to her head and turned away from the woman.

"Potential involvement of a healthcare worker?" came the forensic officer's timid voice.

"Maybe," she answered. "There's no guarantee the suspect is who performed said mutilation. Suspect could be in the health industry, as you said. Or there could be a sick bastard performing surgeries like this in some backroom at the local animal hospital."

Chief Norton turned and beckoned to the worker, who had remained quite a distance away. "What's the fastest way for someone to get to this exact location?" he asked.

Connor Veal, eyes flickering to the forensic team, begrudgingly walked over. A hand swept at the hair that clung to his ruddy forehead, and he bit the inside of his cheek as he thought.

"Well, it's been raining for two days straight, so there really wouldn't be a fast way. The mud here's nearly impossible to get through and stay on your feet. But my security guards stay up most nights, and they didn't see any new car in the parking lot. But––" Veal paused and waved his hand at Chief Norton. "Drayton isn't locked down. We want people to get in and have an experience. We can't do that if every nook and cranny is off limits. So maybe someone snuck in. But they'd have to walk a few miles in the mud to get here."

The chief placed a consoling hand on Veal's shoulder and guided him away from the tent. Cassandra straightened as the photographer walked over.

"See anyone at Saint Andrew's?"

"Yeah. The priest and I had a great talk about God."

"Mills didn't see anything?"

Cassandra gave a dismissive shake of the head, casting her eyes along the shaded edge of trees that gathered around them. She had left her Maglite in the Impala. Any investigations would occur beneath the flimsy light of her cellphone. The distant sound of voices filtered through the woods to their left.

"I'm surprised. Crawford was so sure someone would show up."

Cassandra hummed in response to the woman's speculations. Talk of the early morning funeral frustrated her, leaving her closed off from the photographer's attempt at friendly interest. Her eyes returned once more to the edge of the nearby trees. She crept forward as though unwilling to leave footprints in the mud. A slick, grassy slope separated two trees like a jagged scar cutting a smooth expanse of skin in two. The tangled remains of lichen and moss sat turgid at the slope's base before disappearing into dark swampland. She crouched down, her eyes meeting the dim glass reflection of another gaze.

There sat a sodden stuffed lion, slumped sadly amid the underbrush. It had large glass eyes colored a warm brown, and a porcelain nose connected to a curly, threaded smile. One of the lion's limbs had a stained paw, as though having been wet more often than the rest of its body.

"Where's the kid?" Cassandra asked, projecting her voice across the clearing. She waited, crouched, as Chief Norton hurried over.

"What?"

She motioned to the stuffed lion. "There's a child here. Has it not already been found?"

"Are you serious?" Chief Norton questioned, his face becoming stern with alertness.

"Right now, I am."

"A stuffed lion doesn't mean the child was here," he said.

As Chief Norton spoke, Cassandra knelt low amid the undergrowth, searching for something unknown. After a moment, she rose and peered into the treeline. A few leaves and twigs were askew, as though something had rushed through them. The haggard canopies overhead grew thicker as Cassandra left the clearing. Cramped and dim, the surrounding trees and bushes glowed a pale silver as her flashlight found remnants of the earlier rain.

"Wake?" the photographer called, her own Maglite leveled at the break in the trees. There came a rustle from the darkness. Calling for the detective, she scrambled up the slope and leveled her Maglite into the opening. Cassandra was kneeling on the ground with something large and wriggling in her arms. She rose swiftly with her hands out as though to pass the item directly to the photographer but paused.

Detective Cassandra Wake held a young girl, perhaps four-years-old, under the armpits. Her face was pallid, but her grip upon the child was firm and unyielding. Quietly, she stepped past the photographer and emerged once more into the clearing.

"That's a child," the photographer said slowly. Cassandra stood still, arms stretched out before her. They were tensed, hard and steady like lines of iron. The little girl's feet kicked in the air, and she gave a light laugh. Across the clearing, Chief Norton's head whipped around.

A frenzied conversation began that resulted in the girl being sat on a silvery shock blanket spread on the ground. Chief Norton had taken out his keyring and let the girl play with it, as they had already bagged the stuffed lion for evidence. SVU had been contacted, and a pair of officers were on their way. He sat directly before her, attempting to draw her attention away from the crowd of people rushing about. The photographer and a single forensics officer had moved to the crushed grass patch where the girl had been found.

"Wake," Chief Norton called. His voice was urgent but quiet, like a harried man intent on remaining calm. "Gloves. Now."

She stepped forward, having never left the child's side. Wordlessly, she pulled a latex glove onto her right hand, only then taking the slip of paper offered by Chief Norton. It was a thin, cream piece of notepad paper, like the pads placed beside phones in hotels. It read:

Beatrice, Sister of Giovanni Singer

The blood fled Chief Norton's strained face, and he whispered a curse into his handkerchief.

"It was in her jacket pocket. I found it just now."

"Who are Beatrice and Giovanni Singer?" she asked.

He remained silent, instead fumbling for the radio at his belt. After a curt greeting, he sent a succinct thread of orders into the mouthpiece. Cassandra went to the nearby forensics bag and slipped the piece of paper into a plastic baggie.

"Who are they?" she repeated.

He did not answer. He sat back on the blanket and offered the little girl a tentative smile. The forensics team bustled around them like a tempestuous stream over three immovable rocks. She glanced down at the baggie, feeling its plastic crinkle under her fingers. After a moment, she sat beside Chief Norton and listened to the dull murmur of childish play, her gaze fixed on the massive cypress tree and the body abandoned between its roots.

2

─────────────

Chapter Two

T he dry, rhythmic scratch of chalk on a blackboard snapped Giovanni Singer from his reveries. A gel pen fell from his restless fingers. He glanced covertly about, watching the intense profiles of his fellow listeners. He had been up since three in the morning for some reason or another, the specifics of which no longer seemed important. Dim, intelligent eyes peered out from a tired face, blinking as the professor continued from the front of the room.

"It's different when you think about pre-existing theories instead of questioning the premises they are based upon. We all know utilitarianism. Maximize the good. Save the five over the one, other things equal. The quantitative value of things seems quite easy to determine. But what about quantitative values that aren't as immediately clear?"

"Like what?" one of his fellow students asked, gaze shifting from the professor, the blackboard, and back to her notebook.

"Time," the professor supplied. He sketched a horizontal line along the board, labeling it *time*. Then came a vertical line, the professor labeling it *value*. "Theoretically, it's better that a good thing last longer. Assuming the positive value cannot be overindulged, it would be best to listen to your favorite band for fifteen years rather than five. On the other hand, it would be better that a war last for as little time as possible.

"But the question arises, what if something of supreme value lasts only momentarily? Should anyone ever choose that, instead of engaging in something of lesser value, but by its length of time, ultimately more valuable?"

He demonstrated each situation by drawing a respective box. The first, a high-value thing of short duration, was a tall, thin vertical box, while the latter was a squat but wide horizontal box.

"Why would anyone choose that?" the professor repeated, examining the semicircle of students stationed about him. There came a distant rumble from the hall as students filed out of their classes. They each eventually stood, notebooks and laptops shoved haphazardly into their bags. Muted conversation sounded behind Giovanni as he slipped out of the room and into the bumbling crowd.

A fresh blue sky greeted him as he reached the sidewalk. He closed his eyes and drew in a deep breath. There came the hostile horns of cars shoved close together on the street. It was the first day for students to move out. One father was territorially gripping a wheeled cart, presumably waiting for his child to check them in. There came a cough from behind him, and he turned, noting the curious student from earlier.

"I thought that was a great last lecture," she said, eyes also trained on the cars. "What do you think Professor Heinlein meant by that? By a momentary thing of supreme value?"

Giovanni smiled at her, shaking the exhaustion from his mind like frost from strangled tree limbs. She was a younger graduate student, two years into her doctoral program rather than his five. He pointed to the father and his cart.

"Love," he said. "Better to have loved and lost than never loved at all. Or that's what Tennyson thought."

"Love doesn't stop at the drop of a hat," she answered, tightening the bag strap on her shoulder. "You can't measure it like you measure an amount of people. There's no exact minute when love dies."

"Give or take six months, then. If you wish to think like that, what's the exact point at which something momentary becomes something long-lasting? The difference between a thousand minutes and a thousand-and-one is still sixty seconds."

He began walking once more, the sun having brought a warm flush to his cheeks. He gave one last glance over his shoulder, pausing as he noted a timid look on the girl's face. With his eyes, he questioned her abrupt change of mood.

"It could also be life," she said.

"What?"

"It could be life. Momentary but of supreme value. A good twenty-five years versus a mediocre eighty."

Something hateful shriveled up within him, and whatever vestiges of friendliness he had conjured rushed from him like air in a dark, vengeful vacuum. His hand tightened painfully at his side. Without a word, he turned and began again toward home. The blaring noise of car horns and laughing families streaked by. The fall of his sneakers was strong and constant against the pavement, the only sound in an otherwise quiet mind.

His destination, the place which he called home, was a crowded apartment located above a backstreet bakery. It stood three blocks from the College of Charleston's Addlestone Library. Rounding the last corner, he noted the rather conspicuous presence of a pitch-black Dodge Durango parked at the bakery's backdoor. His steps faltered, and for a moment, he considered turning back around. Plastered on the vehicle's side was a white and blue decal, the words *CHARLESTON POLICE* printed in obnoxious capitals.

"Singer!"

There came his roommate's voice across the parking lot. He glanced about, locating him at the bottom of the ugly wrought iron staircase that led up to their apartment. Beside him, leaning on the thin, crumpled railing, was a woman about his age. She wore an Ohio State sweatshirt despite the blazing heat, and her hands were tucked deep into its front pocket. She withdrew one as he drew nearer, offering it in greeting. When he did not take it, she gave a noncommittal hum and straightened.

"Detective Cassandra Wake. According to him, you're Giovanni Singer. That true?"

"Yes," he answered curtly. "What do you want?"

"Philosophy PhD candidate should know how complicated that question is."

"With me," he amended. He watched as his roommate–– a part-time baker in the shop below their apartment–– retreated upstairs with a whispered excuse about having to get back to his "pastries and things."

"I want you to tell me about your sister."

"You've got plenty of first-hand sources right in your department. Ask them."

Her eyes followed him as he rushed up the steps, a flurry of metallic creaks sounding under his sneakers.

"Don't want to ask them. I'm asking you."

"Ask me something about Victorian literature. I've been trying to get on Jeopardy."

"Where were you the night of April 23rd?"

He blinked and wiped his sleeve against his brow.

"What day was that?" he asked.

"Yesterday."

His mouth hung open for a moment, as though he were awaiting the tardy firing of neurons in his brain. He watched her before his mouth crept into a bitter smile. There came a breathy snort, which he tried to smother with his knuckle.

"This isn't a humorous matter, Mr. Singer."

"That perspective really puts a damper on life, Detective Wake," he said, a tone of faux sternness in his voice. "It also puts an ignorant limitation on humor."

She waited a moment, and he abruptly felt overcome with shame, as though he were a disruptive child being chastised by a teacher. His shoulders slumped forward, and he gestured for her to continue.

"There was a victim found on the outskirts of Drayton Hall Plantation. While investigating the surrounding area, we located a child. A little girl. There was a note in her pocket."

Deeming further explanation unnecessary, she produced her phone and handed it to him. His eyes finally leaving her face, he took her phone and examined the image on its screen. After a moment, his hand dashed up to scratch behind his ear.

"There's no point to this," he said.

"Do you know any connections your sister could have to this child?"

He scowled at the ground between them. "Whoever named that kid after my sister was playing a cruel joke. It has nothing to do with me. You have to be new here, or you'd recognize her name. For God's sake, it was in your own department."

At the detective's stoic silence, he became flustered, hands gesturing weakly at his sides.

"Do you believe in ghosts? My sister's been dead for nearly five years. It was a famous *incident*" –– he enunciated this last word with great venom –– "in Charleston. Nearly everyone was involved in a search party or something like it. I'm telling you, they mentioned her name for some sort of fame. Your department always paid attention to Beatrice."

Following this explanation, he delved into a terse but polite silence. He answered the rest of the detective's questions succinctly but mindlessly, as though he were already far away from the conversation and its implicit violence. After twenty minutes, he watched as the Dodge Durango pulled out onto the street. With a sharp, defeated breath, Giovanni Singer hurried up the last of the steps. The warm smell of fresh bread filtered up into the clear sky, and a few melodious birds chattered overhead. He paled at the rise of the new day, and with a trembling hand, he pushed into the quiet darkness of his apartment.

"Turn the goddamn thing off!"

Michael Heyward loomed over a small, pinched-face man like a hound snapping at a cornered squirrel. The patrol officer's face burned a breathless red, the saturation of which made the dirty blue of his eyes seem even bluer. His anger wasn't aimed at the security worker, not really. Drayton Hall's security system seemed, through a series of unrelated accidents separated by many years, completely and utterly incapable of fulfilling its job.

"Sir, I really don't appreciate your anger––"

"I'm sorry," Heyward said. His words came brusque and tight. "It's not you. Turn it on. Please."

"It's not a flashlight. You can't hit it and hope for the best," Cassandra said. She leaned against the security shack's far wall. It being a shack, the wall was still quite close to Heyward and the poor worker. She did not appreciate Heyward's anger, had thought it unlike him. But the more time she spent with her fellow officers, the more she became aware of a seething undercurrent of frustration surrounding the case. It was a tender, barely healed wound for the Charleston Police Department. Asking him to calm down would only make it worse.

"I'd like to hope for the best. Really. But life seems intent on proving me wrong today. So I hope for the worst fucking news you've ever heard," Heyward said, his face slowly but surely returning to its usual tan.

All eyes turned to the staticky collection of computer faces situated precariously on a folded plastic table. They were covered in a thick layer of dust, and whatever images that might appear were hardly discernible from the grainy slurry that immediately filled each screen. The computers released a shrill, irregular hiss, like a balloon slowly leaking air. The worker, taking this sound as a negative sign, laid his hands flat on the table and let out a low sigh.

"Ma'am, please. It's not going to work."

The worker turned his beseeching eyes to her, having decided Heyward was a lost cause. She straightened and stepped between them.

"I don't think you understand," she said. "Who's coming to Drayton Hall when word gets out a pregnant, defenseless woman was brutally murdered here? She went out expecting a fun trip, and what? Got killed? And despite this terrible loss, the workers of Drayton Hall didn't care. You couldn't care less about anyone besides yourself, right?"

"No," the worker answered quickly. "That's not true."

"Yes," she insisted. "Yes, because if you care about other people, you make sure they're safe. Especially when it's your job. You make sure the security cameras work. You make sure the screens connected to them turn on. And you make sure your eyes are on the screens so that if something like this happens, we can stop it."

No one spoke any further, and her eyes would not move from the blurry computer screens.

"Fix it," she said. "It's not my career on the line."

The next fifteen minutes were filled with awkward, frenetic fumbling, abrupt apologies, and muted curses. With a startled exclamation, the worker demanded they turn their eyes to the computers. There was no point. They had been watching nothing else.

Through the static came a large, dark mass. Part of it opened, and Cassandra realized they were looking at the side of a black truck. A lighter, oblong figure slipped out of the truck and stood surveying the clearing for a few seconds. Another vague figure, as solid as a shadow, came around the truck. They stood together for a moment before moving toward the treeline.

She watched as the truck sat in grim silence. If they continued watching, they would pass the time during which the homicide occurred. They would see the supposed killer return and drive off.

"That's news," Heyward said. His face gleamed with a pride she recognized well–– of the lead working out. Somewhat.

She looked up from her contemplation and found Heyward and the worker engaged in friendly conversation. Whatever irritability that had welled between them was abruptly and truly terminated. Her eyes returned to the screen, and she watched the truck sit motionless, tensed as though expecting it to start and peel out of the parking lot without a driver.

"Play it again," she ordered the worker.

He complied, and they watched as the truck door opened and the figures stepped out anew. Five times she had him rewind the tape, her face blank and eyes keen.

"We're looking at the passenger side, right?" she asked.

Heyward nodded. "You can see the cargo bed and the brake light turn on for a second."

"So this person," she pointed at the first figure that appeared, "is the passenger. And the second figure is the driver."

"Yeah," Heyward confirmed. "Presumably, that passenger is our victim."

"That's the pregnant woman we found here in Drayton," Cassandra repeated to herself. She leaned forward, humming to herself.

"What is it, Wake?"

"Her hands aren't bound," Cassandra said, simply and without weight. It was as though she had merely noticed a leaf stuck in her hair. Heyward moved to stand beside her and ordered the worker to rewind it once more. It was true. The passenger's hands swung conspicuously at her sides. If one did not take the context into account, it could appear as though she were almost skipping with excitement.

"She had severe ligature marks on her ankles and wrists," she said. "But they had healed. They had been left alone prior to her murder. It didn't occur to me–– the question of how the victim physically reached the cypress tree from the parking lot. She went along willingly."

"How long was she chained up somewhere?" Heyward's question left an uneasy silence in its wake. "Such severe ligature marks, but they're healing."

Quelling her thoughts for a moment, Cassandra shook her head and gestured at the screen. "I thought security cameras were actually supposed to capture something. Can someone touch up this video?"

"We're not getting a full face. Not a chance," Heyward said.

"Just a touch up."

Heyward and the worker fell again into friendly chatter. She moved closer to the screens as the pair squeezed out into the oppressive humidity of Drayton Hall Plantation. As a midday silence crept overhead, Cassandra realized she was cold, almost insufferably so. She shoved her hands into her sweatshirt pockets as Heyward turned to get her attention.

"We're going to get the supplies to make a copy," he said. Upon receiving no answer, he waved the worker off and stepped back inside.

"What?" he murmured.

"This six-second window. Right after the driver comes around the back of the truck. They're standing there for six seconds. The passenger starts walking without the driver. The driver just stands there." She fell silent for a moment. "I can feel their eyes on me. It feels like I'm in a staring contest."

"A staring contest?" Heyward repeated to himself, half-bewildered.

"It feels like I just blinked."

They remained standing together; Cassandra watched the screen, and Heyward watched her. There came the noise of nearby voices, and the outside world returned to press in upon them. Heyward wandered away, reigniting conversation with the curious worker. Her eyes remained locked on the blurry screen, willing the grainy images to still, to become clear. An overhead AC unit kicked on, and Cassandra's concentration broke like a string finally snapping after being pulled too taut.

She glanced up, startled to find a friendly pair of eyes upon her. Chief Norton stood in the doorway, the toes of his duty boots scraping the hard concrete floor, heels squelching in the muddy grass. A sodden handkerchief twisted between his fingers. After a quiet moment, he cleared his throat into his elbow. Cassandra half-expected him to wave her away, trapped again by the polite anxiety that had seized him upon the child's discovery. Instead, he straightened and stepped back, gesturing for her to rise and accompany him.

"Beatrice Singer was a uniformed officer for CPD while I was a few years into being assistant chief. She was twenty-five. On December 17th, 2017, she pulled over a suspected DUI. The woman produced a pistol from her glove box and shot Beatrice Singer twice. We're not sure where exactly, but it's likely she was shot once in the head. We know this–– her car's dashcam caught most of it. It cut off too soon... When we got to the crime scene, Beatrice's body wasn't there. And when we went to the suspect's house, she wasn't there, either. Neither has been found. Giovanni Singer was Beatrice's brother. He nearly tore the department apart when we couldn't find her."

They had crossed the sliver of grass wedged between the security shack and parking lot. The chief's car, one of the few vehicles remaining in the gloomy parking lot, watched with its vacant headlights as they trudged through the mists of Drayton Swamp. Dim yellow lamps lit up gravel walkways like white snakes in the darkness, curling in oft-frequented paths through the distant trees. The sharp smell of salt had grown softer as night fell. Cassandra glanced into the treeline as he threw the car door open and fell heavily into the driver's seat. A flood of garish white light burst from the car's overhead lights as he turned the ignition. It fell through the car window, spilling out onto the mud and crawling over the steel toes of her boots. Grimacing, she stepped backward, listening to the gentle scud of gravel kicked up with each movement.

"He hates me, and I can't blame him. I wouldn't have gotten anything out of him. He's been pulled more times than I'd like to admit for criminals wanting their fifteen minutes. Mention Beatrice Singer's name, everyone starts thinking we've found her or Kira Rushton."

He paused abruptly, his eyes pinned to the steering wheel between his hands.

"Kira Rushton? That's the DUI who Beatrice pulled over?" she asked.

He nodded and swiped a hand at the sweat bead that hung from his nose.

"DNA's being run through CODIS right now," Chief Norton said. "We'll figure out what to do with the girl, but I don't want her name getting in any papers. Singer won't tell anyone. You know what-- we shouldn't even mention the note. There was a body and a child. That'll work."

After a quick nod and an assurance that she would be at the office by seven-thirty, Cassandra retreated to the edge of the parking lot, lifting her hand in a weak 'goodbye.' She watched the inside light of his car click off. He slipped into the dense darkness of the long entrance road to Drayton Hall Plantation.

Cassandra stood gazing into the dark long after his car disappeared. It was a cruel effigy of their early-morning funeral. The same black night, the same warm, thick air, the same old trees. A different body. That detail seemed the most important, the most damning. She combed a hand through her hair and released a deep breath into the night.

Mills's Chevy Impala sat two spots away. The young officer would drive her back when she asked, had most likely been waiting hours for her to make the request. It was time to go home, she could admit. At least for most people. Some officers were interviewing workers who had recently arrived for the night shift. With a curt glance at the car, Cassandra turned and began the trek again to the distant smattering of LED lights situated around a tent. The dim blur of a few officers moved in and out of sight, solid as shadows lurking in a pitch-black room. A nauseating resignation grew heavy in her chest. In a few hours, it would be morning.

3

Chapter Three

The bakery beneath Giovanni Singer's apartment was a rustic bread shop, the sort of which usually operated out of street-corner bodegas and hole-in-the-wall counters. Four to six bakers rushed behind the white-and-red tile counter, mixing, folding, caught in the mad dash of daily work. Giovanni occupied a thin wrought-iron table wedged against the wall, his legs pulled in tight as customers hurried past. His left hand flipped deftly through pages so thin they were nearly translucent, while his right hand scribbled comments on an undergraduate's final essay. In the mindless bustle, he could actually think.

All four of Giovanni's roommates were bakers. Their small flat burst to life around three o'clock in the morning, as that's when they all woke up to start their shifts. His room sat closest to the staircase; the sickly yellow porch light blazed through the night, and as each man scrambled down the steps, their quick shadows dashed across his eyes. Each abrupt awakening tumbled like a shock of frigid water over his head. Pulling the duvet over his face, he would wonder why he had not taken up baking, as well.

There came the shrill whistle of a coffee machine and the discordant creak of the bakery's backdoor swinging open. He glanced up. Cody Lenniker's beaming face glowed sallow in the pale overhead lights. The lanky man was Giovanni's only roommate not currently working behind the counter. He held a bundle of creased, bone-white envelopes, which he gestured about with like an extension of his arm. Under his breath, he read aloud the recipients.

"They're all bills. Bills and ads. They want my soul. They want my soul, and they want to sell it for pocket money. Here's a philosophy question for you, Giovanni. Who bills the bill guy?"

"That's a federal infrastructure question."

The younger man sat down, splayed like a long animal in the opposite chair. He effortlessly shuffled through them, examining their addresses before throwing them down. The monthly water bill fell across the essay Giovanni was grading. He leaned back, pulling the pair of glasses from the bridge of his nose.

"This is illegal, you know," he said.

"What is?"

"Looking at my mail."

Cody made a warning noise as though cautioning a child. "You already tried getting me with that. I haven't opened them. I'm designating them to the correct people. Someone would have to do it eventually."

At Giovanni's blank look of disapproval, Cody paused and cleared his throat. When he spoke again, his voice was soft and solemn.

"I registered for, uh. Registered at Trident Tech. Thought you could help me pick out some classes."

A strange warmth grew in Giovanni's chest, flooding up into his face. He straightened his spine and offered the younger man a dim smile. Cody Lenniker wanted to be a pediatric doctor, had been saving for three years now to fund an undergraduate degree.

Little words had been offered about his roommate's family, and Giovanni had not dared to ask. Cody watched him with atypical hesitancy. Giovanni couldn't for the life of him understand why.

"What major were you thinking?" he asked evenly.

"Biological sciences. I'd do two years here then transfer for a bachelor's in Charleston. You'd be a doctor by then. Not a medical doctor, I mean––"

Giovanni cleared his throat. "If you'd like, I can look them over. But I'm not the expert on the necessary classes for a biology degree, Cody."

"No, I know. I know. But it would be nice if someone else had some input. If someone else. You know."

If someone else cared. Giovanni nodded down at the papers before him. A hand scratched idly at his temple, needing something to busy itself with. His fingers were like ice against his forehead, and he jerked them away as though burned. Clearing his throat, he took a particular envelope and turned it over.

"What's this?" he murmured.

"What do you mean?"

"Letter to me with no return address."

Cody reached across the table and took it from him. In an instant, he had slid his thumb between the crease of the envelope, splitting it open. A slim slip of paper fell onto the table between them. The younger man took it before Giovanni could even think of moving, and his eyes dashed across the words, drinking them in.

"So that is actually super illegal. You said so yourself. One would consider that self-incrimination."

"You weren't gonna open it. Would have just stared until you forgot about it."

Cody's words were absent and mindless, as though his thoughts were somewhere else. Irritated, Giovanni took up the discarded envelope, searching once more for any provided information. Something fluttered through his fingers. His chair screeched back as he bent down to retrieve whatever had fallen.

"Giovanni," Cody said, tone strangely firm.

"What?" came Giovanni's voice from beneath the table.

"Stop it. Get back up here."

Wheezing, he paused, pulling himself back up with a grimace. Whatever amiable response ready on his lips fell away as he noted the look on Cody's face.

"What?" he repeated.

"It's a newspaper headline."

"Someone die?" he said humorlessly, hands squeezed together in an anxious knot.

Cody shrugged and began to speak, his voice quiet and devoid of jest:

"'Body found in Drayton Swamp with alive baby. Connected to Beatrice Singer?'"

His throat grew tight. He knew perfectly well that the news would hinder his so far futile efforts to extricate himself from the situation. It would take mere days for a renewed intrigue to rise regarding the fates of his sister and Kira Rushton. Every time said intrigue arose, it felt like a modern grave robbery. People who had no interest in Beatrice alive obsessed over the mystery of her death. And he could do nothing to stop them. Could no longer protect someone who had long been dead.

"It'll blow over," he said, and bent again under the table. He found what had fallen–– a small rectangle of film. A Polaroid. It was a blank, unappealing gray. Undeveloped and ugly. An insistent chiming sounded from his right pocket. He answered the phone and put it to his ear.

"Hello?"

"Mr. Singer, this is Detective Wake from CPD's Violent Crimes Unit. We talked earlier at the bakery. I would like to discuss some recent developments in the case involving the child known as Beatrice Singer. What's your current availability?"

His gaze slid down to the Polaroid in his hand. A subtle but profound change came over his alarmed expression. Basking in the warmth of his grasp, the Polaroid had developed. Thoughtful eyes clung to the Polaroid like slippery hands to an ever-crumbling cliffside.

"Mr. Singer?"

"I'll be there soon," he said, nodding to himself. The temptation of a new task gleamed brightly in his mind. He did not wish to remain sitting there, neither to stand still nor walk. He would give anything to be at the department now, in a mere second, before the next breath could escape his lungs. Despite his galloping mind, his body remained stuck to the chair.

There came an extended pause from the other line. After a moment, he heard her release a deep breath.

"Your desire to help is appreciated," she said.

The detective's voice was cautious, observant, and Giovanni cut the call. Without a word to Cody, he stood and in an instant was out the backdoor. His fingers flexed on the Polaroid before he slipped it into his pocket. The image burned like starlight against his eyelids.

A red-haired woman peered out from the gleaming Polaroid. After a closer examination, Giovanni saw that she was clean but ragged, like a plant kept too long from sunlight. Her cheekbones were gaunt, and her hair was thin. She looked down at her lap, where a young girl sat. Giovanni had not seen the girl before, had only heard of her, but he immediately recognized the woman. Someone had scrawled their names on the Polaroid's white edge. In sharp, concise lines, the Polaroid read:

Kira and Beatrice, February 2023

Cassandra sat silent in the spacious main boardroom of the Charleston County Police Department. It was a shockingly cold and sterile room, with dark cinderblock walls and a glaringly white overhead light. Only a fourth of the large mahogany table was occupied. Chief Norton reigned over the table's far end, a stern-faced gargoyle glaring at the opposite wall. Three senior officers, including Michael Heyward, surrounded him. She listened to the unhurried tick of the clock.

She had just returned from the Coroner's Office. The smell of latex and decay still hung from her clothes and hair. The woman, still unidentified, had shown no signs of malnutrition despite the circumstances under which she was discovered. Her chest had been methodically peeled open, examined, then sewn shut. She watched quietly as the coroner and her assistant bathed the woman. Dark rivulets of muddy water trickled down her pale skin, gathering in trembling circles on the metal table.

Someone had spilled ink on the conference table. The tip of her finger touched the blots, tracing unintelligible shapes into the reddish wood. There came a thwack of paper against wood, and she glanced up to find a thick, crumpled newspaper splayed on the table.

"I thought I made it very clear," Norton began, jaw tight, "that some details of our Drayton homicide do not get out."

Silence enveloped the room. They watched as blood seeped into his face, his eyes sweeping over them in solemn accusation. Slowly, one of the senior officers stretched across the table and shook out the newspaper, scanning its front page.

"What the hell?"

"What?" Heyward leaned over, examining it in turn.

She had seen the headline that morning, had swiped it from the front desk of the Coroner's Office. Nonetheless, she took it from Heyward when proffered. She raised her eyebrows as though in concern, aware of eyes on her. A long breath stole from her lungs as she read, and they filled again with the stench of death.

"Body found in Drayton Swamp with alive baby. Connected to Beatrice Singer?" she read aloud. The pages were rough against her fingers as she unfolded them, spreading the whole paper wide across the table.

"The media's gotten to it," Heyward murmured, leaning over her shoulder. "There's a name going around."

"Name?" she asked.

"The Stillborn Killer."

"That's not even accurate," she said, frowning. "There wasn't an actual baby. Don't they typically make up a name after the second or third murder, anyway?"

"That's my issue," came Norton's resounding voice from the end of the table. "They believe this is the second murder, what with the little girl we also found in Drayton."

"They think that little girl is connected to Beatrice somehow?" Heyward questioned. "That's bullshit. There were a dozen-plus crimes this year with rapists and carjackers claiming they'd tell you where Beatrice Singer was for a reduced sentence."

Cassandra met Chief Norton's eyes across the table. They were bright and angry, and she felt the tickle of cold sweat on her temple as he turned away. One of the senior officers cleared his throat, gesturing to the paper.

"We know who was aware of the note. We question everyone and find the leak. The story's out. We can't change that. But we can prevent another betrayal like this. The media's gonna fuck us over for a while."

"Are you sure it's that easily quantified?" Cassandra asked, examining her ink-stained fingertips.

He paused and glanced in her direction.

"What?"

"How do we know all the people who were aware of little Beatrice?"

"I sure as hell didn't tell anyone. And I sure as hell know Norton didn't. Neither did Heyward nor Robertson." He gestured to each officer as he spoke, his shoulders hunched forward.

"Who does that leave, then?" she asked quietly.

"No one is accusing anyone," Norton said, clearing his throat. "This meeting was not intended as a trial. I will discuss future actions and decide on a better intelligence process––"

"Sorry, Chief," came a voice from the doorway. "Something came up."

The tall, pale figure of Lieutenant Virginia Crawford came into view. She fell into the seat beside Zeigler, smiling amid the tense atmosphere.

"There's something inevitable about trials. They happen even if you don't want them to." She picked the newspaper up and folded it. "To answer Wake's question, the only people left are her and me. You meant to accuse her. But you forgot you were also accusing me."

"I didn't mean anything by it, Virginia."

"Lack of foresight is no excuse. You know that from the criminals you've put away. It's easy to throw blame at Wake. She's new. But not everyone in this department is as bullheaded and shortsighted as you. You have an obvious bias that's not conducive to a proper investigation whatsoever. Fix it, Zeigler. Now."

There came a heavy silence, the sort that envelopes the crumbled landscape of a city after it is bombed. The senior officer's face burst a shameful red, impossible to miss even as he turned away. His fist was a white ball on the dirty table.

"That's completely out of line. You sound like Singer's brother. Talking about bias and quantification." His words were unclearly leveled at both Crawford and Wake, his eyes sweeping between them like two hateful pins of light. "I thought we were done with that. When he finally left us to do what we could. But apparently not. It seems like––" Before he could continue speaking, a knock sounded at the door.

Mills appeared in the doorway, his eyes wide and searching. He brightened as his attention seized on Cassandra.

"Detective Wake, someone's requesting to see you immediately. It's important."

"Who?" Chief Norton demanded, clearly irritated by the interruption.

She gestured for Mills to turn back to the hallway, pausing for a moment to answer.

"Giovanni Singer. I needed to talk to him about collecting DNA samples. Rule out the possibility that he's related to the child––"

"He's not here for that," Mills interrupted. "He's got something."

"What do you mean 'something?" Cassandra asked.

Mills blinked at her and stepped back, half in the hallway. "Something. That's what he said."

In a moment, she was in the hall, striding out of the department's depths and toward the front desk. She appreciated Mill's dramatic entrance, despite the inherent foolishness of it all. He was six months younger than her but had started at a later age; he still contained the youth and enthusiasm of a relatively untested officer.

She found Giovanni Singer sitting in a hard-backed chair by the door. He stood as she entered. There was a slip of paper clenched in his hand, and he lamely offered it to her. It was the same headline from the morning's newspaper, cut out in a neat little rectangle. She took it and stepped back, a hand raised and gesturing down the hall.

"I know, Mr. Singer. It's among the many things I want to talk with you about."

"Can we speak in private?" he asked.

In response, she began once more down the hall. After a few silent moments, she opened a nondescript door to the right and let Giovanni enter before her. It was a minor interview room, no larger than a dignified broom closet. Its walls were made of dark cinderblocks, similar to the boardroom's walls. It was meticulously lifeless. Any trace of color had been relentlessly pursued and subsequently bleakened. An AC unit wheezed and shuddered to a start in the adjacent room, and even it seemed quite ready to give up. She sat across from him and examined the clipping.

"I can't imagine any of this is making your life easier."

"That's not why I came here," he said. "It's happened many times. There's-- here."

His hands were flat on the metal table before her. He removed one, and in the exposed space was a Polaroid. It was placed in a small plastic baggie.

After a moment, she picked up the baggie and examined the single line of words.

"What is this?" she asked.

"One of my roommates found it in the mail pile. Left in an envelope with no mailing or return address. It was in there with the newspaper clipping."

Strong, hasty footsteps sounded in a seemingly endless back and forth before the door, and muffled voices conversed merrily in nearby rooms. The brittle tick of a clock echoed somewhere above their heads.

"You don't seem surprised," he said.

"I am. Not for the reasons you suspect, but I am."

He drew a knee to his chest, the other hanging off the chair.

"What reasons do you suspect me of having?"

"This Polaroid suggests that Kira Rushton, your sister's suspected murderer, is alive. It also suggests that she is somehow related to the child found at a recent homicide scene."

"Those are incredibly valid reasons to be surprised, I think," he said.

"They are. But it addresses something I already wanted to talk with you about," she said. "We tested little Beatrice's DNA against CODIS, as well as a few other public DNA databases. We weren't expecting any results for weeks, but her maternal DNA matched with a woman guilty of several DUI offenses and drug-related arrests. The little girl left in Drayton Hall, called Beatrice Singer, is the daughter of Kira Rushton."

After a moment of silence, she continued:

"The Polaroid left in your mail this morning confirms, at minimum, the presence of a relationship. We are forced to believe that the Drayton Hall homicide is connected to what happened to Kira Rushton, as well as your sister."

"Is she Ronald White's daughter, then?"

Cassandra had spent the past four days dragging heavy archive boxes from their cobwebbed shelves in the depths of the station. Her eyes burned from the damp, dusty air, and her shoulders ached from hours bent over affidavits and case reports, her Maglite the only consistent source of light. However, her exhaustion had been rewarded by a complex familiarity with Beatrice Singer's apparent murder and disappearance, as well as the subsequent investigation. She had expected Giovanni Singer's question, as Ronald White was the long-time partner of Kira Rushton prior to her disappearance.

"Yes. Little Beatrice is the biological daughter of Ronald White and Kira Rushton. He gave us plenty of hair follicle and saliva samples when contacted and brought to the station."

This information was, at the moment, unknown to anyone besides Cassandra and Chief Norton. She had lied quite easily about her motives in talking with Giovanni Singer. That would do nothing for the sentiments of distrust and dislike leveled at her, would even give her critics a leg to stand on. She straightened and quelled her thoughts like a kennel master glancing sharply at his hounds.

"I was surprised because someone wishes for you to be aware and involved in this case. It is not enough for a homicide to occur. You must know of it. That is why someone purposefully dropped this newspaper and Polaroid into your mailbox."

"Someone also wants the media to be involved." He glanced at the cut-out headline on the table. "Someone leaked."

"What an astute observation, Mr. Singer."

"Do you know who?" he questioned.

"All knowledge degenerates into probability," she said. He stared at her for a moment. His shoulders lightly rocked, and she realized he was kicking his foot beneath the table.

"Didn't take you for a Hume enthusiast."

She hummed and leaned back. Overhead, a vent breathed forth frigid air into the room.

"If someone sent a headline and Polaroid to you, couldn't they just as easily have gone over to the Post and Courier and done the same? I don't believe anyone leaked. It was merely an attempt to incite distrust within the police department."

"And has it worked?"

His questions were like bolts of lightning that flashed across the dim space between them. A queer restlessness took hold of her body, clenching her fists and straining the lean muscles in her thighs and calves. She wanted to stand but thought better of it. At her silence, he cleared his throat and sat forward.

"The guy who did this. If he wanted to get my attention–– to get everyone's attention–– he could have shown me a Polaroid of Beatrice. But he didn't."

"We can't force our rational deductions onto the decisions made by psychopaths."

"But he very well might not have a Polaroid of Beatrice. This shows that Kira Rushton is alive. It might very well show that Beatrice isn't–– that she's dead."

His voice had grown caustic and defiant as he reached the conclusion. His eyes flashed with anxious shame, and his hands that were splayed across the table flew back into a tight knot in his lap.

"Stop leaping to conclusions," she said sharply. "You're looking for reasons to feel worse. It seems you have plenty of those already."

His face relaxed into an expression of stunned defense. Taking advantage of his momentary reticence, she spoke hurriedly:

"Why do you think it's a man who did this?"

"I didn't think," he said. "If you'd like to claim this person for the women, be my guest." He leaned forward and peered into her face. "You don't think so, then? You think it's a woman?"

"Extreme attention has been paid to the absent infant. The suspect does not kill women merely to kill. They only want the child. I believe if the killer could obtain children naturally, this homicide would never have occurred. But they cannot steal a child from the hospital's nursery, or remove a fetus from a mother's womb, as in the case of Reagan Simmons-Hancock. Absolute control must be present during the gestation period of the child.

I fear the suspect has tried many times to achieve their goal and has failed. They are trying to replicate something that can only be achieved through a child. Now, should the suspect be a man, why not merely impregnate multiple women and monitor their pregnancies? Although he might simply be unable to do so."

Giovanni lifted a hand and pushed back the dark hair that had fallen over his eyes. He frowned and shook his head, sitting back.

"A woman being murdered doesn't eliminate an entire sex from your investigation. You said the murder isn't significant in and of itself, so the woman wouldn't be, either. The killer might view this as an experiment, and the woman is the factor that resulted in failure."

Cassandra hummed in response. She nodded for him to continue.

"And if the killer were a woman, why would she not become pregnant herself? The murder is important, otherwise they'd skip them altogether."

"You're forgetting infertile women, Mr. Singer. But I'll forgive you that. The killer wishes to produce a child like a chemist wishes to produce a wanted reaction. It wasn't a sexual crime. The victim was cared for, almost affectionately so. The only act of violence was the woman's final end, her murder--"

"If there were previous experiments, why were they all failures?"

Cassandra rolled her shoulders and stood. She did not know why she had spoken so truthfully with him. It upset her, not in that she had betrayed the department, but herself. It was highly ill-advised to share such information with an unknown third party. She watched him for a moment before slipping the Polaroid into her back pocket.

"I have absolutely no clue." And with that, she pulled the door open. A strong burst of warm air flew into the room. The sterile hallway light fell upon her face as she threw a string of instructions over her shoulder. Before she could hurry away, urged by a strange dismay, Giovanni Singer had jumped up and stood beside her in the doorway. His eyes were aflame with interest. He was of a shorter stature, coming to an inch below her forehead. He offered her a hand. She took it slowly, forcing a strained smile.

His mouth opened, but before he could speak, Chief Norton and a pair of officers tore through the hallway. They were engaged in rapid, ruthless conversation. The chief paused as he reached Cassandra and put a hand on her shoulder.

"ID for Drayton homicide. Follow me." He glanced over at Giovanni and offered a slight smile, his stern expression wavering for a moment. One of the officers behind him pulled a pager from his belt, and the triad began again down the hallway.

Giovanni's eyes returned to Cassandra. She nodded once, and he watched as she disappeared in the direction the chief had gone. A shrill phone rang from the front reception desk, and he was torn from his reveries, like a weight knocked abruptly from its shelf. He smiled at the receptionist and strode out.

4

Chapter Four

A troop of young boys on bicycles scattered across the balding
lawn as Cassandra's car pulled into the parking lot of the Kiln
Apartment Complex. It was a squat, ugly complex composed of
flimsy plastic railings and cheap slats the color of urine. A few men
sat smoking on narrow, slanted balconies overhead. She smiled at
a pair of boys who remained. They stared blankly up as she passed,
ignoring her attempt at friendliness.

A low archway opened between the two main buildings; overhead, three stories of whitewashed walkways rose and connected
the buildings, like a bridge between two solid banks of pale sand.
She strode under the archway and turned to the right, standing in
the mouth of a thin, open hall. The distant chime of a struggling
elevator sounded down the hall. A dark and dank crevice opened a
few feet to her left, and there she found an unlit set of broad concrete steps that climbed up into lifeless gloom. Cassandra sucked
in one last breath of fresh air and began up the stairs.

They had identified the Drayton homicide victim as twenty-
five-year-old Clara Thompson. She had disappeared eleven
months prior after making a late-night gas stop after work. A
QuikTrip employee had found a half-full pack of cigarettes strewn

across the asphalt, one still smoking. She was a welder's apprentice with aspirations of repairing freight vessels in Charleston Harbor. She left behind a fiancé of two years, Alex Wendel. That was who Cassandra currently sought. Supposedly, the fiancé lived in Apartment 373 of The Kiln Apartment Complex. She glanced up from her thoughts as she came to Wendel's door. A knock, then fragile silence.

"Who is it?" came a voice through the door.

"I'm Detective Cassandra Wake from the Charleston Police Department. You received a call from us earlier this morning."

There was a flurry of steps before the door creaked open. A pale slice of light fell through the doorway and across Cassandra's right boot. The door wobbled back and forth, as though it could not decide whether to let Cassandra in, before slowly swinging open. Standing illumed before a thinly curtained window was a short, hard-eyed woman. She spared a sharp glance at Cassandra's badge before stepping back and gesturing to the next room.

It was a combined kitchenette and living room, cramped from the sheer amount of furniture stuffed within. The walls, a pale blue, were filled with mismatched paintings and rustic sketches; some peered out from ornate, gilded frames, while others were stuck with pushpins to the wall. A pouchy gray couch sat before a modern white coffee table, and two unique love seats were shoved against the back of the couch.

Cassandra could not hazard a guess as to the floor; rugs of varying shapes, colors, and sizes lay sprawled across in an attempt at haphazard cohesion. They overlapped like a map that no one could hope to decipher. She stepped carefully over a particularly patchy rug and sat on the couch, opposite the woman who had chosen a simple wooden chair.

"I'm sorry we're meeting under such unfortunate circumstances. You're Alex Wendel?"

"You told me Clara was found at a plantation," the woman said. "That true?"

Cassandra crossed her legs and dropped her bag at the foot of the couch. Wendel sat in the blue shadow of a window collared by gauzy gray curtains. Her eyes gleamed in the room's dim light, and Cassandra straightened her spine as her gaze grew heavy.

"We ran fingerprints through our database, and they matched with an Identago check Clara Thompson completed for a previous employer. Her description matches verifiable photographs we obtained. We have good cause to believe the homicide victim we found in Drayton Swamp is Clara Thompson."

"Description?" Wendel asked. She leaned forward and shook her head, as though dispelling her thoughts. "She went missing eleven months ago. You found her at a–– at a park? She was outside? How would you get fingerprints from a skeleton?" Her voice was weak but accusatory, demanding a happier explanation.

"Clara Thompson was not in the severe stages of decomposition. It is estimated she was found within twelve hours of death."

"Twelve?" Wendel breathed, staring blankly at Cassandra.

"We believe she was alive for the past eleven months." She paused and uncrossed her legs. After a moment of frustration, in which she could not decide on the correct words, she asked:

"Did Chief Christopher Norton tell you any of the circumstances of her death?"

After a terse shake of the head from Alex Wendel, Cassandra rolled her shoulders back and softened her voice.

"Clara Thompson was found nine months pregnant. We can only conclude that she became pregnant after her disappearance.

Do you know anyone who could have been involved in her disappearance?"

It was a long period of silence before Alex Wendel rose and wandered over to the kitchen. There was a light clatter of plates being removed, and the dull, hollow swing of cabinets opening and closing. She returned with a small plate of brownies in her grasp. Holding up a hand, she slipped again into the kitchen and came back with two identical glasses of iced tea. Upon placing the food and drinks on the coffee table, she stepped back and attempted a gentle smile.

Cassandra watched her clenching hands and knew that Alex Wendel wished only for something to occupy her thoughts. She had supplied both the brownies and tea merely to avoid examining her memories of the forsaken past. A strained laugh issued from Wendel's mouth. She nodded at Cassandra and sat again in the hard wooden chair.

"I know it's a bit much. You were looking at the furniture. It's mine and Clara's. She always liked the new stuff, the cool, upgraded things–– I wanted a pretty home. Old and warm."

Her eyes ran over the cramped, colorful room like hands fumbling for a missing knickknack. Cassandra followed the woman's gaze and could see only the sterile frigidity of a house haunted by the now unattainable hopes its owners had once held.

"I can't just throw them out. She'd be so mad. So mad." Her face grew red, and she rose once again, collecting a yellow knitted blanket from a nearby sweetgrass basket. She sat and wrapped the blanket around her legs.

"We didn't live here together. I got this apartment after Clara disappeared. We lived in a horrible apartment building down near West Ashley High School. It was between two really great neighbors, so we thought it'd be safer. And–– and we didn't tell anyone, you know–– if people asked, we said we were roommates. But no one believed us. They burned the plants on our balcony. Someone even stole the card table we had out there for breakfast. We'd eat breakfast out there, but with the table gone–– Clara got a new one, later. But still."

"Who stole your card table?" Cassandra asked, taking out a small notebook and setting it on her lap. She scribbled a few hasty lines before glancing back up at Alex.

"I don't know who stole the table," Alex said, puffing out a short, amused laugh. "But there were some men who would smoke outside every night. There was a communal barbecue place, but no one ever used it. Some of the neighborhood men would bring out folding chairs, like the ones parents take to soccer games, and watch everything. They never cleaned up after themselves. The grass was burnt where the cigarettes fell. Clara was furious–– she thought they would start a fire one day."

"Did these men ever talk to you?"

"I mean–– they whistled and yelled. They'd throw cigarette butts at us if we walked by. But the worst days were when they just watched. It was like they were all thinking the same thing, but no one had the guts to do it. They were cowards. Disgusting, useless cowards."

"What do you mean by 'thinking of the same thing?'" Cassandra questioned.

Alex's voice, which had wavered and grown inaudible at times, was firm and venomous:

"Rape. They all wanted Clara. She was beautiful, but that wasn't it. She would flip them off. She'd walk right up to them and tell everyone to fuck off. Tell them how ugly and worthless they were. They wanted to hurt her because she wasn't afraid of them."

Cassandra paused her writing and glanced up. She put the notebook down and reached for the glass of tea, its moist iciness numbing her fingers. She murmured a 'thank you' before meeting Alex's eyes once more.

"Do you have any definitive reasons to suspect these men?"

"They disappeared after she did. I saw them sometimes, and I talked with their wives. But they never sat at the barbecue area again, catcalling women and smoking. The grass grew back, so I know they weren't there."

Cassandra stood, ignoring the rising sense of intrigue growing within her. Her hands itched. Silently, she set the tea down and released a low hum.

"Do you know the names of these men?" she asked.

"Most of the men passed through–– the neighborhood wasn't one you tried to stay in. It was usually four men. I can only remember two. Not their names. It was too long ago. They played in a local church orchestra. I thought it was crazy how different they could be. One night they'd be screaming at you, and the next you'd hear them practicing their violins through the open window."

"Do you know which orchestra?"

Alex paused, covering tightly closed eyes with her hands. After a moment she nodded, opened her eyes, and unwrapped the blanket from her legs.

"The name was strong. It was funny since the building was almost falling over. It was their practice building. The acoustics were better than all the other options. It was the Triumph Church Philharmonic."

Giovanni Singer waited on the collapsed porch of an abandoned house in Folly Beach. He sat with a straight back, his palms pressed to his knees. He watched a family walk to a gleaming Audi parked down the street; they wore vibrant swimming suits that still dripped ocean water onto the hot pavement. They smelled of salt, and their laughter dissolved in the warm midday air.

With a grunt of effort, he unbent his knees and stood. To his left, away from the street, rose a tall crown of beach grass, its slender green stalks bleached from the insistent sun. The grass sheathed a sturdy little pier that jutted out to the edge of the water. Giovanni's eyes found a gurgling spigot, the kind that sprays on sand-stained feet. Its handle remained turned despite there being no feet. Water sprang to the sand, and the sand hungrily gulped it down. A puddle burbled on the sand before slowly sinking out of sight.

He tore his gaze away and crossed the street. The brick step that he had sat upon for a half-hour was two blocks away from Ronald White's house. Giovanni had never ventured to speak to Kira Rushton's partner. It would have been like conversing around an enormous boulder and attempting, in vain, to ignore it. He could not look upon Ronald White and forget what his partner had done. He shook these thoughts from his mind and drew himself up as White's house came into view.

The house was an oblong, yellowish shed that seemed half-sunken into the ground, as though it were living and had slowly decayed over the years. A cherry-red door sat atop a plastic step that wobbled about on cheap, squealing wheels. Windows like fever-dulled eyes followed Giovanni as he sprang up the steps and knocked.

He ran a hand along the dry red curlicues of paint that hung from the door. The exterior's wooden slats bristled out like staticky hair. Neighbors had pried wood from the walls for fires and construction. He turned and saw White's mailbox lying splintered on the sidewalk. When he moved to knock again, the door swung open. A thin-eyed, thick-jawed man stood for a moment with his hand shading his gaze. With a noise of recognition, Ronald White beckoned him in.

They entered a low living room that smelled of damp, sour laundry. The house seemed filled to the brim with dust rather than air. Dozens of water glasses sat upon the room's surfaces: a squat black coffee table, the television stand, a side table that seemed to resemble a frog dressed in a waiter's suit and tie. Dust floated on the surface of each glass like an airtight seal. Giovanni's steps stirred up acrid, rotten air; his face flushed red, and stubborn tears came to his eyes. He pinched his nose and sniffed.

"Pollen," he said, and sat where Ronald gestured. He began to speak, but a shrill burst of static interrupted him. A radio sat by the older man's recliner. Giovanni picked a few familiar abbreviations and code numbers out of the static. It must have been connected to the local police channel. A minor crash was being reported at the intersection of Vanderhorst and Pitt. He cleared his throat and began again.

"I'm Giovanni Singer. Beatrice Singer's brother. I was wondering if we could talk."

"About?" A glass bowl of pistachio nuts appeared in Ronald's lap. He fiddled with a shell and slipped the green bead between his lips. Giovanni noted that the entire right side of the older man's face bulged and would not move, as though it had turned to stone with disuse. His pale pink lips flapped together as he chewed.

"About Kira Rushton. I know you were partners for many years before her disappearance. Could you tell me about the night she disappeared?"

He cracked another shell and slipped it between his lips. After a moment, the nut slipped out from between his fingers, and Ronald released a hoarse curse. It fell to the floor and rolled into the thick film of dust beneath his recliner.

"I've told everyone everything. Nothing new."

"Yes, but I've only ever read about it. I just want your words. Everything you remember," Giovanni said.

Ronald gave a dismal shrug. His thick gray brows looked as though a cloud of dust would shake loose from them should he shrug any harder.

"I remember different things all the time. There's no point in asking me. It's why I couldn't help with finding Kira."

"Or my sister."

"Or your sister," Ronald readily agreed. He looked at Giovanni as though for the first time, eyes wide and gentle. After a moment, he shook his head and slowly turned about, feeling for the television remote's secret location.

"I really can't help," he said.

"Please," Giovanni said quickly, voice tinged with desperation. He flushed at his obvious panic and paused, pulling in a slow breath. "I don't care if you help. I'm not trying to find anything out. I just want to listen to whatever you remember. All fifty versions of it."

Ronald ceased his mindless sifting and sat back once more. He lifted the pistachio bowl and held it out to Giovanni. He waved it away, but at Ronald's persistence, he took a handful and slipped them into his pocket.

"You know Kira liked drinking. But she didn't do more than that before me. I'll take the blame for that. I never thought she'd drive while doing it. Sometimes I'd have to go to Charlotte or Sarasota for work. I'd just gotten back from Florida. She'd been out since I was home, and I fell asleep waiting for her to come back. I must have been asleep a few hours when Kira got home."

"She came back?"

"They didn't believe me when I said it. They said I died."

Ronald leaned close, his face tight and conspiratorial. His eyes were wide and gleaming. Giovanni felt as though he had to reassure a child that the abnormal shadow they had seen was no monster, no witch come to boil them alive. He cleared his throat and sat up.

"Did you?"

"The hospital said I'd overdosed on oxytocin. Except I'd never done that before. It needs a prescription. And I didn't have that. You think I went looking for oxytocin? I didn't even have it in the house. They didn't believe me. They found me dead on the bed over there."

He pointed to a distant corner of the house. He burned a flushed red, a ruddiness that clashed unpleasantly against his white hair. His mouth trembled. The glass pistachio dish wobbled in his grip, and Giovanni lunged forward to catch it.

"They don't believe you. They don't believe anybody. I'd never had any of that. Never. And Kira was there in the doorway, and she wasn't moving--"

"You really saw her?"

"You don't believe me?"

"No," Giovanni said nervously. "Yes. I do believe you. Just clarification. You saw her standing in the doorway of your bedroom?"

"I saw her. Not her face. But she was standing there with a big coat on, and I thought it was weird that she didn't shine. She always wore these cheap sequin dresses to bars. She didn't shine at all. She didn't move. She was so drunk she shot a cop—"

He glanced at Giovanni and quickly continued.

"She was really drunk, that's what I'm saying. How was she standing so still?"

There crept a disturbed silence over the room. Giovanni slapped his hands on his knees, as though to disperse the melancholy mood, and jumped up. He gestured vaguely to the place where Ronald had pointed.

"Could I see the bedroom?"

They moved down the house's singular hall, which in all measured only six feet. Dust caked every surface in Ronald's bedroom. Dirt had found every crease in the comforter; it appeared to be made of crepe paper from the way it lay lifeless across the thin, misshapen mattress. A weary fan, situated in a corner of the room, rotated its sputtering head back and forth to no avail.

Ronald had hurried in, attempting to make the bed, to untangle the curtains and wipe the dust from his bare wooden wardrobe. Giovanni would not enter. He laid a gentle hand on the doorframe, unwilling to leave any physical evidence of his presence there.

"This is where she stood? Right where I am?"

At Ronald's affirmative answer, he leaned his head against the frame and gazed upon the bed. Kira Rushton had stood here minutes after she murdered Beatrice. He wondered if his sister's blood had been cleaned from Kira's face in the bathroom they had passed. If the older woman had examined herself in the mirror and truly realized what she had done. Stuck in his reveries, Giovanni did not realize Ronald was staring at him in sharp scrutiny.

"Are you standing straight?" Ronald demanded.

"What?"

"Are you standing up straight? Don't slouch."

Giovanni drew himself up and glanced behind him.

"Why? What are you thinking about?"

"Kira–– when she stood in the doorway, I couldn't see that picture behind her. Her head covered it."

He pointed to the picture on the wall behind Giovanni. It was a portrait of a dark-haired young woman, perhaps of Ronald's mother. She wore a thick red dress, and her hands were crossed on her lap. Alterations had been done to make the woman appear as though she were suspended in a dark fog. The picture peered over Giovanni's head.

"My head doesn't even cover it. How tall was Kira?"

"Kira wasn't tall," Ronald said. "She was hardly five feet. But that night she was tall enough to block the picture."

Ronald glanced at the door, and Giovanni realized something had been discovered without him. He stepped into the bedroom. The feeble light that had filtered through the curtains moments before was gone.

"If you didn't have oxytocin in your house, where'd it come from? How'd you overdose on a drug you didn't take?"

Ronald passed him and plodded to the front door. There came an expectant silence as he watched Giovanni hurry after him.

"If I didn't have the pills, someone else must have brought them. And if I didn't take them, someone else must have made me."

Giovanni moved to go through the door, but Ronald grabbed his wrist. His grip was firm, and his palm was icy. Without thinking, Giovanni attempted to shake him off but could not.

"Leave this alone."

They stared at each other for a moment.

"No," Giovanni said.

"I was like you. I just couldn't believe that my life had been ruined so randomly. So quickly. For no reason besides Kira drank too much, and no one stopped her from leaving. It's not worth it. It's not."

"What made you believe it, then? Why did you stop looking?"

Ronald released his arm, and it felt like an octopus untangling itself.

"Nothing. One night I went to the store and tried to buy some rope thick enough to hold me. Couldn't afford it."

Giovanni glared at him. He felt himself shrivel with disgust at the dust, the clammy palm, the withering fan, the old portraits, and most at the ugly man before him who didn't know what to do any more than he did. He drew himself up and pushed past Ronald onto his yellowing lawn.

"I won't do that," he said. He wished to run down the street, to escape Ronald's immobile, stone-like face; instead, he wiped his hands on his pants and stood for a moment in silence.

"Kira's stuff. Did she–– did she have journals? Diaries?"

Giovanni longed to speak directly to the woman who had thus far hidden behind dense reports and testimonies. He had deliberately evaded any mention of Kira Rushton as though averting his eyes from something too intimate, too vulnerable for his examination. Above all, something ugly within him had been cultivated by a vague but intense hatred for the woman who had shot his sister.

Perhaps a journal would justify his resentment. Perhaps Kira Rushton was morally abysmal, thinking only of her own pleasure and advantages. She might have abandoned friends who sought only to aid her, fought those who sought only to love her. He longed to be proven right, to find that his five years of hatred were not only necessary to his peace of mind but also to the good of society. His character was not one that tolerated such furious sentiments. At times, he felt as though something inside him were rotting.

He looked up the porch to Ronald's face. In the daylight, he could see the wrinkles that cragged his face like a field left fissured by drought. He realized the old face was upturned for the first time in a smile.

"Gone in the garbage. All pulp."

"All of her belongings?"

"If they weren't thrown away, they were sold."

"To whom?"

"People. One here, one there," Ronald said. "You won't find anything. You better watch out, kid. When your time comes to get some rope, you'll find it."

5

Chapter Five

It took Cassandra three days to crosscheck the entire Triumph Church Philharmonic 2021 records with property owners in Cooper's Dell. The analysis took a mere half hour; however, the Triumph Church had shut down in 2022 following a series of disastrous flash floods. She had obtained an old performance program of the orchestra's rendition of Gustav Holst's *The Planets*. Six members of the orchestra had resided at one time in Cooper's Dell. Three were women, and of the remaining men, two were deceased. The sole survivor, a fifty-six-year-old by the name of William Serk, still lived in Cooper's Dell.

Cassandra had just slipped a notebook into her pocket when Serk's front door swung open. It opened limpingly–– the frame had swelled in the heat, and someone was pushing quite forcefully against the other side to get it open. Cassandra pulled it further, ignoring the grating moan of the old wood, and peered into the stuffy gloom revealed in its stead. Behind the door was a tall, gaunt girl in her early twenties. Her face was gray but splotchy, and her hair, a light blond, seemed nearly translucent. She offered Cassandra a tight smile and stepped aside.

"Who is it?" called a hoarse voice from behind the girl.

"Who–– who are you?" the girl repeated, glancing quickly at Cassandra with the look of a chastised child.

"I'm Detective Cassandra Wake of the CPD. Is William Serk here?"

"He's here," came the voice again. "What's CPD want with him?"

A faded floral divider obscured the living room from view. Dust and cooking grease stained its crinkly folds, marking their own sort of sordid flowers. Upon rounding the divider, her eyes fell upon a rather ugly man, whose skin was pallid from lack of sunlight but reddened with an alcoholic flush. He sat in a squat leather chair, its arms marked with abrasions and tears. A gurgling air tank sat beside the chair, releasing an intermittent whistle when he moved.

Serk was a bald man whose forehead gleamed with an insistent sheen of sweat. His face was extraordinarily ragged, a bundle of bones rough with graying whiskers. His stomach bulged like a misshapen stone beneath his stained t-shirt. His wrists were fragile and discolored, and Cassandra was struck by his likeness to an upended cockroach.

"I want to talk with you about the disappearance of Clara Thompson," she said. "Are you willing to answer my questions?"

He laughed, and the air tank laughed alongside him, spluttering and whistling. Sweat had gathered around the clear tubes in his nose. He lifted a hand and wiped at the shining lines tickling down his face.

"I'm willing, but I don't remember nothing. There's no point in being here."

He spoke quickly but in a loud whisper, as though he had plenty of enthusiasm but not enough breath. His eyes darted about like they were chasing flies in the dim room; they came to rest on the girl, who thus far had remained behind Cassandra.

"Make something for us, then. Go on."

The girl seemed grateful to disappear behind the divider. Cassandra drew herself up as Serk returned his attention to her. He gestured to a threadbare sofa and watched as she sat.

"What do you want to know?" he asked.

"You've lived in Cooper's Dell for seventeen years now. If anyone knows anything weird happening, it would be you."

Serk offered her a grin before flushing red and releasing a thick cough. His gags crunched through the air. She glimpsed the bristly back of his head and the gnarled line of his spine as he folded at the waist, coughing with his mouth uncovered. A thick pair of jagged lightning bolts marked his left shoulder blade. Beside it, faded and sun-damaged, was the outline of a naked woman, the sort of woman that truckers have stickers of on their eighteen-wheelers. He straightened and caught his breath.

"Eighteen years, girl. I've been here almost as long as you've been alive, I'm guessing. Well, I never really talked with her. She lived on the other side of the complex." He raised his hand and pointed to the distant door of Clara Thompson's former home. "She filed some complaints about me. Not about me. No. The grass. Our cigarettes burnt up some grass in the yard out there."

"You and some friends smoked a lot in the yard, then?"

"I know what you're thinking. Nothing illegal." After a shallow, gurgling laugh, he resumed: "Me and some men would stay up a little late and talk. Just about a bunch of stuff. Gave us some time to smoke and drink, and the women got to gossip and all that."

"You were married?" she questioned.

"Still am," Serk said. His eyes darted over Cassandra's shoulders, and she turned to see the tall girl standing slightly obscured by the divider. Realizing she had been spotted, the girl hurried in with a pale enamel tray in her hands. It was laden with cheap plastic glasses, a pitcher of iced lemonade, and a tray of sandwiches. The sandwiches held thick tomato slices slathered in mayonnaise and black pepper. She set the tray down on the card table at Serk's right side.

"Ever had a tomato sandwich?" Serk questioned. He bit into a sandwich but kept his gaze on Cassandra. A smear of mayonnaise remained hanging from the whiskers above his lip.

"Can't say I have," she answered. Her eyes followed the girl until she disappeared into a dark corner of the room, presumably through an unseen doorway. "I was raised in Ohio, but my family was from Romania."

"I've got some family up there. Cold."

"Ohio or Romania?"

"Ohio, girl."

Cassandra nodded but chose to remain silent. After a moment, he wiped his hands on a napkin and cleared his throat. He took the plate and, struggling, pushed it onto the edge of the sofa. She pulled it closer and nodded in thanks.

"Most everybody sat and smoked with us at one time. Everyone was invited. But there were usually four of us. Me, Tony Weaver, Danny Litch, and..." He paused and closed his eyes in thought. "Fred Ellison. He was in the orchestra with Tony and me."

"You were in the orchestra? What did you play?"

"I was first violin. I've taken lessons my whole life. Just haven't gotten around to playing again. Fred played the trumpet. But we just sat together. You can sit with anyone. Doesn't mean you know them."

"You weren't friends?"

Serk sniffed and sat back, leather cracking under him. "I didn't dislike him. It was just hard to really, actually like him. You give someone a chance, and then they're talking about the Crusades and stupid philosophy shit. Old fucking books and old fucking people."

"Did he talk about those subjects often?"

"No. He hardly ever spoke. And that made it worse when he did. What little time he spent talking, he used it on stupid things like that. His mouth would barely be open and I'd already pray for him to shut the hell up. If you think one of us did something weird, it was Fred."

She sat stunned for a moment at his brazen admission. A slim, dirt-caked window was on the wall behind Serk's head. Blue mid-day light had darkened into dim tidings of an evening storm. When she spoke again, her voice was low with intrigue.

"Why would you say that?"

"We all sat together. But he'd sit sideways, so he looked at the sides of our faces instead of straight ahead. But he wasn't looking at our faces. He always looked up and to the right. And you know who lived there?"

"Clara Thompson," she answered.

"And her roommate," Serk added conspiratorially. "Did you know about the roommate? Everyone thought they were together. Like a married couple. You could ask her a few things. She'd know more than me."

Rather than acknowledge his suggestion, she leaned forward and raised her shoulders, as though asking a silent question.

"Do you think these rumors could have resulted in her disappearance?"

"They weren't rumors, girl. Fred climbed onto their balcony one night and looked right in. Said he saw them dancing like a husband and wife. He thought Clara saw him, and he broke some table getting out of there. Had to sneak back and clean up the pieces."

There came a great rumble from outside the window. Harsh wind beat against the glass, intermingled with incipient splatters of rain. The bleak gray sky crept through the window and fell in twisting shadows across the floor. At the noise, Serk set the tray aside and wrestled his feet from the rest.

"I don't have anything else to say. Hope you have an umbrella. I didn't know there was supposed to be rain today."

"Before I leave," Cassandra began, "what philosophers did Ellison talk about?"

"What?"

"Old fucking books," she repeated. "Old fucking people."

He frowned, and his face, for a moment, seemed impossibly cold and hard.

"You're in the wrong neighborhood if you want to ask questions like that. He might as well have been speaking to the wind."

He sat back, and even the respirator remained silent, its characteristic splutterings conspicuously absent. His shirt sleeve had ridden up to reveal a thick, gleaming watch on his left wrist. It winked in the dying light. It was brazen and gold, with a bold round face and small gilded digits. A cruel amusement arose within her. What use did this man have for keeping track of time? For what reason did he rise in the morning?

Tearing her gaze away, she rose and slowly made her way across the room. She passed the shadow of the girl, who had emerged from some hidden doorway into the shade that hung like smoke about William Serk. For an instant, Cassandra paused, examining the girl's face, before turning and reaching for the handle of the front door. She was met with its unwieldy bulk and pressed her shoulder into the wood. It came undone with a gasp.

She stopped and stood on the ugly, two-by-two concrete porch. A strange warmth filled her chest as she stepped onto the slick grass of Serk's front lawn. The flash of distant lightning sparked in countless puddles scattered across the yard. Thunder roared in the direction of the highway, now hidden by a belt of slender fir trees. Instead of returning to her Dodge Durango, she turned and walked to a small concrete clearing that crouched, as though hiding, between the two squat rows of apartments.

Faded blue plastic chairs huddled in a semicircle on the platform. Two red brick grills sat in varying stages of disrepair behind the backs of the chairs. She walked around the platform with her head bent, her gaze cast ever downward.

Alex Wendel had been correct: the grass on all sides had grown back. It was a bland, pea-colored green, the shade a sailor's face turns amid bouts of seasickness, but it had grown, nonetheless. A great rumble of thunder sounded directly overhead, terminating any thoughts she had of continuing her exploration. As she began toward the parking lot, a white spot flashed in the corner of her eye.

She walked over and crouched beside the furthest left chair. They had been bolted to the platform, most likely after numerous thefts by the neighborhood's inhabitants. Crushed beneath the back leg of the furthest chair was a drenched cigarette butt. She leaned back on her heels and stared at the cigarette. A single raindrop hit her forehead and rolled down the bridge of her nose.

Any signs of William Serk's evening sessions were long gone, torn asunder like scraps of clouds into an uncaring, uninterested sky. Some would consider it an evil thing that the world could go on its cruel way, even after witnessing such crimes as the abduction and murder of Clara Thompson. It seemed that the world could only absorb so much hardship, like soil in which crops shall never thrive again. It was not a hideous phenomenon, but an invaluable gift, that life could go on after death, just as joy could succeed the greatest despair. Cassandra rose and began again toward the Durango, pressed on by the profound but gentle assurance of the gray sky and drowning grass that squelched under her boots.

The strange warmth filled her lungs, and she released a haggard laugh. A pale hand swept the water from her face. A slight smile crept to her face and would not leave, trembling with the effort to ease the joy from her expression. She gave a shuddering breath and twisted the keys in the ignition. Despite her pleasant expression, she would give many years of her life to never see the hideous scene of Cooper's Dell again. Soft rain streaked her windshield as she began toward the department.

Sic. Slide. Sic. Slide. She stretched her consciousness out like a piece of fabric, like an animal twisting and straining its muscles after a long rest. She sat on the motel room floor, breathing slowly and deeply. She had swept that morning, but dust still clung to her palms when she braced them against the tile. A light breeze came in from the raised window. The sharp scent of rain filtered in, coating the air that passed routinely through her lungs. She closed her eyes and leaned back.

Her thumb moved mechanically over the spark wheel of a tarnished chrome lighter. It was small, barely peeking out from her loosely closed fingers. The rhythmic hiss filled the silence. It had long emptied of any lighter fluid, becoming a mere object of fixation for her thoughtful moments. She dropped the lighter into her pocket and slowed her breathing.

There came the sound of muffled voices from the room next door, bleeding out amid the distant commentary of a televised baseball game. She knew them to be a young couple from New Jersey. The husband had gotten a job as a long-haul trucker, but a failed drug test had made their temporary stay at the Harbor Motel a year-long slog. If she strained harder, she would hear the flux of their raised voices, the content of their monotonous argument. And monotonous it was—they argued every day like clockwork. She figured they could have at least invited her for dinner once or twice, with how much she knew of their marital lives.

Her eyes flew open, and she drank in the bland motel walls, the patchy couch and darkened television. Footsteps dashed up the concrete steps outside, and a hand crashed against the door. She rose and crossed the room, flipping on a light as she let Mills in.

He pushed past her, a foil-wrapped Pop-Tart hanging from his mouth. His eyes found hers, and he began an undignified monologue, crumbs falling in a dry spray from his lips.

"You're disgusting, you know that?" she said, retrieving her bag from the couch.

He crossed to the connected kitchen and opened the fridge, peering inside. His voice was clearer when he spoke again.

"We've all got problems. Some people are assholes. You think I'm disgusting. Do you have any breakfast stuff?"

"You always look," she said. "And you never find anything."

"I read there's this theory about lowering standards. When you keep checking the pantry, you're not looking for something you didn't find the first time. You're checking if your standards have lowered."

"And have yours lowered yet?"

"Not this much," he said, closing the fridge. He bounced on his heels and shoved his hands into his pockets. "Have you got the camera? Heyward reminded me to ask."

"Yeah. Yes. Let's go."

Mills hurried out to the parking lot, and Cassandra turned, twisting the door's flimsy lock with her key. A few yards away, the neighbor's door swung open, and the husband stepped out, his face dark and thunderous. He stood for a moment outside, braced against the door, before glancing up at Cassandra. He offered her a weak smile.

"So you are real," he said.

"At the moment."

"You're so quiet," he said. "It's hard to believe you're ever here. I–– I'm sorry if we're loud sometimes. A lot of the time. You never know how thick the walls are."

Cassandra shrugged, slipping the key into her pocket.

"I hardly hear anything at all. And I was thinking the same thing. I'm so loud, you must hear me."

"Never," he said. "Never."

She hummed as though interested in the observation. She heard the wife's footsteps nearing the door, and she watched as it swung open, nearly sending the husband toppling over backward. She watched tanned hands grasp gently at his shoulder, and he turned to go inside, having almost forgotten their conversation already.

"I hear the Orioles are doing fine this season," she called after him, already turning. "Maybe we can have a potluck or something if they ever get to the Series."

He paused, his head swinging back as he registered her words. He grimaced, nodded, and threw the door shut behind him. Her gaze lifted across the parking lot. Mills stood waiting next to his Impala, arms crossed in a gesture of impatience. Quietly, she crossed the remaining asphalt and slipped into the Impala's passenger seat.

"What did he want?" Mills said, crumpling the foil wrapper in his hand as he started the engine. It rumbled beneath them, and she pressed a hand to the seat's upholstery.

"Nothing with me," she said. Silence settled around them, and she listened to the light scrape of Mills's hands against the leather of the steering wheel.

"Why do they stay together?"

"Who?"

"My neighbors."

"The ones that scream all the time?"

At her reticence, he glanced over. She nodded.

"I don't really know, Wake. My brother fights his wife all the time. Says it's like she kills him every morning and brings him back every night. And I asked the same thing. He said it was a privilege to have someone, even if they annoyed the hell out of you."

Her eyes followed the flash of traffic out the window.

"Which I think is wrong. Obviously. But people don't love in the same way, I guess. Maybe that's all they've got."

"Does Lieutenant Crawford know Giovanni Singer?"

She watched as Michael Heyward bent carefully over a tray of eTone film developer, his eyes obscured by a bulky pair of night vision goggles. His deft hands were hidden in a pair of orange rubber gloves. After a quiet moment, the tweezers in his hand clamped around a sodden bit of film and delicately turned the entire photograph over. Having accomplished this task, he sat the tweezers down and wiped the gloves on a rag at his waist. Without a glance to his surroundings, he bent once more and began work on the next tray.

"Why would she?" Heyward asked, distracted.

He completed his tasks with such concentrated diligence that the contents of the images, which he worked so ardently to procure, nearly went unnoticed. A previous batch hung freshly dried on a clothesline stretched above their heads. The photograph directly above Cassandra's head revealed the bland, gray face of the side of the Charleston Police Department office building. On the bottom right corner of the photograph was a blot of faint color—— the tarnished green awning of the Indian cuisine restaurant next door. Another depicted the blurry faces of a crowd of passersby. Cassandra raised a hand to touch one but received a sharp nudge from Heyward's boot.

"Singer said something. Made it seem like he knew her."

"I know that Crawford worked with Beatrice for a while. They entered a few years apart. Beatrice wanted to be a detective from the very beginning—— like you. She never got it. Crawford got lieutenant, though. That's something."

Despite her determination to focus solely on the developed film, she could not help but notice Heyward's bouncing shoulders. They moved in a subtle but noticeable rhythm, spurred on by a song she couldn't begin to guess. The officer's ears were covered in a pair of flimsy headphones, a pair with thin, tangled wires and thick orange foam pads on each ear. He flipped another photograph before pulling the headphones off. For a moment, she could hear the energetic beat of Lalo Rodriguez's "Ven Devórame Otra Vez" dissolving into the silence.

"They're amateur work, but they're not bad," he noted.

Cassandra had taken an antique Kodak from the boxes stuffed under her motel bed. She had received it post-marked in the mail alongside the lighter, having been unable to attend the reading of her uncle's will up in Cleveland. Thus far, it had been nothing but a hinderance to her habit of moving residences every other year.

They needed a film camera, and Cassandra Wake had one. At various points about the office, she had crouched, adjusted the various dials, cupped a careful hand around the lens, and taken over forty random images. Heyward overlooked the process of film development.

Lab results had recently come in about the white powder found on Clara Thompson's body. It was a powder film developer, the likes of which were dissolved in tubs of water and used to expose the results of darkened films. Most major brands used the same chemical makeup, so it was impossible to trace any particular purchase of developer back to a local photography store. However, particular development processes for color film required specific chemicals. Should their sample film develop similarly, they could potentially trace select manufacturers for a chemical purchase.

"So you're saying I should quit my job and pursue photography full time?" she asked, her nose almost touching the surface of the developer in the nearest bin. It shivered with each rhythmic move Heyward made as the next song spilled out of his ancient headphones. She shrank back, her nose wrinkling.

"What?" Heyward glanced over.

"That's so strong. The vinegar."

"Yeah. The film delivered to Singer smelled like it, too."

"That's different," Cassandra said. Her fingers ran lightly along the edge of the lighter in her pocket. "Cellulose acetate film, if treated poorly enough, can develop something called Vinegar Syndrome. It gets brittle and breaks easily. Smells like vinegar."

"Why the hell do you know that, Wake?"

"I worked at the local cinema in high school. We had poor management. Cellulose acetate film replaced cellulose nitrate. That stuff was too flammable. We had a bunch of abandoned film reels that couldn't be played because they were too worn down. Some kids would steal handfuls of film and start trashcan fires with them."

"Some kids," Heyward said, grinning. "Never Detective Wake, though, huh?"

"My uncle wasn't religious, but he would have called for an exorcism had he caught me burning a movie. He was into those things. Big Noir guy. Smoked a pack-a-day to be like Bogart and Mitchum."

"And was he?"

Cassandra bared her teeth in a mockery of a smile.

"Bogart died of esophageal cancer. Mitchum of complications with lung cancer. Adrian Wake died of oral cancer. That's the closest he ever got to being some big Noir guy."

"Closer than some of us will ever get," Heyward said, shrugging. He slipped the foam pads of his headphones over his ears and recommenced his slow, methodical work. Cassandra braced herself against the counter. She eyed the clothesline of dripping film, the smell of vinegar sharp in her nostrils. Killers often took mementos, and it wasn't the most shocking thing in the world that this suspect chose photographs. Direct evidence that something had occurred. A timeless moment in which the victims still lived. The Vinegar Syndrome, however, directly contradicted the very purpose of a memento. A photograph meant to capture something forever; ruined by poor care, a photograph that would never last.

She released a harsh breath and jumped off the counter. Heyward did not look up, and Cassandra did not find it necessary to distract him any further. She pushed through the door and down the hall. The smell of acetic acid clung to her clothes, and after a quick decision, she shrugged her jacket off. As though watching her, an AC unit kicked on overhead. A faint breeze rolled through the labyrinthine department, but Cassandra was long gone, slipping out into the bright midday sunlight.

6

Chapter Six

The next day, Cassandra found herself bent over a glass case, unblinking and unmoving. The Charleston Museum was holding an end of the school year sale, with tickets being a third of their usual fifteen dollars. There was a permanent photo collection by Laura Bragg. They were scratchy, yellowed squares of film that depicted various scenes of South Carolina plantations around the early-twentieth century. Sunlight fell through the tranquil limbs of an old magnolia tree, glittering across the smooth face of a pond. Magnolia Gardens. A spray of coarse, bleached grass climbing up the side of a slim house. Harrietta Plantation.

Her visit had been an abrupt idea spurred on by the possibility of a lonesome evening spent bent over case files. There were no photographs of Drayton Hall Plantation, none that she could see, at least. A young girl, no more than seven years old, pushed against her to peer into the glass case. Behind her, throwing a weary reprimand into the air, came her mother with a baby strapped to her chest.

"I'm sorry, Miss. She knows better. Sarah, you know better, don't you? Apologize," she said.

"You were standing there for so long," the girl bemoaned, garnering a sharp glance from her mother.

Cassandra laughed and stepped back.

"Didn't realize it was so long. Sorry."

She turned and regarded the bustling but subdued crowd that filled the Charleston Museum. An older couple sat on a nearby bench, carrying on a hushed conversation beneath the general buzz. Young boys streaked past, ignoring the frantic protests of their parents. The smell of chemical cleansers soaked the air, not too harsh as to damage the fragile historic paint, not too pungent as to put off the visitors. Strong enough to thoroughly complete their job.

For a moment, the crowd cleared, and she glimpsed a wooden square of benches. On it sat a single man, his eyes narrowed but unfocused, as though he were chewing on a rather complicated thought. He could easily have been another exhibit, a man turned to marble like the artifacts and busts he sat between. The surrounding noise dissolved into warm silence as she observed him.

He did not appear to be observing anything in particular. Her rather obvious surveillance had gone unnoticed thus far. She stood frozen in the crowd until something connected in her mind. She strode toward the distant wooden island, toward Giovanni Singer.

With every step closer, her certainty grew that Singer would glance up, would discover her pointless trek. She did not wish to speak with him; rather, she quite vehemently wished to avoid any conversation tonight. But her feet trudged on, and quietly, politely, she sat beside him on the bench.

She noted the subtle flash of his eyes, the straightening of his neck. He pulled a knee up to his chest. Neither made to break the silence. She watched his mouth curve into a slight, grimacing smile.

"There are no photographs of Drayton Hall in this collection," he said.

"I didn't ask."

He hummed, his fingers playing against the fabric of his trousers.

"Just an observation." After a hollow instant, he ventured again: "Was this your idea? Seems like a Crawford thing."

"Please. If you want to talk, give me a minute." Frowning, she glanced at the profile of his face and straightened. "What do you know about Lieutenant Crawford?"

She was taller than him when they sat. He did not have the best posture, nor did it seem to matter to him how he appeared. His chin rested against his chest, rising with the rhythmic ebb of his breath.

"Have you seen the armory?" he asked.

She inhaled and glanced about the large room. A sprawl of signs and labels hung on the wall and over doorways. To their distant right, over Giovanni's head, was a sign indicating the referenced room.

"No. I haven't seen anything yet."

"I saw you staring for nearly half-an-hour," he said. "A half-hour of nothing."

"And what was your half-hour spent doing, if you were just watching me?" she questioned. She felt an uncharacteristic irritation rise within her and fought to quell it.

"It's a particular aim of mine to do nothing for thirty minutes a day. Good for the soul."

She nearly laughed, a cold flush coming over her. Thirty minutes of nothing felt particularly harmful to her soul, or whatever Giovanni Singer referred to as such.

"I disagree," she said.

He nodded. "It takes great skill to master the art of doing nothing."

"No, I don't think so. It might be the one thing we're all too good at."

"No," he replied quickly, with a sudden urgency in his voice. He sounded as though he were lecturing something pedantic and trite to a room full of disinterested college students. "No. I leave you alone for five minutes, you get bored. You begin admiring the wallpaper. You start to write a grocery list in your head for the next week. And you know how important thought is to the human experience. We must forsake thought for a half-hour so the day does not kill us."

"You sound quite thoughtful, Mr. Singer."

"Yeah, well. Yeah." He sat up and blinked rapidly, the bright overhead lights bringing tears to his eyes. A pleasant silence grew between them, and Cassandra let the burble of the crowd wash over her. A touch on her shoulder, light as air, had her looking over into his curious eyes.

"The girl. Is she all right?"

"She's been situated with a foster family. She's not ready for adoption yet. Not at all," Cassandra responded. She had seen young Beatrice Singer only once since Drayton Hall. She had accompanied a pediatric therapist on an initial checkup; she had stood like a gargoyle behind the therapist's shoulder, her eyes mindlessly fixed to the little girl. She was remarkably little–– not malnourished, just naturally small. She had worn a large T-shirt boasting the emblem of some local burger shop. She had brown eyes and brown hair. Someone had braided her hair into a single plait that hung over her shoulder.

"Could I see her?" he asked. He stared at the dull concrete floor, a fierce blush coloring his cheeks and the tips of his ears. It was as though he knew the answer already, had known it before even contemplating the question. Her palms had suddenly gone clammy. She ran a hand over the denim of her jeans.

"You're getting a doctorate, right, Mr. Singer? You want to teach?"

At her obvious avoidance of the question, Singer offered her a crooked, rueful smile. His eyes were cold despite the warm expression on his face. He slapped his hands once against his thighs, the universal gesture that ended a conversation, but he did not get up.

"Oh, I want to do everything. It's difficult. With all the world before you, you can't really decide what to do."

"Like the fig tree," Cassandra offered, determined to maintain her amiability despite his false cheer.

He watched her for a moment, motionless as stone. His hands were like blocks of ice on his knees. Giovanni Singer had the general character of someone whose knees would constantly bounce with nerves, but they were conspicuously still.

"You say that so cheerfully," he said.

"Would you have me be morose?"

He leaned forward, fingers tightening on his knees.

"You read," he said.

"I do."

"Do you know the story Shadow out of Time by Lovecraft?"

She thought for a moment. "I don't believe so."

His hands came loose, and in an instant he was standing. He gestured loosely, constrained by a sharp but directionless ferocity. Words spilled from his lips like blood.

"There's this race. The Great Race. They sort of, uh, mindswap smart people through the generations. The victims have incredible amnesiac episodes because they're not *there*. The protagonist, see, he's a professor. And he's giving a lecture one day and *poof*

He collapses. For five years, he struggles to remember. He travels around and tries desperately to figure out what happened to him. And one day, out of the blue, he collapses and starts speaking. What's he saying? He's continuing the lecture from five years ago. For five years, he was somewhere else, stuck between one syllable and the next. A paper jam of the soul. Stuck on that one sentence that no one was ever listening to. A five-year-long stutter of the consciousness..."

He fell into abrupt silence. Neither spoke.

"What were you doing that night?" she asked softly.

His hands slipped into his pockets, and he glanced over his shoulder to the fluorescent *EXIT* sign.

"It was a Sunday. Hadn't been going to church for years by then. I was waiting. We were waiting."

"We?"

"And I'm still waiting. What happens to someone who waits for something that never comes? Was never going to come, ever."

With that, he turned and crossed the museum floor. She watched the door fall heavily shut behind him. After a moment, she rose. Her eyes found the *Armory* sign. Polaroid images flashed unacknowledged in her mind. The museum surged against her senses like a salt-fringed tide, and she sucked a breath through her nostrils, drinking in the life about her.

Sheathed in the shade of Hampton Park, Giovanni Singer walked cautiously across a bright, grassy hill. He had not dressed appropriately for the weather-- humid heat clung to his thick trousers and woolen jumper. His face was pale but slick with sweat. His eyes traced the clumped bunches of grass that occasionally rose underfoot. Only once did he glance up, pretending to take off his glasses and wipe gingerly at them with his sleeve. With a noncommittal grunt, he rubbed at his forehead and picked up his pace.

Under a nearby copse of trees sat a pair of dilapidated picnic tables. They were meant to provide seats for parents who watched their children scramble about the adjacent playground. A single man waited at the table, his shoulders hunched as though attempting to conceal his face. Giovanni knew the man's face, and he thought it silly for the man to think he needed concealing. No one knew either of them.

The older man had a shock of white hair and a face that twitched irregularly. The right side of the man's face hung limp, as though suspended in time-- its lack of motion made his irregular, twitching blinks even more noticeable.

"Engaging in the usual fatherly activities, I see," Giovanni said. He frowned at Ronald White and sat down on the edge of the bench, far from him. Truthfully, he was thankful the man had reached out. He wanted to see the girl, wanted to see the mysterious child who bore his sister's name. The desire made his skin tingle and his eyes ache. He had not wanted something so badly in many years.

"Be quiet, please. I'm not supposed to be here," Ronald murmured, his eyes fixed on a distant point beyond the trees. Giovanni followed his gaze to where it rested on the abysmal playground. A handful of children ran about, crawling up short ladders and dangling from hot metal monkey bars. Their clumsy steps kicked up sprays of woodchips that sometimes skittered over into the grass. He noted a small, brown-haired girl engaged in a game of kickball.

"That her?" he asked, voice lowered to appease the older man.

"Yeah."

"Oh."

He drummed his fingers on the crooked wooden board that constituted a tabletop.

"Tiny."

"Just like Kira," Ronald said. His eyes flickered over to Giovanni but in an instant were again on the little girl. A breath shuddered through him as he decided to continue. "They need proof of sobriety. So I can meet her."

Giovanni hummed. "Then get sober."

"I am," Ronald said, his voice biting but weary. "It's a lengthy thing. You need to meet a lot of times before they'll trust you." He dragged his hands over his face. "It wasn't— I didn't just start drinking after Kira disappeared. It's been a while."

It was not a question of ease. Giovanni knew the man was terrified. Loneliness had been a fatal balm to the man's tender soul. An assurance that no one would see him for what he had become— a condemnation that, should he ever improve, no one would ever stick around to notice. An odd excitement arose within Giovanni, and he ran a hand through his hair, ignoring the swelling in his chest. He was glad that Ronald White suffered, even took a malicious pride in it. He cleared his throat and shifted on the bench.

An abrupt cheer sounded through the air, and Giovanni saw a flash of red flying through the trees. The kickball landed with a dry thump at the edge of the picnic table. He jumped up and rounded the table, thinking it best to avoid Ronald coming face-to-face with any parent or child. As he bent to pick it up, he felt an extra set of eyes on him.

It was a young boy, no more than twelve. He had crept through the trees in search of the kickball and had found it clasped in Giovanni's hands. Giovanni offered him a strained smile and received a cautious one in return. Uttering a quiet apology, he threw it underhand to the boy, who caught it and tucked it under his armpit. The boy did not turn away, and Giovanni felt his face flush, as though he were a child caught out of bed by a disappointed parent.

"Sweating like a pig," he said weakly. "Didn't dress for the occasion."

Instead of leaving, the boy offered an intrigued smile. As though reciting a script, he said:

"Some pigs can run a mile in seven minutes."

"Faster than me, then. Do they race pigs?" At his clumsy words, he heard Ronald give an exasperated sigh. "Although I guess you have to be aware of a race to–– to race. Otherwise, you're just running. Which sounds silly. Saying the only difference between running and racing is the thought of it. You like pigs, then? Yeah?"

The boy seemed unfazed by his unrelenting discomfort. He gave a shrug and rolled the kickball between his fingertips.

"They're sad."

"Why?"

"Well," the boy began. "Pigs love their babies. But when they're killed for meat, they have their babies in cages. They can't turn around to see them. Ever. The babies are just there wondering what's all happening. And the pig can't turn around to tell them."

Giovanni stood in silence. He figured the boy had thought much longer and harder on the lives of pigs than he had. He bounced on his heels and clasped his hands behind his back.

"Well, can pigs wonder? They're probably not wondering what's all happening because they can't wonder like us humans do."

"But they feel pain," the boy said, eyes fixed on Giovanni's face.

"Yeah. Yes. They do."

"So they're feeling just as much pain as we do without knowing why. Which makes it worse now."

"The other kids must be waiting for the kickball," came Ronald's voice to his right. He glanced back before nodding fervently, his hands clasped ever tighter behind his back. "Best be getting back, boy."

The boy stared at Giovanni before stepping forward and offering his hand.

"I'm Henry," he said.

Giovanni took it, barely giving it a shake before retracting his hand and shoving it into his pocket.

"Giovanni."

Henry nodded as though confirming something.

"You're Beatrice's brother."

"What? Where'd you hear that?"

"Newspaper. Your sister is Beatrice Singer. Like my sister."

In an instant, Henry turned and trotted back to his game of kickball. He seemed unperturbed, as though their conversation had never happened. Giovanni watched as he gave a shout and crouched, readying himself to catch a wayward kick.

"Good fucking job," Ronald said from the bench. His head was in his hands.

"I was walking in the park and happened to catch their ball," Giovanni said, waving his hand as though to disperse the anxious cloud about him. It did not disperse — it never truly did — and he bleakly watched Ronald rise and begin across the grass.

"Where are you going?" he called.

"If that boy mentions two odd men prowling around the playground, there'll be an officer here in five minutes ready to pin us for something. I'm not supposed to be here. They won't let me see her."

Ronald climbed the grassy hill like a worm wriggling up a brick wall. His face was the color of a rosy latex balloon, and as his cheeks puffed up with each breath, Giovanni could imagine a balloon-like squeal issuing forth. The thought nearly made him laugh, and he coughed into the crook of his elbow. Noting the man's irascible glance, he winced and cleared his throat.

"Ronald!" he called, waiting for the man to give any sign he'd heard. "How'd you know she'd be here?"

The older man couldn't outpace him, but Giovanni did not want him to feel trapped. He dragged the soles of his shoes against the grass slowly, thoughtfully, as though he found it the most interesting thing in the world. After a long moment, he reached Ronald and continued at a crawling pace, a step behind him.

"That's her foster brother. Henry. He takes her to play with the neighborhood kids some afternoons after school. I got lucky today. Sometimes it's just him."

"Lucky," Giovanni murmured to himself. He recalled the previous conversation, the uncomfortable silences. The fact that some pigs could run a sub-seven-minute mile. These thoughts fresh in his mind, he concluded that Ronald White's idea of luck had nothing to do with his own.

"Will it happen again?" By *it* he meant their meeting at the picnic table with the intention of seeing little Beatrice Singer. It wouldn't be a daily thing-- hardly even a monthly thing. He did not want to acknowledge the hope such a possibility inspired within him. He felt as though there had been a monumental wall separating himself from his sister and the people who had loved her. With the young girl, no matter how gruesome her appearance in his life, it seemed a chink had opened up for him to squeeze through.

"Well, you told me you didn't know anything about this stuff going on."

"I don't."

"He recognized you."

"That was–– that hardly even makes sense. He recognized me from the newspaper. It's not my fault newspapers like having my name on them. It's weird but not impossible."

Ronald whipped about, startling both Giovanni and himself with the action's suddenness. He peered into Giovanni's face, his eyes balefully bright. Two veiny hands rose to sweep back his thinning hair.

"You know what I think, Singer?"

Giovanni ceased his slow pace up the hill. He recognized the man's tone and the manner in which he flung words down at him. It was the sort of fight siblings engaged in. The eldest, better with words and stringing them together, would dive into an argument and flee before a response could be formulated. There was no philosophy in the world that could settle a fight such as this. His eyes closed, and a sharp breath rattled up through his lungs.

"No, of course I don't."

"I think you know shit. You know fuckall. You don't know why any of this is happening. My daughter knows more than you, and she's four."

"Daughter," Giovanni repeated, staring at the ground with a cheerless smile.

"Yeah, she's my daughter. No one can deny that. I won't have you making fun of me. Whoever did this–– they might think you're her brother, but you're a nobody. I'm her dad. And you'll respect that. You think you'll find answers with my daughter? You only find them because of me. You only see her because of me. Got that?"

Giovanni clasped his hands behind his back and straightened his spine. After a tense moment, he nodded and rocked back on his heels.

"Do you need a ride back, Ronald?"

"Not with you," the older man said, turning and shuffling down the hill. A small dirt parking lot sat at the foot of the hill, bordered in with a thick chain drawn through crooked wooden poles. He watched as Ronald struggled over the chain and began down the street.

The sky was soft and bright. Sunlight filled the air, falling against Giovanni's face. Heat seeped into cold flesh. A frigid sheen of sweat had gathered at his temple. He blinked, the sting of sweat in his eyes. A quick hand wiped at his forehead, but his eyes, red and irritated, fluttered shut. Images came unbidden to his mind.

Beatrice's brown hair burned in the warm midday sunlight that fell like water through the curtained window. Her skin was a pale brown, much like his own, but her eyes were a sharp green. Her smile was crooked but wide. She sat at the foot of their couch. He was bundled in a handful of thick woolen blankets despite the fierce summer heat that raged outside. His lungs burned as though sucking in frigid air, but his skin was taut and gleamed with sweat.

"You'll be in trouble when she finds out," he said hoarsely. The 'she' was his mother. "They could arrest you."

She laughed and looked down on him with the familiar condescension of an elder sister.

"Arrest me? For what?"

"Truancy," Giovanni said, sitting up. Blankets fell from him like chains from an escaped prisoner. He intended to continue his tirade but erupted into a rasping coughing fit.

"You don't even know what that means," Beatrice said. She pushed him down and rearranged the blankets, tucking them beneath his chin and around his shoulders. "Besides, they usually arrest adults for that. It's considered neglect or something. And if our dad gets arrested, huh? Who's gonna look after you? Who's gonna pay for you?"

"I'll look after you," Giovanni said, his eyes like bits of implacable stone in the soft, round face of a child. "I'll look after you, and you'll look after me. We'll pay for each other."

She watched him for a moment, her hand on his blanketed foot.

"How about I just make this a one-time thing? Then no one gets arrested, and we don't have to sell our souls to the man yet?"

"Who's the man?" Giovanni asked, voice scratchy. "What man?"

"You're an idiot," she said, turning to her backpack on the floor. She rifled through its contents, tossing aside books and folders that were deemed of little import. Finally, she retrieved a slim, cream book and flipped to a random page. She cleared her throat, drowning out his attempt at rebuke, and began to read.

"She's lost her wits, obeys the sorrow-craze of the hurt mind wrenched from her just-captured home..." she began quietly, glancing from the page to his pallid face, half-hidden by the frilled edge of a blanket. He closed his eyes and listened to the gentle murmur of her voice. Giovanni remembered it and mourned. He remembered the edge of her voice, like an infant recognizes the dim outline of a parent's kindly face. He remembered the tips of her hair drifting in the breeze of the open window and the dusty scent of her discarded schoolwork. The memory of Beatrice fell like a slow but irrevocable bomb into the calm of Giovanni's mind. His eyes flew open.

7

———————————

Chapter Seven

It was difficult locating files on Beatrice Singer–– she supposed it was the same reason people didn't need the color of the sky explained to them. One could simply look up. There was not a person in the Charleston Police Department who did not know the details surrounding Beatrice Singer's disappearance. That is, besides Cassandra Wake and Benjamin Mills.

She had not enlisted Mills in this endeavor, had wanted it to stay within the bounds of her own mind. Despite the information being massively relevant to her investigation, she had noticed an invisible but unyielding barrier about the whole mess. She felt as though she needed to work her way up, the way a recently awoken child must accustom themselves to lamplight before glancing at the sun. It was not she who required this gentle handling–– the pain and discomfort apparent in her fellow officers' eyes had unintentionally hindered her efforts. It did not seem to occur to them that another woman had died, leaving behind a vacancy just as big as that of Beatrice Singer.

A muffled sneeze erupted from her unlit corner of the department's records room. The records room was a crooked, cramped cavern the shape of a lung. Ancient but undissipated cigarette smoke hung in the air overhead, and an unrelenting fly darted through the haze about her. She was not huddled away in some nondescript, forgotten corner of the building; rather, she could hear loud, cheerful voices and heavy footsteps every other minute. One might say she was hiding in plain sight, but Cassandra would vehemently deny it. There came a breathy *whoosh* as she dragged another file onto the table before her.

Her fingers skimmed over dusty, neglected reports. They were messy, having been thrown together and subsequently forgotten. There were most likely copies on the relevant officers' desks, gathering dust in those offices, too. Her eyes grasped at a half-hidden document, and she slid it out with a deft movement of her fingers.

"Missing person report," she murmured to herself, her gaze sweeping over the faded print. It had been filed at 12:03 AM on December 18th, the morning following Beatrice Singer's dreaded traffic stop. Filed by Giovanni Singer, the subject's younger brother. Processed by Sergeant Virginia Crawford.

She sat for a moment, staring at the paper. It stared back. After tilting her head in thought, she bent across the table and retrieved a thick manila folder. The missing person report was unusual, having been filed two hours after the time of the known armed conflict. Beatrice Singer had been an officer on duty. Fellow officers would have reported to the scene upon noted lack of communication–– had reported to the scene forty-five minutes after the patrol car's dashcam shut off. There came a minute shift in the air, and Cassandra glanced up to find Lieutenant Virginia Crawford leaning on a nearby table.

"I didn't hear you," she said, her eyes returning to the impenetrable mass of papers strewn across the desk.

"Paperwork will do that to you," Crawford answered. She took a seat across from Cassandra, the wood of the chair groaning beneath her. It sounded like a scream in the dull silence of the records room. Cassandra leaned forward, swiping an irritated hand at the fly that circled about her.

"You were here two months before Beatrice Singer arrived."

"I was."

"You started here at the age of twenty-three in 2014. Two months later, Singer was hired at twenty-two. In 2019, you made sergeant. Five years later––"

"I appreciate the effort you've made to get to know me, Wake. But I'm the last person who needs a lesson on the contents of my own life. I spend too much time with myself already."

"Did you know her? Beatrice Singer. Did you know her well?"

Crawford's face remained unreadable in the smoky haze. Her light brown hair gleamed in the lamplight.

"Yes. I think I did. You can never really be sure. But I think so."

"What was she like?"

"We stayed up late together on patrols. She wanted to be a detective, of course. It was easy talking with her. I think it runs in their genes–– the ability to make anything sound interesting. Even when it should be the most boring stuff you've ever heard. She would talk about flowers, about the mechanics of clocks. Sometimes, if I got lucky, she'd recount one of her dreams."

"They were interesting?"

"Disturbing," Crawford recalled with a breathy laugh. "There was this one. This one I remember every now and then. There was a society where criminals, instead of being kept in jails or rehabilitation centers, were stranded in oceans. Somehow, they usually survived–– they adapted. Drank rain and caught fish. The punishment was that they would survive, but they could never touch land again. And in this dream, Beatrice was a prisoner. She came upon a fishing city with ports and cranes in the water. There was a worker up on land, and the worker recognized her. They had gone to school together, you know?"

Crawford lapsed into thick silence. After a moment, she began again.

"They had gone to school together. And the worker, she went down to the water, went into it with her. And then she brought her up to land. Beatrice said it was the greatest feeling ever, of acceptance and relief. That someone would brave the dictations of society to bring you out of the water. To let you sit for a while in peace."

"Are you all right, Lieutenant?"

"She said the worker was me. And that's something. But–– that's who Beatrice Singer was. She thought I was the worker, but she was. She was strong enough to brave the dictations of society to give you a moment's peace. She would do it for anyone she loved. And the truth is, she loved very easily."

"How long were you partners?"

"Oh, a few years. Things happened. Got married, had a kid. I moved to a desk, and she kept going out."

The creak of leather cut through the air as Crawford shot up. She gestured weakly at the beeper on her belt despite both knowing it had made no noise. Cassandra raised a solemn hand and watched as the older woman hurried out into the hallway. Quick footsteps retreated down some wayward staircase. Left in silence once more, Cassandra cast her eyes upon the tangled mess of aged case files.

She noticed a thin square of paper, hidden like an unwanted announcement behind a thick manila folder bound with multiple rubber bands. With slow fingers, she pried the paper free and waited for the grainy words to come into focus.

"Noise complaint?" she murmured.

The paper marked a supposed noise complaint on April 17th, 2022. Reported by a neighbor, worries that shouting might eventually turn violent. Cooper's Dell, down near the high school. Unit 13b. Anonymous caller. Two officers reported to check the livelihood and domestic situation of two women. Alex Wendel and Clara Thompson. She sat back, the dry shuffle of papers like rough breaths in the silence.

Witnesses reported Clara Thompson shouting about apparent infidelity on Wendel's part. A group of men, having crowded in the communal area, offered to give their own recollections of events. They all were visibly drunk, and their reports were not taken into evidence.

Her head swam as she stood, and her eyes burned against the cigarette smoke lingering in the air. Clara Thompson had been reported missing June 13th, 2022. Two months between. Cassandra Wake was no stranger to shame. The advantages of keeping one's past under wraps did not escape her. But the sacrifice of a life for one's momentary peace? The protection of a secrecy that meant death? They had no right. They had no right to kick the door closed in the faces of those who needed asylum the most. To abandon those who were the easiest to help. Her hand tightened so fast her knuckles cracked.

Without cleaning her mess, she scrambled for her things and fell like a bat into the hallway. The memory of cigarette smoke filled her nostrils as she sucked in a furious breath, and a strange, thick warmth filled her bones as she hurried toward the parking lot.

"You don't remember?" Cassandra asked, voice no louder than a whisper.

"It was a very eventful time in my life," Alex Wendel answered. She cleared her throat as though to dismiss Cassandra's surprise. "We were going to get married. Clara had just been promoted. She always wanted to work on the ships, you know, in the harbor. And she was getting there. It was just so busy."

"Your fiancé went missing, and you forgot to mention you'd gotten in an incredibly public screaming match two months before."

For this meeting, Alex Wendel had situated herself precariously on the edge of a wooden loveseat. The striped cushion on which she sat had frayed edges. Her fingers mercilessly twisted the loose bits of thread. She would not look up at Cassandra, who stood directly before her.

"I was worried it would make me look guilty," Wendel said. Her eyes darted up as her shoulders dropped low in defeat.

"You didn't have to worry about looking guilty. Believe me, you do. No use worrying about it anymore."

"Can you stop standing so close? I know you don't think so, but I'm innocent. I would never do that to Clara."

Cassandra stepped back, her eyes fixed on the pitiful woman.

"I could stand a mile away and you'd still feel like this."

"I don't understand why you can't just take my word for it. I told you who to look into. Those men——"

"We haven't discounted them, Miss Wendel. But we haven't discounted you, either." Cassandra took a photocopied paper from the bag at her feet. "Says here a couple neighbors heard Clara accusing you of infidelity. Did you cheat on Clara Thompson?"

"I don't know who would have said that."

"Then tell me what you were shouting about, or I'll drag you to the station and get a few of my coworkers to question you."

Alex Wendel's face flushed a splotchy red, and she raised her hands in an odd parodic plead. Her fingers twitched in the air, grasping something invisible, before she slumped back into the loveseat.

"Yes, I cheated on Clara. He was a coworker. Nothing special. I don't even talk to him anymore. It was a mistake. You can't tell me you haven't made any mistakes before."

Cassandra retrieved a battered notebook from her back pocket and opened it to a relatively unblemished page.

"Give me his name."

"I hardly remember it. Something French."

"His name," she repeated.

"I don't know. I'm sorry. Please. I swear."

"Your swearing means little to me," Cassandra said, closing the notebook. She crossed her arms and glared down at the woman.

"My report has Clara leaving Cooper's Dell the night of the noise complaint. She come back?"

Wendel massaged her temples before nodding.

"She came back the next morning. Said we could work things out. And we did. I'd made breakfast for her the day she–– the day she was taken. Things had changed, but they weren't over. We were working on it."

Cassandra felt the uneven creak of wood beneath her boots as she shifted her weight. A quiet hum sat on her tongue, caught by vague strands of thought she couldn't yet flesh out. Her gaze flashed to the nearby window, and its nearly white light burned her eyes.

"Do you remember any particular individual who witnessed your fight?"

"Just the men I mentioned before. I truly don't know their names."

"William Serk, Fred Ellison——"

"I don't know!" Wendel cried. "I didn't know their names, and your yelling them at me won't make me remember. You can't remember something you never knew. So—— if that's all."

Her voice hitched as if on a climax, unprepared for which direction the conversation would go. Without a word, Cassandra turned, crossed the room, and spilled out into the hallway. Her face burned, even hotter than the stuffy air outside. Cold palms pressed to strained eyes. A single breath hissed between clenched teeth.

After a moment, she straightened and clicked off the recording device in her pocket. The surrounding hall drained from her consciousness like paint in an unexpected summer shower. Her shoulders rolled back, and her footsteps were measured drumbeats on the concrete steps down to the parking lot.

8

Chapter Eight

Giovanni Singer's father had been an established pastor in the local Baptist seminary. His mother was the youngest daughter of his father's close childhood friend. Prior to their marriage, it was not uncommon for her to call him "Uncle Teo." The implications of this address did not escape Giovanni. Their family had been founded upon the ruins of another. Dinners were distant, like cold and necessary reunions that occurred each night. The shape and form of cautious love that Giovanni recognized emerged only during his father's weekly services.

Giovanni remembered the smooth, dark wood that smelled of smoke and lemon furniture polish. The air squeezed into his lungs, always thick with incense and sweat. It was like walking into a vat of steam. He would stick his clammy fingers under his collar and sweep at the sweat already gathered at his neck. His mother, hardly a day over twenty-four, would stride in every Wednesday and Sunday, Beatrice and Giovanni following obediently behind. With stern eyes, she would clasp Giovanni's hand in hers, daring him to tug anymore at his starched and creased outfit.

They got engaged the morning after the last funeral rites had dissipated over the grave of Beatrice's mother. His father, a small but loud man, had exhibited no shame, no hesitation in moving on. He imagined his sister as a little girl, her hand hanging loosely in their father's. She would have worn a plain black dress—— neither starched nor ironed like it later was. Their father was a careless man outside of religion. He figured sufficient precaution regarding his soul outweighed the urgency of wrinkled shirts and stained dresses. Giovanni's mother had cared for Beatrice not out of obligation but out of a fierce desire to avoid embarrassment. It would not do to have a bedraggled, unkempt stepdaughter. Not when your husband had such momentous public pursuits to dedicate himself to.

His father became unrecognizable at the pulpit. His face would crease and harden, would glow like flame in the thick incense. His voice spiraled through the wooden pews, so loud and deep that Giovanni could believe he was talking straight to God. He spent hours deep into the night hunched over a reading desk, his threadbare Bible thick with dog-eared pages and scribbled translations. Giovanni enjoyed listening to the sounds of his father working, and he would stay up with him, sitting with sleepy eyes and a blanket folded about his knees. These late nights were the only time he could truly stand his father; as soon as the sun rose, someone else had taken his place—— someone he wanted nothing to do with.

A few rare nights, perhaps fifteen nights out of ten years, his father would rise, smile at Giovanni, and produce a slim wooden case. He would unfold a plastic card table and, with thoughtful hands, assemble the chessboard and its pieces. They played until the early morning. It was in these quiet nights that Giovanni felt as though his father had finally put work aside and chosen, just for a moment, to love him more than God.

A small leather notebook always sat open on his father's lap. He would chew on the end of a cheap pen, and every half-hour-

or-so he would write something down. He had assumed it was an attempt at anticipating the coming moves, at counteracting the defeat that Giovanni would surely reign upon his opponent. It was many years after his father's death when Giovanni finally found the notebook. He had searched for it with the cautious reserve of someone unaware of searching–– of someone seeking warmth without realizing they were cold. He had tentatively flipped through the pages. They were filled with rapid, half-formed notes for the next week's sermons.

He sat at a concrete table, the stone seat hard and unyielding beneath him. A bland chessboard had been carved into the table. One usually had to bring their own pieces–– someone would undoubtedly snag a bishop or knight, and the entire game would be upended. Someone, however, had forgotten their small wooden set on the table. Giovanni held a queen in his hand, pressing the pad of his thumb into its simple crown. He closed his eyes and basked in the warmth of the dwindling afternoon.

"Mr. Singer?"

There came a gentle voice from across the table. His eyes flew open, settling upon the hesitant visage of a young boy. Henry, he remembered. Beatrice's foster brother. The boy wore a grass-stained jersey. A pair of long, rolled navy socks hugged his ankles. A dirty, sunken soccer bag hung from his right shoulder.

"Henry," he answered, smiling. "What're you doing here?"

He sat at the edge of Hampton Park. Hardly anyone milled about, as the sun was still bright overhead, and the handful of concrete tables were far from any shade-giving trees. Three notebooks lay carelessly about the table, filled with anxious lecture notes and half-formed lesson plans. Unlike his first interaction with the boy, he had no ulterior motives in seeing little Beatrice. This had been a complete accident. He glanced over the boy, allowing himself to indulge in intrigue. In the momentary silence, he could hear the wind rustling over the discarded papers.

"I walk through here after soccer camp. Saw you and figured I'd say hello."

"Just sitting here," Giovanni said, gingerly placing the queen down on a square. His palms pressed flat against the hot concrete, and he examined the thin bones of his knuckles, unwilling to let his eyes linger any longer on the boy.

"I'll sit with you," Henry said, sinking down onto the opposite bench without awaiting an answer. He seemed impossibly small behind the thick concrete table, a knee carelessly drawn up and pulled into his chest. There was a phone in his hand, and it was connected to a pair of thin white earbuds that hung around his neck. He slipped his bag from his shoulder and rummaged through its contents.

"Aren't you going anywhere? I don't want your parents to worry," Giovanni ventured.

Henry shook his head and put his bag down at his feet.

"The camp is down at the Citadel. It ended early today. They'll know I'm here. Just waiting to be picked up." He regarded Giovanni with a neutral, curious expression, and his hand sought a wayward pawn on the table.

"Could you teach me how to play?" he asked, glancing at Giovanni before looking away. For the first time, obvious anxiety tinted the boy's words. Giovanni straightened, a flash of cold heat rushing to his hands. It wouldn't do, not with his close association to the boy's foster sister. He shook his head to himself, filled with a familiar sense of embarrassment and shame. Without thinking, he moved to clear away the papers, tucking the notebooks into a bag at his feet. His fingers nimbly assembled pieces across the board. After a quiet moment, he glanced up and offered the boy a smile.

"Of course. Always."

The boy had already been exceptionally brave in asking him. It wouldn't do to get involved in Henry's life. It wouldn't do any good to contaminate anyone beyond himself. Any association with Ronald was an unfortunate stain he endeavored to tolerate. He inconspicuously examined the boy while he sat out each piece. Images flashed across his eyesight like lightning illuminating a dark horizon.

He remembered another elder child swept aside in the excitement of gaining a younger sibling. He remembered the roll of his mother's eyes, the nonchalant gesture of a woman dismissing his sister's worries and interests. A public demonstration that the girl was an unnecessary and unwanted addition to the household. Pulled along like a weight scorned by those she burdened, eventually scorning herself, too.

It would not do to get involved, but he would not punish a child for mustering the bravery he could not. His fingers tightened on a pawn, and with a long breath, he emptied his mind and grinned at the table.

"Chess is about a lot of things. It's a simple battle, you know. But not really. Nothing can be forgotten or overlooked. Even a pawn has the potential to defeat a queen. You've gotta figure out all the mistakes you can make and try not to drown under them all. And you just keep choosing the right mistake..."

The low, warm murmur of conversation filled his mind, and the world stumbled to a halt.

At two-thirty in the morning, Giovanni's phone sent a blaring ring through the apartment's sleepy quiet. His roommates had not yet risen–– it didn't take them long to pull on their work clothes, to chase the sleep from their eyes and dash down the rickety stairs outside his window. He had not been asleep, had not yet managed the insurmountable task of taming his racing thoughts. Following the blaring ring, he cursed, shot up, and scrabbled for the glowing phone.

"Singer? Are you Giovanni Singer?"

"I could be the fucking President of the United States, that still doesn't give you the right to call me at two-thirty," he said. He felt as though he should be furious and acted accordingly. Truthfully, he was desperate to escape the empty night. There came the dismayed groans of his abruptly awoken roommates from the adjacent bedrooms. "Who's this?"

"I'm sorry–– I didn't realize how late it was. I wanted to apologize."

He recognized the quivering voice of Ronald White. The man no longer sounded accusatory or bitter. His voice was light and tentative with shame. Giovanni got out of bed and blinked furiously into the dim gloom of his room, his mind churning but registering nothing.

"Apology accepted. Is that all?"

There came a bang from his door. He crossed the room and swung it open, his palm over the phone speaker. Cody Lenniker stood glaring in the hall. He had one striped sock on, and his face was a sleepy pink.

"How about you don't get calls at two-thirty, huh? How does that sound?"

The boy was irritated out of his typical congenial humor. Giovanni nodded and glanced over his shoulder, catching the vague shapes of his other roommates racing to and fro like insects exposed by the sudden removal of a rock.

"I'm sorry," he said. "I thought my phone was silenced."

Cody gave a grunt in response and shuffled back to his room. Muttering under his breath, Giovanni closed the door and held the phone once more to his ear.

A stunned silence filtered over from the other end. "You don't even know what I'm apologizing for."

"What?"

"You said you accepted my apology. You don't know why I'm saying sorry."

"All's forgiven."

"Will you––" there came a strained breath. "Will you stop acting so careless? I acted cruelly at the park. I want to make it up to you. You asked a while ago for Kira's journals. I didn't pay much attention to who everything went to. I had a storage unit that eventually sold from lack of payment. The stuff's been moved around a bunch."

"Do you have any way to contact the new owner? I can't get into that unit without authorization," Giovanni said. "I'm not a detective. Don't have a badge or warrant to flaunt around."

"That owner died," Ronald said. "She died recently, and the latest unit is up for auction this morning. I suggest you buy it."

Giovanni paused, the phone wedged between shoulder and ear. He crossed the room to his wardrobe and pulled out a wrinkled T-shirt.

"Any other suggestions?" he asked.

"Cash. You pay upfront in cash. Unit 54. Zenith Storage in Goose Creek."

The call disconnected. Unbidden, a smile came to his lips. He glanced about but noticed nothing besides the uncomfortable chill of the early, early morning. Slowly, as though realizing his situation, he refolded the disturbed shirt and crossed the room again, standing before his bed.

After a minute, he turned and slipped into the hallway. His footsteps made no sound as he reached the counter. No one had started a new pot of coffee, and the near-empty container of instant coffee grounds had been stuffed behind powdered creamers and squished filters. He hummed and reached for the overhead cabinet, retracting a slim glass. He shuffled to the sink, filled the glass with lukewarm water, and dumped in a handful of grounds. Bracing himself against the counter, he downed the glass. He sniffed the musty apartment air. Giovanni closed his eyes and listened to the clamor of his roommates getting ready for the day.

9

Chapter Nine

Cassandra came upon Zenith Storage amid a shroud of rain and sickly artificial light. A gaunt sign peered down onto the street, its yellowish fluorescent face igniting oily puddles across the parking lot with light. Ugly, ripped letters announced the arrival of a Halloween sale, the message left untouched as the seasons changed. Electric bursts of lightning crept through the pitch outline of clouds overhead. Zenith Storage sat like a white prison beneath the roiling sky.

Zenith Storage was a cramped, one-story building made of beige cinderblocks and flimsy wire fences. The floors were pale blue concrete, pocked and pitted with irregular holes rapidly filling with rain. Whatever grass grew about the building was stale and dead, choked beneath the downpour. She glanced about, wiping at the dripping locks of hair stuck to her forehead. On each corner perched an outdated security camera wrapped in multiple layers of duct tape. They were most likely fakes meant to instill fear in any potential wrongdoers. A stream of rain splattered against the back of her jacket, and she shivered uneasily.

"Detective! I hope I didn't wake you."

Her steps came slow and measured as she neared the huddled man. He wore a threadbare rain jacket, the sort with tight shoulders and short sleeves that young men retain from adolescence. His fingers were white on the handle of a glistening umbrella. Noting her predicament, he moved forward and held it over her head.

"I'm sorry," Giovanni said. "I thought you'd bring an umbrella or something."

"Don't bother, I like the rain. Please. Stay dry."

His face tightened, and only after another nod did he retract the umbrella. Instead of returning it over his head, he closed it and held it under his elbow. After a moment, he cleared his throat and bounced on his heels. Before he could speak, she gestured for them to continue walking. They came upon an unlocked wire gate. With a grunt, she heaved, dragging the gate a foot to the left. Metal scraped against wet concrete like a hiss beneath the rain. Giovanni slipped inside, his head tilted down to avoid the surge of water falling from a gutter above him.

"Unit 54?" she questioned.

"Yes. Yeah," Giovanni said. He reached into his jacket and retrieved a plastic bag filled with fifty-dollar bills. He feebly wiped the sheen of water from the bag. Cassandra watched his eyes and the shine of rain and sweat on his forehead. He murmured something that drowned beneath the rain.

"Excuse me?"

"The office is over there. Give me a minute."

The gleam of his red jacket dissolved into the darkness like a haggard breath swallowed by the wind. Having lost him in the gloom, she turned and regarded the bleak hall of aluminum doors. Giovanni Singer had explained everything over the phone, ultimately fumbling into a nervous inquiry about her availability. Something about not wanting to die alone in a storage unit.

Scraps of plastic and debris flew down the middle of the alley, where a thin strip of wind funneled in from the gate. After a moment, she turned and leaned against the nearest unit, the sole of her boot anchored against the wall. Her shoulders scraped the wet cinderblock, and a slight overhang had the rain falling a few inches from her face. She pulled the hood from her head and listened to the ebb and flow of the night.

There came the distant crash of a door slamming shut, then the slow shuffle of shoes through stagnant water. Giovanni Singer crossed the block like a prisoner shuffling toward the gallows. His hands plunged into his pockets as though seeking nonexistent warmth. He tucked his chin deep into his chest, his reddened nose the only thing visible outside of his hood. As he reached her, he took one hand from his pocket and showed her the crumpled, now empty, plastic bag.

"They robbed me. This is why I didn't go into business. Don't they know I'm naive and destitute?"

"They know. It makes them want to rob you even more," she said, gesturing for the key he had retrieved from his other pocket. He handed the key over and nodded vaguely toward an unlit block.

"It's been a lifelong badge I wear against my will."

"What?"

"Poverty," he said absently. Neither knew very well nor cared what they were saying. "Think it gives me that academic but starved look. I've heard that's in."

Cassandra paused and raised a hand to the unit beside her. In red, flaking numbers, it read *54.* The door was made of crenulated aluminum, crumpled on the right side like the drooping curtain of an old stage production. An ancient iron lock hung from a thin handle at the crumpled end. She dropped into a squat and slotted the key into the lock. Bits of rust showered from the lock as the key turned with a crunch. She grabbed one handle, waiting as Giovanni went to the other. Simultaneously, they heaved upward. The door yawned open in a shuddering screech of metal.

"Stay behind me," she said, unclipping the Maglite from a stretched belt loop on her jeans. Stepping into the unit, Cassandra winced, the sour and stale air instantly burning her nostrils and eyes. Behind her came gagging noises. She leveled the Maglite at the nearest smattering of boxes. Air sat thick in the unit, and she felt as though the very stench weighed down her extended hand.

They stood stunned amid the junk. And junk it was. The small unit seemed to be a cavern constituted of trash and broken trinkets, like a broom closet filled to the brim with a soggy cardboard fortress. Green puddles of water gathered below some leaking boxes, and her boots scudded through them as she ventured forward. A beaded cord dangled from the ceiling and fell against her face. She pulled it once, twice. A sickly light flickered overhead.

It did little to illuminate the unit, rather casting a small yellow cone of light around Cassandra, who stood directly beneath it. It would not be easy finding any relevant documents, a frail hope she had maintained until stepping into the unit. The light had not revealed two neat cartons full of papers or journals. It merely impressed on her mind how utterly unpleasant the unit was. She pressed a hand to a nearby cardboard box, seeking to ascertain some sort of organization. Her hand sank straight through, and in the dim quiet, she heard the skitter of insects fleeing from her intrusion.

Cobwebs gathered on her fingertips as she ran them along the heaps of trash. A busted dartboard peered out like a red face beneath her Maglite, and a quick investigation revealed a plastic tub filled with old Chinese calendars. When she heaved the box back to its original position, a small trunk clattered to the floor. She fumbled with her Maglite and saw a sodden bundle of books sprawled across the wet cement.

Giovanni had the books in his hands before Cassandra could even kneel. He clenched three in his left hand, another splayed open in his right. His glasses were white and opaque with steam. Sighing irritably, he hooked the bridge of his glasses with his thumb, swiping them from his nose. He blinked blearily into the dark.

"That's odd," he said, mouth pulled tight in a strange smile. "Agamemnon. Funny."

"How so?" Cassandra questioned, pausing as she heaved a load of boxes from their precarious tower.

Rather than answer, Giovanni flipped through the pages. His attention had been caught. With a hushed voice, he read:

"The hour arrives when I speak no more riddles. Then you will be the witnesses how close I trod, how well I smelt, the train of your old guilt."

"Stop that," she said, dragging a deep breath through her nose.

"What?"

"You're creeping me out. Read something else."

Her work had revealed the sleek green lid of a long metal chest. She pressed her palm against its side and gave it a push. It hardly budged. A rusted iron lock, similar to that hanging from the unit door, kept the principal latch firmly shut. An abrupt chill ran through her. Noticing her silence, Giovanni set the books on a nearby tub and crept over.

There came rustling behind her, and she turned to find a thick-handled hammer in Giovanni's hand. He gestured for her to move and, lining the hammerhead with the latch, brought the hammer down in a quick, heavy arc. It flashed against the latch with a spurt of sparks. He drew his arm back and hit the latch once more, coughing as a plume of rust and green paint flakes burst upward as the latch clattered to the concrete. He stepped back, his shoulder touching hers. The hammer remained clenched in his hand.

Neither spoke. A cruel wind groaned against the ceiling overhead, and for a moment she imagined countless phantasms outside, whimpering to come in from the rain. She knelt, dried her hands against the denim of her jeans, and gently lifted the lid. It opened like an old tomb, moaning sour, sacred airs into the unit. She reached over, only releasing the lid when it clicked against the cinderblocks behind it. She peered down, glancing into the abyssal eye sockets of a skull.

A great dread burned within her as she held the skull's gaze. She rose and stepped back, chest heaving. They both stood as though watching a body lowered into the ground at a funeral, polite but distant, frozen to the slick concrete beneath them. To her right, Giovanni laughed.

"Please be quiet," she said, narrowing her eyes against the sour stench of rot.

"Detective," Giovanni said, his young face torn in a distraught smile. "Detective. Look." A pale finger indicated the fathomless depth to the left of the skull within the trunk. Placed neatly beside the bleached bone was a Polaroid. She dropped to her knees and leaned forward. It depicted the haggard face of a young woman, younger than Cassandra herself. A dark brown pixie cut. Tanner than either Kira's Polaroid or Clara Thompson's family pictures. Her eyes moved to the jagged sentence penned on the Polaroid's white border. It read:

Una Boland, October 2021.

Subtly, hardly distinguishable from the rot filling the unit, arose the faint scent of vinegar. Cassandra stood, grabbed Giovanni by the wrist, and strode from the unit. In an instant, a phone was at her ear. The rain had slowed to a frail drizzle, and the dissipating steam slipped softly into her heaving lungs. As she spat brusque instructions into her phone receiver, she watched Giovanni Singer slump against the cinderblock wall. The hammer fell from his fingers. Her legs like lines of lead, she trudged over beside him and sat down. They awaited the arrival of distant sirens, the shrill, mechanical screams already audible in the dissolving quiet.

Thirty minutes later, five rain-swept patrol cars sat outside Zenith Storage. Their flashing blue-red lights steamed beneath the wide moon. Cassandra stood outside the office from which Giovanni Singer had initially purchased the unit key. Its windows were crisscrossed with broken glass panes that gleamed with a yellowish light. Ancient newspapers had been pasted to some panes. Ink smudges blurred where headlines had melted from paper to glass. The building manager, a bristly old man, had printed out a copy of the transactions regarding Unit 54 and its maintenance. Folding the paper into thirds, she slipped it into the inside pocket of her jacket and continued toward the smattering of cars.

Walking between the lit gate of Zenith Storage and the patrol lights, she sank into the darkness with a heavy breath. She raised a hand to her face and pinched her nose between thumb and index finger. The sour smell of vinegar clung to her like burrs to a sleeve. She figured that was better than the stink of death that seemed to permeate the entire block. That thought provided her little consolation.

The rain had stopped, and with it, a great wave of thick heat had dropped like a black cloud over them all. Her hair, previously wet with rain and mist, now clung to her forehead with the sweet, warm smell of sweat. Her breath softened as the stench of vinegar abated, the air cooling in the damp darkness. The sound of strained voices came from behind the nearest patrol car.

"What were you doing here?" came a sharp accusation.

"Thought I might find some interesting antiques," came Giovanni Singer's tired but humorous response.

"Yeah. Yes. Thought a body would go well with your old books?"

"That's cruel," Giovanni answered stiffly.

"I'll be nice when you tell the truth."

Cassandra shuffled through the voices she knew like a man frantically searching for the right card in a deck. The answer did not come.

"I won't be telling you anything if you keep speaking to me like that," he said.

"Giovanni," the voice began. "Why are you here?"

"I was here to buy a storage unit. There was a body in it. You're welcome, actually."

"Detective Wake reported that it was you who found out about this storage unit. That correct?"

"I didn't find anything out. I heard things. They weren't correct things, mind you."

"Don't you know how suspicious you look? Please, just think. How guilty you look."

"I'll concern myself with how suspicious I look," Giovanni spluttered. "As for you, that's none of your business."

"It is. It is," they repeated, "when I'm a high-ranking officer in the police department that deals with these homicides. It is."

Cassandra took a few paces back and pulled the paper from her pocket. Unfolding it, she emerged from the darkness a ways out, her head bent as though in thought. Her boots passed through the brackish puddles that marred her path, and she glanced up to find two pale faces watching her apprehensively.

"Good morning, Lieutenant Crawford. Singer."

Crawford's eyes snagged on the paper in Cassandra's hand.

"Got the payment transactions?"

"Yes, well." Cassandra settled on the heels of her boots, breathing in the warm night. "Yes, I did. Seventy-five dollars a month charged to a prepaid card. Can't trace any accounts." Noting Giovanni Singer's obvious interest, Cassandra beckoned for the lieutenant to come closer. Together, they turned their backs to the patrol car's open door, in which Giovanni Singer had reluctantly settled.

"They were required to put down a name and birthdate for the unit, though."

"Well?"

"Fred Norris Ellison. A former inhabitant of Cooper's Dell around the time of Clara Thompson's abduction."

Lieutenant Crawford peered down into her face.

"What's wrong?" she asked, her voice low.

"Fred Ellison has been dead for almost a year. Not some mysterious drowning, not some explosion where his body couldn't be recovered. He died of pancreatic cancer on August 5th. Not even two months after Clara Thompson went missing."

The lieutenant straightened, and Cassandra knew her eyes lay on the distant gate of Zenith Storage.

"Someone's been using his name as some sort of moniker."

"They knew we'd find this unit. Knew we'd figure out who supposedly paid the bill every month. But they did it anyway."

"They did it anyway," Crawford agreed, rubbing her hands together and stepping forward. "We've got Heyward and Mills dealing with the cameras. Isn't much hope since it was so long ago. These sorts of cameras delete footage for storage after a set amount of time."

Cassandra raised a hand in a polite wave. She turned and met the curious gaze of Giovanni Singer. He still sat in the open backseat of the patrol car, his rain jacket hanging from the seat like a mechanic's oily rag. He waited for her to draw closer before he spoke.

"Agamemnon. I said it was funny. Do you know why, Detective?"

Something hard and cold reared up inside her when he spoke. Her hand curled into an icy fist in her pocket. He represented to her all the incomplete, minute-but-infinitely significant details everyone seemed to know but her. He addressed her with the arrogant but nervous manner which transformed conversations into minefields. His nervousness seemed not to originate from the content of his words but from the fact that he had to speak to someone corporeal, someone alive and able to actually listen. He spoke with the ubiquitous fear that someone would hear.

"What, Singer?"

"It follows Agamemnon and his murder by his wife Clytemnestra. Having just returned from the Trojan War, Agamemnon arrives with Cassandra, the prophesying daughter of Priam. Thought it was an interesting coincidence."

"It is," she said, her mind elsewhere.

"But there was–– there was another book. A collection of short stories by Nathaniel Hawthorne. You know, he had this one about a garden and a daughter. Rappaccini's Daughter. Do you know that one?"

"No, I don't think so."

"I read it in undergrad. There was a man, a curious inhabitant of the room overlooking a garden. Giovanni. Then a garden and a girl who took care of all the strange plants within it. Beatrice. I thought that was funny. Thought it was convenient."

She believed him, having already recorded and archived the books visible thus far within the unit. A team was currently stationed in the unit, removing, examining, and filing every bit of trash and every collection of junk bottled up around the body of Una Boland.

"And can that really just be a coincidence? Two insane accidents? I won't lie to myself to remain unafraid."

She turned and looked across the parking lot. A hand dashed up to swipe at a trail of sweat sliding down her temple.

"Ronald White told you about the unit?" she asked.

"Yes."

"He doesn't trust police officers. I've read his past interviews. He blames us for his stroke. I've tried twice to hold a peaceful conversation with him."

"And?" Giovanni said, his eyes on the rain-darkened concrete.

"Figure out how he knew about the unit. Maybe he can make you lunch."

Giovanni did not reply, and she began without a word back to the crooked gate. She gestured to the emerging figure of Benjamin Mills. His face appeared impossibly young in the draining lights, and his uniform gleamed in contrast to the myriad of aged, darkened shirts and safety vests that surrounded him. She pointed a thumb back over her shoulder.

"Take Singer back to his apartment. It's above that bread bakery right next to the College of Charleston. Good morning, Mills."

"I'll hope for a better night. Stay safe, Wake."

10

Chapter Ten

G iovanni Singer did not like to rush into things–– in fact, any action completed without sufficient forethought seemed to ruin his whole week. As evidenced by yesterday's events. And the entirety of the prior month. Despite this habit, he did not sit outside Ronald White's house for very long. He had started his car–– a groaning, ancient thing–– right after his last meeting finished with a rather talkative undergraduate stuck in summer school. He had driven in silence, his face like ice in the impossibly thick heat.

The aluminum stairs wheezed under his heavy steps. A hollow knock sounded as his fist pounded the door, and its noise sent a dense pit of dread into Giovanni's stomach.

"Who is it?" came a cautious voice.

"Open the door, Ronald," Giovanni answered. A chilled hostility sat dormant within his words, and as though to reinforce his seriousness, Giovanni gave another hurried knock. "It's your daughter's long-lost brother."

The door swung open. Ronald stood in the doorway, a plastic cane clasped in his hand. His bulging face twisted in a strange show of pain. A pale, veiny hand hung in the air, caught between a gesture of welcome and dismay.

"Don't you say that, Singer."

Giovanni stepped back, observing the older man's state of panic. The hand hung between them. After a moment, he gently pressed it down and smiled up at Ronald.

"We need to talk. Sit."

He swept past Ronald and cast a cursory glance about the living room. There remained the grim solitude, the disturbing lack of life that welled from the dank crevices of his house. Heavy, cold air settled across every surface, and Giovanni felt his shoulders tense against a rising shiver. He eyed the graying, pouchy couch he had sat on during their first meeting, reluctant to sit and become part of the lifeless house. He felt Ronald's eyes upon him and, tensing his jaw, sat on the couch, crossing one leg over the other.

"How did it go?" Ronald ventured. He had closed the door but would not step further into the room.

"How did what go, Ronald?"

"The journals. Did you find the journals? Did you find what you were looking for?"

"Who told you Kira Rushton's things would be in Zenith Storage?" Giovanni asked. His eyes were on the far wall, narrowed as though looking at the sun. Truthfully, he felt as though somehow the house would seep into him, would imbue him with whatever clung so dreadfully to Ronald White. Unacknowledged within his own mind, Giovanni feared he had already long possessed the same disconcerting lifelessness.

Uncomfortable with the silence, Ronald crossed the living room. However, instead of sitting in the recliner adjacent to the couch, he shuffled to the dusty kitchen table. A lopsided ceramic bowl, gleaming with a dull pink sheen, sat in the absolute center of the table. It contained old receipts and creased power washing advertisements, the sort of mail one never uses but forgets to throw away.

Ronald stood, examining the bowl, before grasping it gingerly in one hand. His gaze pinned to the bowl, he slowly made his way to the recliner. With a muffled grunt, he fell back. The recliner's cushion choked out a gasp of air as his weight sank down.

He noticed Giovanni's eyes upon the bowl, and he offered him a wry grin.

"Kira made this. No one ever expects a drunk to have hobbies besides drinking. But she loved making things with her hands. Knitting, baking, ceramics. People want to define Kira by the worst thing she ever did. But that's not how we usually see other people. We're lucky enough to have our worst deeds kept in the dark, revealed only when we choose."

Giovanni acknowledged the blatant avoidance of his question with a toss of his head. There was a queer pleasantness in Ronald's words, as though he were teasing Giovanni. It wasn't a cruel jibe or a challenge to disagree. The older man wanted to talk, and for some reason, he wanted Giovanni Singer to listen.

"I know it's silly–– you have no obligation to be nice to me. I just... when you love someone, you want to protect them. Not just from bad people, but from the judgement of good people. Even if they deserve it. Kira might have done horrible things, but she wasn't a horrible person. Have there never been bigots who donated to charity? Or killers who comforted upset children?"

Giovanni frowned, and his eyes gleamed in stern reprimand. They were the brightest lights in the room. He leaned forward, sharp words ready on his tongue.

"And when the saint murders someone you love, I expect to see you defending his moral rectitude."

At these words, Ronald sank back into his recliner.

"You think Kira is wrongly remembered for her worst decision. You think this is because unfair media representation, something like that? The truth is, she could have saved a thousand children from starvation. She could have built palaces for the homeless and produced medicine for the dying. But I don't care. I don't care who she was or why she was like that. She killed my sister. That is the beginning and end of my interest."

"Well," Ronald began, swallowing down his initial words. He glanced at Giovanni and gained some resolve. "That's obviously not true. You asked to see Beatrice. No matter what you want to believe, Beatrice is Kira's daughter. As long as you want to be in Beatrice's life, you have interest in Kira."

"I won't see her again," Giovanni said. He glared at Ronald, daring him to question the statement. He longed to see the girl for some unspoken, unexamined reason. She made some silly, foreign hope rise within his chest, as though a mere conversation with her would give him the answers he'd striven so long to uncover. But she was a four-year-old child. And his beloved sister was five years in the ground.

Recognizing something in Giovanni's expression, the older man nodded and tipped the bowl's contents into his lap. His crooked fingers sifted through the bits of newspapers and brochures before finally lifting a creased, yellowed envelope. It had been torn open long ago, and the enclosed letter fell into his palm after a gentle shake.

"The night after you visited me, I got this letter in the mail. I thought they had the wrong address. But there is no address–– no return address or destination."

"Someone dropped it off," Giovanni said, his eyes on the letter.

"Like the letter tied to my daughter. Like the Polaroid given to you of Kira."

"How do you know about that?"

Ronald struggled to sit up, a few of the newspaper clippings falling to the floor.

"After you told that detective of yours, the police station contacted me again. Said they had proof that Kira might still be alive. It wasn't that difficult to figure out who the *anonymous recipient* was."

He grimaced and, squeezing the letter between the tips of two fingers, held it out for Giovanni to take. It was smooth and fragile in his hands, written on clean, weighty paper. It read:

Kira is alive. If you wish to see her again, buy Unit 54 at Zenith Storage in Goose Creek, South Carolina. Notify no one.

"You know," Giovanni began after a period of silence. "I don't think this letter has anything about *me* doing any of that."

"Singer, please--"

"And it doesn't give you a hint about what's in the unit. What if someone just wanted to kill you? What if someone just wanted to kill you, and I walked in? And money." He scoffed, his face contorted in an odd mixture of regret and pained humor. "I'm a full-time student living in Charleston. You won't need to send me to my death in some creepy storage unit. I won't be eating for a month, anyway."

There came a pained noise from Ronald White. He abruptly rose-- as abruptly as one such as Ronald White could rise-- and began again to the kitchen. Bits of paper and advertisements fluttered to the floor. A familiar gleam of film caught Giovanni's eye.

"I don't want you to die, Singer. Please. I was cruel. That's why I called to apologize. It didn't even occur to me that someone could be trapping me–– trying to hurt me. I never would have sent you there. Please."

"What are you doing, Ronald?" Giovanni asked. The older man fumbled about the kitchen, opening drawers and closing them again with agitated sighs. There came the clatter of a plate on granite tabletop, the quiet clink of silverware being rummaged through. A refrigerator door opened, and the yellow lightbulb cast a sallow light over Ronald's face. Light caught the sweat on his skin and the look of animalistic fear bright in his eyes.

"The least I can do. Let me. I shouldn't have told you about the unit. I didn't think anything through." He had gathered the components for a sandwich and was smearing some mayonnaise across a flattened heel of bread. As though struck with a chilling thought, the older man paused and looked over his shoulder.

"And what was there? I–– I told you the journals were there so you would go. That's what you were looking for when you first visited."

Giovanni knelt on the ground, his hands carding through the discarded papers. A flimsy slip of film hung loosely from his fingers. Ronald's words washed over him like water across impermeable stone. His eyes flicked up as Ronald repeated the question in a louder voice.

"A dead girl, Ronald. There was a dead girl in Unit 54. Her name was Una Boland. You told me a woman had died recently, and that's why the unit was going up. Do you wanna bet they're the same woman?"

"A dead girl?" came a dull reply.

"Yes," Giovanni murmured vacantly. His eyes were fixed on the Polaroid in his hand. "The thing is–– I looked her up. Una Boland was missing. Not dead. But you knew she was dead, somehow. Or if you guessed, that's a pretty good guess. I need you to tell me the whole truth. Or I'll call the police the second I step outside."

He felt Ronald's eyes on him, and as though answering the unspoken question, he flipped the Polaroid over and displayed it for the older man to see. It was a Polaroid identical to the one he had received in the mail. Kira Rushton's fiery hair hung limp about a milk-white face. A little girl–– Beatrice, his mind flared–– sat with a gentle smile on the woman's lap. It fell from his fingers and settled again on the floor. His hand remained frozen in the air, intent but unable to grasp further.

There was the distant thud of a plate being set on the table, then the creak of old bones as Ronald shuffled over. He lowered himself to the floor beside Giovanni before retrieving a separate square of film.

"That's why I was talking about worst moments. About Kira's worst acts. Because she didn't kill Beatrice Singer. She didn't kill your sister."

He held another Polaroid between his fingers. Giovanni saw the obscured profile of a woman lying atop a mattress. The fringe of her dark brown hair spilled through neatly wrapped bandages that covered her face and neck. She wore a blue hospital gown. Her elbows were thin, white sticks that jutted sharply out of the gown's wide sleeves. Beneath the image, scribbled in similar handwriting to the letter, were the words:

Beatrice Singer, December 20th, 2017

Sunlight filtered through a gauzy blue curtain, and shadows shimmered across the floor as though seen through a lens of water. Half the room sat in placid darkness, the sort that falls naturally through the phases of an uneventful day. Miriam Boland, her face like that of an angular bird, had not spoken for over two minutes. Cassandra uncrossed her legs and rose. Across the room lay a long, low table made of gleaming wood. She drew near, noting the faint scent of citrus furniture polish. A collection of cameras sat on the table, recently dusted and cleaned.

She first recognized a small Nikon SP, its chrome face blinking and winking in the light. She turned, hands tucked into her jean pockets, and glanced once more at the solemn woman caught in thought.

"Do you use these? They're incredibly well-cared for."

At the woman's blank stare, Cassandra gestured to the row of cameras.

"Seems like you're proud of them. With them up front and all."

"They were my daughter's cameras," Miriam Boland answered. "We gave her one for Christmas every year."

"Yes, she was interested in photography. I remember. She was visiting her grandparents in Tallahassee."

"It was a seven-hour drive straight through," Miriam said, nodding. "Una left two days early so she could photograph some spots around St. John's River. And she never showed up."

Bright, polished wood creaked under her boots as she crept along the table, examining each camera.

"Do you know what camera she took to Tallahassee? One of these?"

"They didn't find it," Miriam said. "It was the one we got for her eleventh birthday. An Olympus Trip 35. It had a strap–– one of those straps for the camera to hang around your neck. It was orange. Had Clemson pawprints on it."

"She was twenty-two. Just graduated?"

"Yes. The summer right after she got out of school."

Cassandra rounded the couch and sat again, directly facing the older woman. She sighed and leaned forward.

"The trip was rather abrupt, I hear."

"She had been planning on doing something like it for months," Miriam said.

"She left in the middle of the night."

"That's just who Una was," came a level response.

"Your neighbors recalled a slammed door waking them up at three o'clock in the morning. Heard your raised voice."

"I was there, Detective. I was there. You don't have to recount everything." Miriam's voice came strained but monotone, as though she lacked the energy to articulate her frustration. "We had an argument, and she left. And there's not a day that goes by that I don't regret it. We had problems, but everyone does. No one said life was easy."

"What was your fight about?"

Miriam scoffed and fell silent. Her eyes flashed to Cassandra before falling to her lap, pinned on her twisting hands.

"Was that a funny question, Mrs. Boland?"

"Of course it wasn't. There were a few fights. Fights about different things. None which seem important now that she's gone."

"How would you describe your family dynamic?" Cassandra asked.

The two women sat in stubborn silence. Cassandra's eyes rested on Miriam's face, watching a restless dismay surface once more in the twitch of her mouth, the flush of her tan skin. She crossed her legs, gaining the older woman's attention.

"My husband died earlier that year. Three months before Una left for Florida. And no one prepares you for things like that. No one prepares you for things beyond imagination. But it happened. Neither Una nor I acted right. I wasn't kind to her when she needed it. So she left for my parents' place. I was going to apologize when she got back."

Cassandra glanced about and was struck by the sheer lifelessness around her. The white-slatted walls sloped inward like pale sunken cheeks. The house was clean, impossibly clean, the sort of impersonal sterility that characterizes displays at furniture and household goods stores. A distant clock ticked, its gentle but persistent murmur like a singular voice in the silence. The air was heavy and humid, and the house sat silent beneath the weight of a million unspoken apologies. The remnants of raised voices had sunk into the foundation like pitch mold. A breeze played with the distant curtains, and as the wind rose, the house seemed to gasp forth a dying breath.

"I'm sorry," Cassandra murmured, unable to look away from the woman's grief. "I'm sorry for your losses."

Miriam nodded. She glanced around the house as though noticing it for the first time.

"I clean so that everything is presentable. I eat so that I can get around. But when I'm done–– who am I presenting for? Who am I walking around for, anymore? I can't apologize to anyone. I can't read over Una's essays or sit with my husband on the balcony. No one I love can come back home."

11

Chapter Eleven

It was eleven o'clock in the morning, and Hampton Park glittered beneath a bright blue sky. Giovanni Singer sat at a cobweb-dusted picnic table, the wood beneath him still wet with morning dew. Papers lay scattered across the table. Random books dug from the depths of his bag acted as paperweights. His thoughts had grown too loud and insistent for the bleak walls of his office. He breathed in the dewy warmth of the surrounding shade. He glanced over to the far end of the table. Henry sat with a knee drawn up to his chest, his face pressed alarmingly close to an open book.

The boy had appeared rather abruptly, waving away every question Giovanni put forth. His face burned a bright red, and his eyes, when Giovanni caught them, shone clear and watery. Giovanni reached across the table for a particular paper and cleared his throat.

"Reading that close gives you headaches," he said.

"I can't read any other way," came the brusque response.

"Your guardians can't afford glasses for you? Don't they get stipends?"

Rather than answer, Henry closed the book and looked directly at the man across the table. He sniffed and rolled his shoulders back.

"It's the shade. Just a little dark."

Giovanni arranged his papers, not looking over. His glasses slipped down his nose, and with a quick hand he pushed them back up.

"We can move somewhere, if you'd like."

"No, I don't want to read, anyway."

He shifted on the bench, spreading the papers about. The boy's obvious distress upset him, made his thoughts wander from the earmarked copy of Nicomachean Ethics balanced precariously between his knee and the edge of the table. He fumbled for a pen. With his left hand, he scribbled a series of citations on a notepad. With his right, he flipped between pages.

"What are you reading?" Henry said.

"Nicomachean Ethics. It's by Aristotle."

After a moment of silence, Giovanni glanced up to see Henry's gaze still fixed on him. He straightened, his shoulders aching, and let the book hang open on his thigh.

"What makes for a good life?" he asked, watching Henry expectantly.

"What?"

"What makes for a good life? When you're old and looking back on life, would you think your life was good or bad? And what makes it so?"

"I'm not sure," Henry said, his face drawn tight in confusion.

"No one is, Henry. But Aristotle thought it was human flourishing, a thing called *eudaimonia*. Finding out what someone is good at and doing it. One also has to be virtuous, which consists of finding the mean between two extremes."

"Extremes?"

"Vices. If someone runs a race and they go too slow, they'll get in last place. If someone runs too fast, they'll get tired too quickly and hurt themselves. You've got to find the right pace to go at it. Aristotle thought you could be too brave and too generous. Too much of a good thing. But you could also be cowardly and stingy, so you gotta find the middle spot."

"How do you become good, though?" Henry asked, voice low as though he were discussing a secret. His face was bright again, his eyes hard and focused on the table.

"You practice. Fake it till you make it. You do virtuous things until you become virtuous. Aristotle called it habituation. It helps if someone teaches you to find the means. No one has to do it alone."

"What if—— what if someone isn't really bad, but they do bad things? The habituation thing. Can they still be good?"

Giovanni's hands were cold on the table, and he absently rubbed them against his trousers.

"Why are they doing something bad?"

"I don't know," Henry said, shrugging weakly.

"Well, if they're aware that the thing they're doing is bad and they do it anyway, according to Aristotle, they are not virtuous. They are not flourishing."

"And according to you?"

"What, Henry?"

"According to you, are they bad?"

"I don't think you can label someone as fully good or fully bad. Not really. They can do bad things. But then one must ask if they truly understand what it means to be good or bad. Augustine thought no one truly desired evil. They had a spoiled understanding of the good."

"What about Beatrice's mother?"

The question caught Giovanni like a blow to the stomach. His eyes widened, and his lungs quivered, jolted from their rhythm. Beneath the table, his sneaker jerked forward, scraping against a small pile of dirt and pine straw.

"You shouldn't know about that."

"But I do," Henry said, eyeing Giovanni. "Do you think she's a bad person?"

Giovanni sat hunched against the table, looking over at the young boy. He swallowed and clicked his pen.

"No, I don't," he said. "I think she did something terrible. But is she evil? Is she morally irredeemable? I think we call people evil so we don't have to try and understand them." He straightened, and his face tightened into a scowl. "But should she be punished? Without a doubt."

"Without a doubt?" came a hoarse voice from behind him. He whirled about, pen clenched in his left hand like a wooden stake. His eyes fell upon the hunched figure of Ronald White, plastic cane gripped in his white-ringed fingers. A plastic bag filled with paper towels and food items hung from his wrist. "I thought you doubted everything, Singer."

Giovanni cleared his throat and dragged a hand down his face.

"Except I shall see in his hands the print of the nails, and put my finger into the print of the nails, and thrust my hand into his side—"

"I will not believe," Ronald said, his gaze distant but still fixed on Giovanni's face.

The older man paused and released a grunting laugh. Settling on the bench beside Giovanni, he put the plastic bag over the strewn papers.

"You best be leaving here," Ronald said. Giovanni glanced up, finding the words directed at Henry rather than himself. "Your parents are probably missing you."

"He's a child," Giovanni said, his voice sharp with outrage. "You can't just chase him off like a stray dog."

"It's all right, Mr. Singer," Henry said, rising. "My mom's here. Thank you. For the lesson and everything else."

Giovanni raised a hand in a weak gesture of 'goodbye,' his eyes following the boy until he walked out of sight, obscured by a line of dense bushes. He rolled his shoulders back and turned to Ronald. The older man gestured for him to open the plastic bag. Upon doing so, Giovanni found three containers of Indian take-out. He opened all three cartons and put them before Ronald.

"You sounded like a true academic just now," he said.

"What? That Doubting Thomas stuff?"

"Yeah."

"It's the only book I've read in full," Ronald said, grinning.

"Sometimes you make me want to throw up."

"You wouldn't have anything to throw up. Eat." A jab of the plastic fork clenched in Ronald's hand punctuated the order. Giovanni pulled the closest carton to him and retrieved an identical fork from the bag. Rather than eat, he twirled the fork in his fingers, glancing up at the sky.

"Do you believe, then?"

"In God?" Ronald questioned, mouth full.

Giovanni nodded. He closed his eyes and felt the humid warmth against his skin.

"What else can I believe in?"

"What else?" Giovanni repeated. "There are thousands of religions. Thousands of philosophies. Even then, you don't have to believe anything."

"I don't think those religions or philosophies hold a candle to God."

"Why not?"

"I just don't," Ronald said. "God reminds me that there is a purpose to all I've lost. To all you've lost. If you're looking to pick a fight, let's look back on the conversation I walked in on. You quoted Augustine. I've been reading the things you mention, sometimes. And I remember him being pretty holy."

"It's not the holiness I'm interested in."

"You search in all these writings for answers. For understanding. I think you want to believe in mercy, but the world has made it impossible. You want to forgive Kira, but you've hated her too long. You don't think God would understand you?"

Giovanni opened his eyes and glared across the table.

"I could agree with you on the veracity of the moon landing, but that doesn't mean I understand you."

"Don't understand me, then. Just eat."

They settled into tense silence. Giovanni found himself restless and febrile, irritated by the familiar ease with which he conversed with Ronald White. He disliked the man, disliked his incessant need to assert Kira Rushton's value and worth. He longed to see Henry again, to examine his own conscience without the contaminating presence of one so closely tied to his loss. With a breathy snort, he plunged the fork into the opened carton and scooped some rice into his mouth.

Cassandra despised the thick cinderblock walls of the Charleston Police Department. The floors had no give, and any indicative noise came from the heavy boots of her coworkers. The air hung dense and warm despite the countless constantly running AC units installed overhead. Distant laughter echoed off the pale walls. If one sought its source, they would find empty rooms and empty chairs. A hastily vacated home. The station reminded her of a tightly grasped lung trying to expand, or covered eyes straining to peer through thick black cloth. Reaching for something and realizing one's fist cannot unfurl.

Many times over the week, she would inevitably suck in a harsh gulp of air, having forgotten to breathe or blink. A queer restlessness began in her shoulders, threading down through the lean muscles of her back and triceps. The long, cramped hallways always incited unnecessary suspicion within her. Her gaze constantly flew over her shoulder, as though she had heard the rush of quick footsteps or the inhalation of a muffled breath. She clung to the steady rhythm of her heartbeat and tried to ignore the rest.

To her right, directly behind the closed door of her office, came distant voices. Her steps faltered. She straightened her spine and pushed the door open. Two ruddy faces glanced up from the darkness. Neither had bothered to turn on the overhead light.

"Zeigler," she said, nodding to the officer seated in her chair. A tall, pale man stood behind him. She smiled at him, ignoring the hard, unwelcoming lines of his face.

"I hope you found my office comfortable enough for your meeting."

"It's pretty big," Zeigler said, staring at her. He gestured to the walls like a contractor surveying a lackluster plot of land. "Don't know what you need all this room for."

Cassandra grinned, huffing out a strained laugh. She examined the papers and files on her desk. From what she could remember, there were no discrepancies. Nothing had been moved. Zeigler cleared his throat and, with a dramatic lethargy, dropped a file onto the table. It landed with a hollow *thwap*. Her neatly organized papers fluttered to the ground. Rather than gesture to the introduced file, Zeigler made a sweeping motion at the officer beside him.

"Do you know who this is, Wake?"

She glanced at his face. He had a thin, unhealthy visage and bitter eyes. She cleared her throat and rocked forward on her toes.

"Nope."

"He's on vacation from Columbus. He wanted to stop in Myrtle Beach, but I convinced him to stop here in old Charleston. Thought it would do you good to see someone from your hometown."

"I was born in Viscri, Romania."

"Raised in Ohio," Zeigler said.

"Marietta," she returned sharply.

"Ah, well. I was born in Greenville, but Charleston is my home. You'll learn."

"If you're here to discuss my childhood, I must insist we both have more pressing issues at hand."

"Funnily enough, I don't want to talk about your childhood. You were an adult when you first became an officer in Marietta, correct?"

Cassandra nodded. The door had crept shut behind her, unlocked but unwilling to let in any light or fresh air. Her fingers tightened into fists at her side.

"I just want to get to know you," Zeigler said. He drummed lightly on the edge of her desk. "You haven't been very forthcoming. You can hardly blame me for looking in other directions."

At her extended silence, he flipped open the file and began to read aloud. The cadence of his voice, as well as the constant looks he gave to her ashen face, indicated that he was not truly reading. He had most likely memorized the information already. Had read it many times before.

"Over the course of fifteen months, your uncle made eight welfare checks on your apartment. With the first, they discovered you had changed addresses without telling him. Just up and left. Didn't say goodbye or anything."

"I know what happened. There's no point to this," she said.

"You just kept disappearing. Apparently, it drove him crazy. Gave him an arrhythmia. When the police showed up for the eighth welfare check, they found him dead. Sitting in his chair. Waiting for news of you."

"He didn't die of the arrhythmia, you asshole. He had cancer. I visited him every day. His treatment left him confused. I told the officers about the situation."

Zeigler rose, enormous and hunched in the dim office.

"You don't like it when someone goes and digs up your past. It stings, doesn't it?"

"This is different," she said.

"I don't think so. It's not different at all. You need to back the hell off. Let us handle this case. We can't work with you. Not on this. Everyday feels like how you just felt. And I won't have it."

"What would you have me do?"

"Drop the case. Say you're sick. I don't give a shit. Just get out of my way."

The door swung open behind her, and bright, sterile light flooded the office. She whirled around to find Mills frozen in the doorway.

"I-- uh. I thought we were headed to the Coroner's Office," he said.

Her bag and wallet were somewhere behind the desk, obscured by Zeigler's bent form. They would have to stay there. She waved a dismissive hand at Mills, grabbed his wrist, and strode out of the office. Her grip on his wrist did not lessen even as they spilled out into the parking lot.

"What was that?" Mills said, looking back as though he could still see Zeigler and the officer hidden somewhere in the darkness. "What the hell was that?"

"Nothing that concerns you," she said. Hurt bloomed across his face, and she shook her head, slipping into the passenger's seat. She examined the Impala's interior, intent upon calming the frantic beat of her heart. After a moment, she forced her mouth open and spoke.

"Thank you," she said. "Thank you."

"For what?"

She remained quiet, and after a while, Mills directed the Impala forward and out of the parking lot.

The Charleston County Coroner's Office was a squat, homely cottage nestled at the end of a long driveway. A flat pool of gravel constituted the parking lot, a lot populated by two lonely cars parked in nonexistent spots. Cassandra and Mills had wandered in and waited ten minutes for an assistant to appear behind the vacant front desk. They now sat on a narrow wooden bench, almost like an old church pew, that stretched along the entire hallway.

"The Alexandrians first dissected the deceased around 300 BCE. I mean, those weren't autopsies, though. True autopsies began in the Renaissance. But it wasn't a linear process. Tons of cultures had problems with messing with bodies after death. You could get executed for desecrating a corpse. I mean, remember the Legion guy? Thousands of demons inside of him. He lived in the tombs. Big problem with that."

Mills, his eyes bright with excitement, moved restlessly at Cassandra's side. The young officer, usually exhibiting a reined in, polite enthusiasm, spoke quickly into her ear. The hallway was surprisingly long, with floors of warm, dark wood and walls of deep green. The entire building seemed intent upon maintaining a welcoming appearance, as though the office were aware of most visitors' intentions and was trying to comfort them. Cassandra looked up, her gaze fixed on the opposite wall.

"I didn't know autopsies were such an area of interest for you," she said. "Why not work on a forensics team?"
Mills offered her a crooked smile. "Don't have the stomach for it."

"I'm not sure being a police officer was the best second choice, then," came a voice from behind them. A door had opened, and within it, outlined against white, sterile light, stood a woman. She came forward into the hallway and gestured for them to stand.

"You're Detective Wake, I presume. I got your message about Una Boland's autopsy. Please come in."

She stepped back, and Cassandra motioned for Mills to go first. The room was so clean it seemed dipped in white. Bleak cinderblock walls encased a wide room lit harshly by unceasing fluorescent fixtures. Six tables sat at equal intervals in the center of the room. At the far wall, someone had installed a slew of slim mortuary cabinets. They were all locked, clasped tightly shut against the external world.

"Doctor Lanning," she introduced herself. She was a tall, slim woman, with bright golden hair gathered in a knot at the base of her skull. Noting their interest in the laboratory, she cleared her throat and nodded at a nearby door. They filtered in to find an office decorated in warm green colors, not unlike the hallway they had just come from.

They engaged in quiet, halting small talk, Mills intermittently casting curious peeks over his shoulder at the laboratory. Cassandra straightened in her chair, the loud wooden creak snapping his eyes back to the woman across the table.

"You already knew the dental records matched. Boland worked at a daycare center for a few years as a teenager. She had to get fingerprints taken before being hired–– they also matched."

"I'm sure an ID on the body helps, too," Mills ventured, an attempt at levity in his tone. Doctor Lanning regarded the young officer for a moment before nodding and softening her gaze.

"It certainly does. To start off with, I noted ligature marks on her wrists and ankles. They were older though, most likely already in healing stages at the time of death." A notebook appeared on Cassandra's thigh, its slim pages filling with hastily scribbled notes. "There are no signs of emaciation. The victim seems to have been in average, if not good, health at the time of her death."

She cleared her throat and continued:

"Upon examination of her uterus, we found it to be expanded and unfolded. This indicates the victim was pregnant or had recently given birth. As we did not find a fetus, we can assume the victim gave birth prior to death."

"Could birth complications have caused death?"

Doctor Lanning paused, her head tilted as she considered Cassandra's question. Her hands came up to rest on the burnished wood of her desk.

"I conducted this autopsy fully aware of the situation surrounding her discovery. I am aware of the connections this victim might have to other homicides occurring around the Charleston area, but–– she died of natural causes, Detective."

At the pair's silence, she continued:

"There are enormous risks attached to late-term pregnancy. Even once a mother has given birth, she is still vulnerable. There are no signs of external injury. She might have been forced into horrible circumstances, but I could not truly tell you if they caused her death."

Cassandra hummed and ran her fingers along the smooth arm of her chair.

"Would there be any way to test for oxytocin?" she questioned.

"She was found in the late stages of decomposition," Dr. Lanning said, her mouth pressed in a thin line. "I submitted a sample of the victim's bone marrow for toxicology testing. That might take a while to get back.

"Oxytocin?" Mills asked, looking between the two women.

"It's used in hospitals to stimulate labor. There's a possibility the suspect used it to induce. But we can't be sure the victim wasn't already in the early stages. There's also a chance the labor was manually induced, if it was induced at all–– and there's no way we can prove that."

Cassandra nodded, distracted, before standing and gesturing out the door.

"May I see her?"

The doctor nodded and moved to the door, letting Cassandra and then herself out. Behind them, Mills stood abruptly, a half-formulated question hanging from his tongue. She paused and motioned for Mills to freeze.

"Have you ever seen a dead body?" she murmured.

He grimaced, and for a moment, she felt like a teacher comforting a terrified child.

"In photographs at the academy."

She made a noise of acknowledgement before grabbing his arm, forcing him to meet her eyes.

"Don't touch anything. If you find anything of note, tell me. But under no circumstances do you touch her. Do not take this investigation into your own hands and contaminate potential evidence. But there's one last thing."

She paused and leaned in, her eyes boring into his. He was half-a-head taller, but his shoulders were rounded in an odd childlike shyness. Her grasp on his arm imperceptibly tightened.

"Step out if you need to. Vomit certainly wouldn't improve the experience."

His eyes did not leave hers as he straightened and nodded. A strained determination came into his face, as though he had suddenly resolved something in his mind and was going to act on it.

"Lead the way, Wake."

There came a long, extended rattle, and a bloom of frigid air stung her skin. Dr. Lanning stood on the left side of the open mortuary cabinet. Cassandra and Mills shuffled closer, staring at the woman found in Unit 54.

Bits of dark brown flesh clung like curls of dried paint to pale bone. Vague remnants of cloth twisted between tibia and fibula, climbed through rib bones like vines up an ancient lattice. She had decomposed quickly, as the entire storage unit lacked any sort of climate control. Her right hand flexed eternally at her side, and Cassandra noted the chipped vermillion of her nails.

"Any DNA samples under her nails?" she asked.

"None. This could be explained by her bound wrists. But again, they were older marks. Like she'd already started healing prior to death. We did, however, collect traces of white powder on her hands. Toxicology tests came back negative–– whatever it is, it's not a drug."

Cassandra bent at the waist, hands coming to rest on her tensed thighs. Her gaze was level with the woman's yellowish skull. She recalled Una Boland's trip along the St. John's River. How her grandparents had been expecting her and called when she had failed to appear. She wondered what frantic thoughts had painted the mind of Una Boland prior to her death.

"There was an unknown white powder found on the hands of a previous victim, as well. That powder was film developer. We'll crosscheck both samples."

Quiet, stilted conversation washed over the bones of Una Boland, and soon enough, Cassandra and Mills spilled out beneath the sun. Gravel crunched under her boots as Cassandra stepped back into the parking lot. A thick blanket of heat fell abruptly upon them, like a bucket of boiling water elaborately set above a doorway. She felt the sterile frigidity of the morgue seep from her skin. A skinny band of trees curled about the sides of the Coroner's

Office. High twittering sounded from their full limbs, the gentle swell of birdsong filling the afternoon air.

The office door clicked shut with a light push. Mills, hands deep in his pockets, came to stand beside her. His gaze was focused but cast far out onto the horizon. He drew a deep breath through his nose.

"You did well, Mills. Better than I did with my first body."

"Heyward would have helped in there," he said. His voice came cautious and heavy.

"You helped in there," she said. After a moment of silence, she began toward the distant car. Mills's footsteps sounded behind her. Silence clung to the space between them, and Cassandra felt unmoored, bereft of the solace previously offered by birdsong.

She had decided to drive the moment he stepped out of the morgue. Fumbling for the keys with one hand, she grasped at the door handle with the other. A cough, intentionally loud and brusque, caught her attention.

"Yes?" she asked.

"I don't––" he began before sighing frustratedly at himself. "Do you notice the looks you get?"

"Excuse me?"

"You're so observant with the small things. It feels like sometimes you forget that the small things make up one big thing, and that big thing gets important. Did you know our coworkers have dinner together at least twice a month? I bet you didn't."

"They're people. They eat," she said, her quiet response lost beneath Mills's rising ire.

"That's why Zeigler was in your office, right? He doesn't like you. Crawford sees it, too."

"No, that's not why. Don't worry about Zeigler."

"They don't invite you because they're scared you'll figure something out. Aren't you mad? Aren't you upset that they're so stuck in their ways? They'd rather let more women die than re-member-- than remember..."

"You're upset," she said.

She turned and examined Mills's strained face, the troubled slump of his shoulders. She slipped the keys back into her pocket and attempted a small smile. His gaze did not leave her face, and he did not seem to care about her attempt at amiability. Cassandra realized with a slight shock that his eyes shone with hostility. They stood in silence.

"If you want to go to those dinners, be my guest. I won't bring you along anymore."

"I don't mean that," Mills said. "I don't mean that, and you know it."

"What do you want me to do, then?"

"Eat dinner with me. We don't need them. My girlfriend makes a great steak. And I make a pretty good salad. Just think about it."

She dug her hands into her jacket pockets, turning and looking out across the parking lot.

"You haven't been invited?"

"Of course not. Besides you, I'm the only person who wasn't there. They don't like me either. But at least with me, they don't remember someone else. And it's bullshit. So come over and we'll have our dinners twice a month. Or something like that."

"Or something like that," Cassandra said, nodding. She re-trieved the keys from her pocket and opened the car door.

"So you want to stay on the case?"

His answer came in his swift jog to the passenger door. The seat creaked as he sank down. Cassandra became aware of the thundering of her heart in her ears. She had not realized how much Mills's participation meant to her, albeit subconsciously. The shifting of his weight on the seat signified to the frantic, unexamined part of her conscience that he had chosen to stay.

The car rumbled to a start, and gravel went skittering about as they pulled further down the driveway. Mills reached over and, smiling, turned the volume knob up. A light, soothing tune eased out of the radio.

The abrupt ring of a phone tore through the music. Cassandra gestured for Mills to answer, her phone balanced precariously in a center cupholder. He fiddled for a moment before a woman's voice filled the car. She recognized the voice of Lieutenant Virginia Crawford.

"We've got a paternity match for the Thompson fetus."

"Holy shit," Mills said.

"Be quiet," Cassandra reprimanded, watching the brake lights of a Honda Civic flash in the traffic.

"Do we know him?" Mills asked.

"A registered sperm donor. He's been in Norway since before Clara Thompson went missing."

"Samples last indefinitely if frozen correctly," Cassandra said. "Someone had access to his donation. Were any samples reported missing at major sperm banks near us?"

"No," Crawford said. "Nothing's been reported at all."

"We've been looking for a rapist all this time. It's artificial insemination. We're looking for a medical professional. I'll start on employee lists when I get back."

The line abruptly cut off. Realizing Cassandra would say nothing else, Mills leaned over and turned the volume knob up once more.

Later that night, beneath the cool heat of the moon, Cassandra ran the wooded paths that circled the outer edges of the Citadel campus. She enjoyed running late at night despite the obvious safety hazards. The dark asphalt beneath her shoes flew by, and the warm sounds of a settling city surrounded her. Her breath came hot and steady.

The events of the day flashed through her mind. She pointedly ignored them, sucking air into her lungs and tightening the muscles in her abdomen. She had not thought of her uncle in months, not truly. Memories of Adrian Wake sat in the back of her mind like an ignored tomb. Without intending to, she slowed her pace, hands swinging loosely at her hips. She glared into the gloom of the surrounding trees and caught her breath. He didn't deserve that. Not then. Not now.

She remembered the rare weekends she and her mother would bundle up with the neighboring family in a cramped SUV on the way to Bucharest. Covered heads and knit scarves filled Strada Patriarhiei. She wasn't tall enough to see through the tangle of limbs all around her. Her eyes caught the yellow windows of the Patriarchal Cathedral of Bucharest. The gray cobblestones seemed to shift under her feet, and a cold hand wrapped around her own. She glanced up into her mother's face. It burned bright in her mind, dry and reddened from wind.

Her mother hadn't been sober then. Not that Cassandra, at that time, could recognize the symptoms of benzodiazepine addiction. The impulsive late-night walks excited her, sent the anxious child within her reeling at a chance for true adventure. Her mother would sink from carefree exhilaration to scrutinous sadness. It didn't surprise her. One accustomed to pain no longer flinches easily, no longer frequents the doctor when they should. It was only after extended exposure to her uncle's steady affection that she realized her mother had, over the course of Cassandra's childhood, desired to die.

A flurry of dancers flew past her. They wore thick brown bearskins, the massive, matted heads balanced on their own like living crowns. A thick pink tongue puffed out, frozen, from the bears' black lips. Fragile sunlight clung to the bears' fangs, gleaming coldly in the small clearing. Her grip tightened on her mother's hand.

They danced, jumped, some wrapped in bearskins, others warm and agile in coarse furs. A group of musicians practiced further away, the bright greens and reds of their outfits flying as they moved. A cacophonic mix of music and voices sank over her, and she felt impossibly weighed down by the lively dance. Memories from her childhood came slow but vibrant, as though rising from muddy depths to crystalline shallows. A car's horn blared from somewhere behind the trees. She lifted her head and checked her watch. The early morning had crept in without warning.

Noting the name of the adjacent street, she slipped through the line of trees and crossed onto a small block of shops. The street was not quite empty, submerged in a momentary quiet, already anticipating the ruckus of the coming morning. Warm air clung to the sweat on her skin, inciting a hard shiver. The lit doorway of a small liquor shop swung open, and a tired-looking man wandered out and to his car. She peered into the yellowish windows, most of their glass covered by faded decals of beer brands and sports teams.

She watched the door, considering whether to enter, before turning and wandering down a decently lit side street. An ambulance siren echoed chillingly against the old walls of distant buildings somewhere to her right. She raised a hand to her temple, wiping feebly at the gathered sweat. She walked slowly, steadily.

To her left, hidden in a dim niche between two shops, a homeless man shifted further beneath his blanket. She tore her eyes from his hunched figure and continued.

The night swelled, and Cassandra drew in a harsh breath. She could go home when she stopped walking, when she stopped fleeing whatever distant anxieties plagued the corners of her mind. Warm air filled her nostrils. Subtle but fresh came the scent of bread.

She glanced up, and across the street, across another parking lot, rose the familiar crooked visage of the stairwell outside Giovanni Singer's apartment. In a minute she had crossed the street; thirty more seconds, and she cleared the parking lot. She stood like a fearful creature at the bottom of the stairwell, a pale hand clinging to the withered wrought iron railing.

Footsteps sounded behind her, and she turned, coming face to face with Giovanni Singer and two other men. All three had thick plastic-wrapped loaves tucked under their arms.

"Who the hell are you?" asked the tallest man, his rough manner exaggerated by the quiet of the morning.

"There's no need for that," Giovanni said. He examined her, frowning, before gesturing to a flimsy plastic table beneath the stairwell. It was crooked and frail, most likely where the bakers took their smoke breaks. Quick whispers bounced between the roommates. They halted as Giovanni entered her periphery. He pointed again at the table and walked past her. As he crossed the sidewalk to the table, the two other men slipped back inside the bakery.

Giovanni sat at the table. He wore crimson flannel pajama pants and a sweatshirt despite the humidity. The crinkle of plastic wrap filled the night as he tore open the loaf.

"They give me old bread if I help them with their essays," he said, tone light and conversational. "It's almost not worth it."

"I'm sorry," she said.

"For what?"

"I don't know why I'm here."

"Does anyone?" He turned, gesturing again for her to sit. "You're here. Doesn't matter if you know why. Have you eaten breakfast?"

"It's three in the morning."

"That didn't stop you from showing up at my apartment. So I don't think breakfast is beyond the realm of comprehension."

She sat beside him. He flattened the plastic wrap against the table, using half the loaf as a sort of paperweight. Without her noticing, he had ripped off a small piece and sat it on the edge closest to her seat. She picked it up and took a bite.

"My roommates don't believe in breakfast. They really said that, you know. Breakfast isn't something you just don't believe in. You don't believe in God or binaural rhythms. They won't explain themselves."

There came a light clink of glass, and she glanced over to find a small mason jar beside the bread. The preserves within it were a deep purple. Giovanni twisted off the lid and slid it away; in jagged cursive, uneven and nearly illegible, someone had written *Grape Jam.*

"I snagged that when they weren't looking," Giovanni said, noting the direction of her gaze. "Don't arrest me. I'll cry."

He reached over and, commenting on the cleanliness of his hands, used the discarded lid to scrape some jam onto her bread. He cleared his throat and watched as she took another bite. Apparently satisfied with her reaction, he spread a veritable glob of jam onto his own bread and stuffed it in his mouth. He reached for an-other piece, barely pausing the smooth, light rhythm of his words.

She closed her eyes, relaxing beneath the gentle sound of his voice. When necessary, she offered a grunt or a thoughtful hum, whichever resulted in his own noise of satisfaction. She opened her eyes, pulled her shoulders back, and examined the profile of his face in the dim stairwell light. The lines of his cheeks, nose, and ears, the cut of his eyebrows and the gleam of his glasses all inspired within her an admiration that bordered on reverence.

"I had an uncle," she said.

His eyes remained fixed on the distant end of the parking lot.

"Me too."

"He raised me after I left Romania. He was a good man. No wife. No children. Just me."

"That's more than many have," he said.

"Maybe less would be better. I make a pitiful family."

He shrugged, pulling another piece of bread to his lips.

"He was a good man," she repeated. "I don't know if I loved him. But I tried. God knows I tried. He made my lunch every day. Picked me up from school so I didn't have to walk in the rain or snow. But sometimes he would look at me. When we'd had a long day, or we were fighting. And I knew–– knew more than anything, that he didn't see me."

"What did he see, Detective?"

"I don't know," she whispered. "I don't know."

Silence, devoid of judgment or censure, hung between them. Her hands came up to cover her face.

"I'm just so tired of ruining good people. And–– and when I look at myself, sometimes I think–– I worry that I don't know what I see, either."

A warm hand caught her fingers and pulled them from her face. His eyes were soft and dark as he looked over.

"There's the parable of the blind men and the elephant. One blind man feels the elephant's leg. He says, 'Here's a tree.' Another blind man feels the elephant's ear. He says, 'Oh, here's a fan.' They think they're both lying. They're both wrong, but they're not *not* right. Do you understand? Sometimes we forget who we are because we don't know anything different. We're too close. We need others to remind us."

"You think you can remind me, then? You think that'll fix everything?" Desperation tinted her clumsy words.

"No," he said. "Not everything. I'll remind you when you need it. And you'll remind me."

"You don't know me."

"As it turns out, you don't know yourself, either," he said. She glanced over, noting his slight grin. Three hours remained until she was required at the department. He hummed before moving the remainder of the loaf toward her. He wiped his hands on his flannel pants and settled deeper into the chair.

12

Chapter Twelve

The next evening, a floor beneath the Charleston County Courthouse, the clatter of Ronald White's plastic cane rattled the cardboard boxes of the Judicial Department Public Index. Giovanni Singer, who had his arm intertwined in Ronald's, ran a hand down his face and sighed.

"Sorry," he whispered to the myriad of frazzled heads that popped up from various niches and enclaves. "Grandpa's getting old."

"I'm not old enough to be your grandpa," Ronald murmured, glancing down at the younger man. Rather than continue the conversation, Giovanni retrieved the cane from the floor, slipped it into Ronald's hand, and gestured to a nearby table.

The Judicial Department Public Index was a bleak, lightless floor beneath the Charleston County Courthouse which housed the records of most recent court cases. Flimsy cardboard boxes sat like aging birds on high shelves, glaring down at the few visitors who dared to enter its halls. Flurries of dust swarmed through the sparse canals of light that flickered from the sickly overhead fluorescent fixtures. Closer to the stairway stood a line of blue-screened computers, their frames thick, white, and exceptionally outdated. Ronald peered over his shoulder and squinted against the dust.

"Why aren't we using the computers? It would be much faster."

"That is distinctly soporific and unexciting."

"What?"

"Computers have ruined the pursuit of knowledge. You've gotta read a hundred irrelevant articles before you find one that means anything at all. That's the fun part."

Neither man said it, but the trip had also been undertaken in order to get Ronald White out of the house. The decrepitude and isolation of White's life deeply disturbed Giovanni. White was a physical hindrance, as he moved slowly and would not increase his pace for any reason whatsoever. His clumsy cane and heavy, languid limbs often caught on papers and books, sending their precarious towers down in a storm of dust. But Giovanni had decided he was quite necessary.

"And, by the way, you're certainly old enough to be my grandfather. I don't know if you were trying to flatter yourself or insult me, but it didn't work."

Ronal grunted and, tossing his hand at Giovanni, sank down onto the straight-backed chair closest to him. The older man glanced with a deep weariness at the surrounding shelves of cardboard boxes and stuffy, obsolete files. Some boxes were marked with a slanted year, *2004, 2012.* Others dared any poor victim to guess their contents. He looked longingly at the distant bluish glow of the squadron of computers, a look that did not go unnoticed by Giovanni Singer.

"The computers are hardly any more advanced than an early Dynix. The first fully installed Dynix was in Kershaw, South Carolina. Look it up." He wiped his forehead with his sleeve and turned to examine the nearest rows of shelves and dusty boxes. His chest swelled with an old excitement, one he had nearly forgotten. "I'm saying you're better off going through it yourself."

He gestured toward a distant shelf like a general directing his troops.

"Clara Thompson disappeared a year ago. Summer of 2022. We need to find the most recent mention of Fred Ellison and go back from there. Understand?"

"Who in the world is Fred Ellison?"

"I was sitting with a few officers outside Zenith Storage. They had a supposedly secret conversation. But I was listening. Of course I was listening. They hardly lowered their voices."

"And Fred Ellison?"

"Someone was paying for that unit under his name. But Ellison had been dead by then. So we gotta–– we gotta try and find out who he was. Why this killer chose him."

"The Stillborn Killer. That's what they're calling this guy."

"He's not a celebrity," Giovanni said, waving his hand in the air, a brisk gesture of dismissal. "I'll call him whatever the hell I want."

Ronald held up his hands as though attempting to placate him. "I understand, boy. Lead on."

And so their expedition began. Giovanni lugged boxes from their shelves with a dull crash. Their contents would be deftly divided into two parts, flipped through, and put back in their place. Their stinging eyes soon became accustomed to the underground darkness. The silence swelled with the dedicated rhythm of pages turning and the subsequent scratch of pencil on paper. Whatever enthusiasm Ronald had lacked before, he counteracted with a gentle yet firm determination to systematically crosscheck words and dates.

It was nine-thirty at night, and they were in March of 2022. No mention of any individual by the name Fred Ellison had been made for five years straight. Ronald had found a 2020 welfare check made on a woman by the name Cynthia Ellison, but any relation with Fred Ellison was unknown and unable to be confirmed. He thought of nothing beyond dates, timelines, and the resounding absence of Fred Ellison. His diligent search acted as a form of meditation, not unlike the calm he suspected often accompanied the baking of bread or the removal of weeds from a garden. His movements became light and tender as his mind slipped away.

Consciousness returned to Giovanni between the passing of one second to another, abrupt like a gunshot into the dark landscape of his mind. He glanced up from the folder in his lap and blinked the exhaustion from his eyes.

He was momentarily alone. Ronald could not handle staying still for long periods, so he made frequent trips to the half-filled vending machine a floor above them. The tin remnants of empty cans sat in a neat line on the edge of the table (organized by Giovanni, who was adamant that their workspace remain clean). He pushed himself up, tensed the muscles in his legs, and wandered toward the dark depths of a distant shelf. It was time to go home, he knew. The garish fluorescent lights burned his tired eyes, and the constant stream of jargon had put a permanent furrow between his brows. He paused at the intersection of two shelves and released a breath.

A distant light, nearly indiscernible in the shadows, caught his attention. In an instant, he had moved behind a shelf. His steps came slow but firm as he drew closer.

"Ronald? What are you doing?"

The older man peered intently at a crumpled file. Upon hearing Giovanni's question, his face grew pale and drawn. He lowered the file, leaning away as though attempting to hide it. He watched Giovanni for a moment before relaxing.

"I found something," he said. "You might think it's interesting."

"About Fred Ellison?"

"No," Ronald said, his expression one of intense thought. "About your detective."

The words were quick and breathless, imbued with strange urgency. Ronald's eyes shone uncharacteristically bright, as though his cold, unbothered soul had been abruptly lit and was scrabbling frantically for release. Giovanni straightened and remained silent.

"She only transferred here in 2022. Ten months before my daughter was found at Drayton Swamp––"

"Interesting," Giovanni said.

"Yeah, I know. She transferred here for a reason. Worked at the Marietta Police Department for three years, but there was a public thing between her and a relative. Her uncle. He raised her since she came in from Romania."

"Be quiet, Ronald."

"He was dying, and she was his only living relative. He wanted her to take his things, to manage his estate. But she didn't want anything to do with him––"

"Ronald," Giovanni repeated. "Either you stop reading and stop talking, or I leave you here to walk back. How do you like your chances in downtown Charleston at..." he checked his watch. "Nine-forty-five at night? It's a ten-mile walk from what I remember."

They stood as though engaged in a silent duel. Giovanni saw the enthusiasm drip from Ronald's face, watched the paralyzed twist of his smile become even more painfully apparent. For a moment, he deeply regretted his harsh words. The older man had never smiled like that, had never attempted to share any joy with Giovanni. He shook these thoughts from his mind and held his hand out.

"We're looking for Fred Ellison. That's it. Comply with this rule or leave."

"See, I don't understand that," Ronald began, his face red. "She's allowed to barge into our homes and dredge up every bad memory we've ever had. But I'm not allowed to read about her? It's not like I'd be throwing it in her face. But I have a right to know. Just as much as she does."

"She's trying to catch a serial killer who did irreparable damage to our loved ones. You are furthering some childish ideal that she's digging up gossip. Don't you understand that? You want gossip. You're no better than some vengeful schoolboy."

"Not gossip, then. I'd like to get better acquainted with her. How's that?"

Giovanni felt something solidify within him, and a familiar disgust became apparent in his tone.

"You're pathetic. We're done."

He snatched the file from Ronald's hands and stepped back, as though touching Ronald would infect him with something. He could feel the older man's eyes on him.

"Are you still driving me back? I can't walk ten miles. I'm sorry," he said.

"I know, Ronald. I'll get you a ride. Why don't you go wait up by the vending machine? I need to put everything back in its place."

They traded no more words. Giovanni waited until he heard the slide of Ronald's heavy, uneven footsteps retreating toward the stairs. The file weighed heavy in his hand. There sounded the muffled whir of a distant air conditioning unit. The air seemed tense, like the tons of files and cases were bound to topple over any second. He wiped at his face and, straightening his shoulders, put the file back on the shelf.

He wandered back to the corner table where they had conducted their research. A faint buzzing filtered from overhead. He swatted at the fly that circled about his ears. The waft of air from this gesture sent a paper gliding to the floor. He crouched, picked it up, and smiled.

It was an unobtrusive slip of paper with a dingy newspaper clipping scanned crookedly across it. His fingers ran along the grainy letters, as though they were streaks of dirt he meant to brush off. It read:

"Fred Norris Ellison, 42, of West Ashley passed away on August 5th, 2022. He is survived by his mother, Cynthia Ellison, as well as siblings John, Francis, Katherine, and Lorna. His funeral will be held on the 10th at Dupont Cemetery, 1860 Pebble Road."

Beneath the primary message, in a nearly indistinguishable postscript, was a number someone could call to donate to the family's Christmas fund. Apparently, the family flew to Europe every year for the holidays. Ellison's death had ruined their plans. He stood and cast his hands about, as though he were attempting to find what he was looking for through touch alone. After a moment, he produced the documentation of the welfare check on Cynthia Ellison made in 2020. His eyes sifted through the words but could not find any concrete information. The address at which the welfare check was completed was blacked out. The thick bar of opaque ink sneered at him, and he stared back, dumbfounded.

Quietly, he collected the papers. He returned each file to the correct box, all of which were straightened with a gentle zeal. There rose a deep silence in the depths of the courthouse, the type of silence only achievable in places usually bursting with activity. He imagined the purposeful footsteps sounding overhead, the churning gasp of old printers, and he felt as though he were the only person in the entire world. He recalled the quiet, peaceful moments sitting on the front steps of his childhood home.

Cicadas whirred from the darkened trees. Someone was burning leaves, the smoky air thick on his tongue. The static of a stuttering radio drifted from behind the bleached wooden fence to his right. From an open window came sweet, melancholy music. He recognized Lindsey Buckingham's soft voice repeating the chorus of "Oh Diane," the rhythmic tambourine beats, the rolling guitar chords. An island free from the wretched ties of mainland, a rock impermeable to the crashing river water surrounding it. He had welcomed that feeling then–– reveled in it, even. He was the only person in the world. And he was waiting.

"Sir? We're closing. Can I help you with anything?" The voice was low and timid. Giovanni realized he was sitting at the table, his head hidden in his hands. He had not cried, or if he had, any traces were long gone. He did not know how long he had been sitting there. A cold film of sweat gathered on his forehead and neck. An embarrassed glance revealed a young woman standing beside him, a collection of files tucked under her elbow.

"I'm so sorry," he said, standing. He offered her a strained smile and cleared his throat. "I'm sorry. Lost track of time." After seeing that every box was returned to its place, he hurried to the front door and filed out onto the street.

"Singer," called a voice to his right. He turned and saw Ronald sitting on a wrought iron bench. The bench stood directly beneath a bright streetlight, and he could see moths fluttering in and out of the febrile light.

"Stay here," he murmured, before realizing the older man couldn't have heard him. He felt Ronald's eyes upon him and gave a muted gesture for him to stay put. "I'll get the car."

"Are you all right, Singer?"

He flung a careless hand back, frustrated with the man's questions, with the balmy air, with the crooked brick roads that were impossible to cross in the dark. Both hands came up to cup his face. Quick breaths rushed from between his fingers.

"Stop it," he demanded quietly. "Stop it." His steps had grown less careful and, before he knew it, the toe of his right shoe had caught on the raised edge of a broken brick. He stumbled and caught himself against the coarse bark of a palm tree. "Stop it."

A painful heat rose within his chest, shooting like boiling water into his wrists and ears. It was the unbearable normality of it all. The justification of a world in which he could not and would not believe in. One wasn't expected to thrive without two lungs, without a kidney or a heart. His spine was a brittle branch, and his skull swung listlessly on its end. After a tense moment, he put his hands down at his sides.

"Giovanni, are you all right?" Ronald repeated from behind him. The older man had gotten up, a feat Giovanni surely should have noticed. He turned and bit out a response, his tongue thick and unwieldy.

"Do you think Beatrice is still alive?"

Ronald turned and examined the distant yellow squares of house windows. Their lights splayed like plague-ridden bodies on the ground. His hand came up to rest on Giovanni's shoulder.

"I really couldn't say."

"I think it'll kill me if she's not," he whispered. "I think I'll drop dead then and there. With that photo, you reminded me that I was alive. That I am alive. I'd forgotten."

"You won't drop dead," Ronald said. "I won't let you."

Giovanni laughed and began again down the road. He made it down to the parking lot without any error. Slipping into the driver's seat, he felt the night settle around him. Breathing deeply, he guided the car down a slim sideroad, back to Ronald White's hazy figure on the wrought iron bench. It was late, and he had exams in the morning.

Her second-floor office in the Charleston Police Department stood hardly larger than a broom closet. She didn't require much. When the occasion demanded it, she would present in the principal conference room with its long mahogany table and overabundance of people. An unnatural darkness clung to her office like cobwebs in a tightly closed fist. Papers hung from the walls with crinkled bits of tape. She sat at her desk, head balanced on her right hand. Whatever dismal warmth that once invaded its walls had dissipated with Zeigler's intrusion. In the doorway, intrigued but undesirous to venture further, stood Michael Heyward and Virginia Crawford.

"Una Boland officially went missing the 10th of June in 2021. Her father, Richard Boland, died three months prior from a sudden heart attack. Una and her mother were not on good speaking terms following his death. They fought the 9th, and early the next morning, Una took her car and drove down to Florida."

Cassandra reached across the desk and retrieved a paper shoved unceremoniously beneath her keyboard.

"We can't test Boland's fetus for paternity because she'd already given birth. But let's assume she was artificially inseminated, as well. Let's also assume, as the coroner did, that Boland had been dead around a year prior to being found in the storage unit. That means she died in June 2022, and nine months before that was October 2021. It took the suspect at least three months to get Boland pregnant. Right between June and October.

Then, possibly even before Una Boland died, Clara Thompson officially went missing June 13th. Two weeks prior to her disappearance, a noise complaint was filed by her neighbors. Thompson and her partner had gotten in a loud fight about the partner's infidelity. Nearly everyone in their apartment complex knew some-thing had happened between them."

"What point are you trying to make besides the sheer speed of it all?" Heyward questioned.

"Both victims had incredibly public fights with their loved ones. We've been asking why the suspect feels the need to impreg-nate their victims, and no answer ever made sense. They're choos-ing women whose families were falling apart."

"Because they're vulnerable?"

"Yes," Cassandra said. "Yes, but also-- do you remember the ligature markings? How they were long healed? It's not just about subjugation. I think the suspect is trying to fix something. Or at least, they think they are."

"Fix something?" Crawford spoke for the first time.

"Fix their families. Make a new one. Bring a child into the world and start over."

"So," Crawford said. "Assuming Kira Rushton was the first known victim in all this. Do we know about her family dynamic?"

Heyward released a brisk laugh. "You'd need a family to have family dynamics."

"She had a partner," Cassandra said. "Many would consider that family enough. Anyway, I already checked records for Ronald White and Kira Rushton's domestic violence history. Nothing of-ficial in documentation. But then again, I can't try to understand the relationship between two addicts."

"I'm going by Folly Beach today. I'll stop by. See if he's got some-thing new to say."

"He won't speak," Crawford said. "He hates us."

"He doesn't hate Giovanni Singer," Cassandra said. She had not expected to say it and was startled when both officers turned to her. Crawford drew close. Her face was hard and unreadable, and she towered in the darkness of the small office.

"Don't tell me you made Giovanni Singer your informant."

"No," she said. "He mentioned it at Zenith Storage."

"Why'd he have your phone number, anyway?" Crawford asked. Under her hostile gaze, Cassandra straightened. She watched the slight tremor of the lieutenant's fingers. The woman's unease caught her attention, and she stood, pulling in a full breath.

"Gave him my card when we first spoke. Guess it was the first one he found."

Heyward nodded and slipped back into the hallway, calling a quick 'goodbye' over his shoulder. Rolling her own shoulders back in a light stretch, Cassandra shuffled the papers on her desk. The weight of Crawford's gaze hit her squarely in the back like a piercing arrow meant for the heart. Nonetheless, she was wary to engage in such flagrant shows of emotion. It seeped into her lifeless office like a drop of ink in water. She retrieved her jacket from the back of her chair and moved to leave.

"We're having dinner tomorrow," Crawford said. "Some colleagues. Heyward and Norton will be there, at least. I thought you'd be interested in joining."

"Thank you for thinking of me."

A brief, expectant silence settled between them.

"Well?"

"Can Mills come?" Cassandra asked.

"Of course. But tell him there's a no-uniform policy. No exceptions whatsoever."

Cassandra offered a hollow smile and watched as Crawford disappeared down the hall.

The next night, Cassandra listened as Chief Norton recounted one of the exhilarating (but often-repeated) stories of his two years spent in the Metro Drug Unit. He was an enthusiastic storyteller, whose words were often overshadowed by the myriad of expressive and histrionic gestures he employed. She watched him from across the room. He perched on a cream chaise, directly in the middle of a smattering of seated men. A handful of senior officers listened alongside Cassandra.

The wine in her glass went untouched. The chief's story worked as pleasant background noise to her raucous thoughts, a calamity from which she never truly gained reprieve. A crackling fireplace cast a warm orange glow over the wooden panels of the walls and floors. A smaller group of colleagues gathered in the distant kitchen, most likely supervising (and stealing bites of) the anticipated chicken dinner. She could hear their muffled voices, and they acted as a mist that fell about the dim house, making it seem lovely and soft. It felt abundantly alive.

There came an abrupt pause in Chief Norton's story as a child, perhaps two years old, stumbled into the living room and promptly burst into tears. The older man jumped up, scooped the child into his arms, and sat back down.

"What's the matter, kid?" he asked the little boy.

Rather than respond verbally, the boy buried his face in Chief Norton's shoulder and would not move. After a moment, Lieutenant Virginia Crawford walked in, her eyes soft but searching. A dish towel was slung over her shoulder. Upon glimpsing the boy, she offered the chief a weary smile.

"Evan's a little overwhelmed," she explained, watching him tuck his shoulder in the chief's side. "We haven't had a dinner this size for a while."

"We can be quiet," Chief Norton said warmly. He frowned at his surrounding officers as though blaming them individually for the boy's state, but his eyes were merry and bright. She waved a hand at him, shaking her head.

"He'll be asleep soon, anyway. It's fine."

Everyone had separated into individual conversations, their voices building and collapsing atop each other. Cassandra glanced up to find the chief staring at her. He looked as though he were expecting a response, so she strode forward, careful to avoid the extended legs and swinging arms of her colleagues.

"Sorry. I didn't hear you."

"Didn't say anything, Wake. Are you excited for the lieutenant's wonderful dinner?"

She smiled and turned to Crawford. "Dinner by our very own Lieutenant Crawford. I can't wait."

"There might not be any dinner left. Heyward and Mills have been sneaking bites for thirty minutes now." Crawford ran a hand through her hair, huffing a stray strand out of her eyes. "I should probably get back in there. Was just checking on him." She hurried away, but not before calling over her shoulder. "If it's bad, blame Richard!"

The remaining pair fell silent for a moment, with the chief mindlessly patting Evan's back.

"Richard?" Cassandra questioned.

"I see you didn't introduce yourself to the party's host."

"That's not true," she said. "I said 'hello' to Crawford the minute I walked in."

"You greeted Lieutenant Crawford. Doesn't Mr. Crawford deserve some respect too?"

Rather than respond to the chief's teasing, she examined the boy. He had a shiny crown of light brown hair and plump little fingers that clung to the collar of Chief Norton's dress shirt. He wore a white and blue striped shirt alongside a pair of navy-blue joggers. She tentatively reached forward and took a little brown shoe in her hand.

"Hello, Evan," she said, and watched as he finally pulled away from the chief's shoulder. She grinned at him, and he grinned back, albeit with reddened cheeks and watery eyes. He sniffled as she wiggled his foot. After a moment, during which the chief began a new conversation with a nearby detective, Evan crawled over and plopped himself down into Cassandra's lap.

He soon fell asleep, half of his face pressed into the rough denim of her jeans. She could feel his steady heartbeat and the soft snuffle of each sleepy breath. The evening's crooked shadows fluttered on the floor as the chief leaned over and spoke.

"You're good with him. Any younger siblings?"

"No," she said, watching Evan in her lap. "Not even a cousin."

"Pity. No large families in Romania?"

"Not a large Wake family. My actual surname was Petrescu. Took on my uncle's name after I came to the States."

Neither felt it necessary to continue the conversation. Surrounding laughter sank over them like warm water, and it seemed like a matter of seconds before Crawford stood again in the doorway, declaring that dinner was ready. After a slow minute of wrangling Evan off her lap, Cassandra stood and discretely crept to the bathroom.

The water was cold and refreshing against her wrists. She braced her forearms against the sides of the sink and closed her eyes. The house burst with raucous, joyous friends, all of them glad to be there with each other. Pressing hands, stretched legs, calm and amiable words. She couldn't pay attention, not truly, distracted by the heat of too many bodies within such a close space.

Releasing a frustrated breath into the sink bowl, she straightened and pushed the door open.

She stood in the dark hallway, letting the distant sound of laughter wash over her. Down the hall, hardly visible against the deep darkness, flickered a gentle light. It fell softly through an open door. Her steps soundless, Cassandra walked to the doorway. A hesitant hand latched onto the wooden doorframe. She peered into the revealed room, a sort of office with deep burgundy walls and a noble oak desk fixed between two bookshelves. Her fingers tightened imperceptibly on the doorframe as a drawn face glanced up from its place behind the desk.

"You look like you've seen a ghost," Crawford said, crumpled in a rather raggedy office chair. A frail smile forced her face into merriment.

"I was just waiting my turn. Richard left a plate and some utensils for you, seeing as you'd snuck off somewhere. Me too, I guess." After an extended silence, she added: "The chief told me about you and Evan. Thank you."

She hummed in answer. "How old is he?"

"Two. Almost three, actually. Maybe you could come to his birthday party."

Cassandra did not answer and leaned back, looking into the hallway as though hearing footsteps approaching. There had been no footsteps, no muffled sound of approaching friends. A fragile pain hung conspicuously from Crawford like an effigy doused in fire, like a creature dripping with black mud. Emotion radiated about her, and Cassandra could feel it buzzing against her skin. It set her teeth on edge, made her fingers tighten into bone-white claws. Crawford released a strained laugh.

"I'm trying to be honest with you," she said.

"About what?"

"About everything. You don't deserve our secrets."

In the pale lamplight, Crawford held out a picture frame. It gleamed benignly as Cassandra approached. She took it with two gentle hands, careful to avoid the inadvertent touch of Crawford's fingers against her own. The frame contained a worn, saturated photograph curled at the edges. Three figures grinned out from the photograph. Cassandra's fingers loosened, and breath fell in a long rush from her lungs.

A man with intelligent eyes that glared playfully through thin, professorial glasses. A woman with a strong, angular face and cropped hair. She had only seen photographs of the third woman, or editorials commemorating the anniversary of her disappearance. She was short and had dark brown hair, the same as Giovanni's hair. They had the same smile, childish, wide, and toothy. They stood together like children, their faces bright with love, their arms effortlessly entangled. In a corner of her mind, Cassandra noted the muffled sobs coming from the woman beside her.

"We were engaged," she said. "Beatrice and I."

Cassandra sat the picture frame down on the edge of the desk.

"I know," she said.

"What?"

"Earlier. You said you'd gotten married and had a kid. But that happened after Beatrice Singer went missing. Your child's too young for anything to coincide. I noticed a ring in some of her photos and asked around. No one knew where it came from."

"I'm not-- I'm not ashamed. You might think I hid everything, I didn't tell anyone-- because I was ashamed. But I'm not. It's just easier. Easier for everyone if we started over."

"Does anyone know?"

"You," Crawford said, voice low and mournful. "My husband."

"Jesus," Cassandra said, dragging a hand over her face. A sharp chill had risen in the office despite the comfortable warmth that welled just yards away in the living room. Her fingers ached in the cold, and she shoved them deep into her jacket pockets. "Jesus."

"I know you knew something happened--"

"You were there with Giovanni Singer the night Beatrice disappeared. He said he had been waiting with someone. It was a Sunday, and he had been waiting. He was waiting with you."

Crawford nodded, and lamplight illumed the sharp, distorted planes of her face.

"I haven't moved on. You don't move on. You learn to live differently. And I have. Richard and Evan aren't replacements. They're my family. We can't-- we need to think about other things besides what we've lost."

"And that meant abandoning Giovanni Singer?"

"He won't speak to me," Crawford said fiercely. "I've tried countless times. He doesn't answer the door." She moved closer and grabbed Cassandra's hand. "You're taking his side. But, Detective, there are no sides. We aren't friends any longer, but I still want the best for him. I want him to learn everything he wants to learn. I want him to be happy. And the truth is, he can't be happy if you're showing up every week with news about Beatrice."

"I don't give a damn if he's happy," she said.

"You do. I know you do. You're braver than me. Don't start lying now."

Cassandra did not answer. Words welled up in her throat. In an instant, she wrenched her hand from Crawford's grasp, crossed the room, and spilled into the hallway. She drew closer to the living room, her steps quick but heavy. Warm candlelight fell upon her face, and laughter from the next room made her frown and rear back.

A desperate vision flashed in her mind. A weak and weary traveler caught in a snowstorm. Dark, furious swirls of snow ablaze before her eyes. Hands flail unseen in the dark. And all the snow converges, and all the winds snap. All the dying light falls upon the doors that will not open for her. Panting, she turned, straightened her spine, and slipped out the front door.

13

Chapter Thirteen

The street flickered with weak candlelight. Overhead streetlamps gasped, their bulbs either dead or dying. Pale, mournful faces swam in and out of darkness. Cassandra imagined they were an army of ghosts brought back to mourn and wail in the streets of Charleston. They moved together with a grim turgidity, cattle pushed against each other by walls growing ever closer. Dirty shop windows glared at the slick brick beneath their feet, but even the glass seemed lifeless and cold, working only to dig a wet chill deeper into their bones. Grimacing, Cassandra pulled a rain jacket tighter around her and pushed further into the crowd.

It was a candlelight vigil held for Una Boland, and by proxy, Clara Thompson. Miriam Boland had organized a gathering alongside the local Baptist church. They were to convene at a gazebo. She figured the pastor would initiate a mass prayer, give a mournful eulogy, and stand by as Miriam Boland and Alex Wendel wept. What more was one to do?

The department had let slip false information regarding Una Boland's autopsy. They hoped it would bait a suspect out into the shallows, where waiting hands could, hopefully, snatch them up.

Cassandra trudged along in the drizzly heat, sweat curling the tips of her hair.

Her eyes scrambled from face to face. The rain wasn't helping—participants hunched down to avoid wayward raindrops, their heads covered with caps and jacket hoods. She wasn't in uniform. There were plenty of officers stationed around the vigil, as was common with public gatherings of any sort. Lieutenant Crawford stood somewhere at the crowd's front. Mills surveilled the crowd to her left. A handful of officers were responsible for her right and back. A radio hung from her belt, hidden beneath a baggy jacket. Their gathering contained a peculiar silence, the sort of silence produced by anticipation and shot nerves. Her radio crackled to life, connected to a rickety earpiece wired under her shirt.

"Keep your eyes open for suspicious persons. If you notice any-one, do not cause a scene. Divert the individual to your fellow offi-cers where questions can be asked. Pursue only if suspects attempt to flee."

She recognized Crawford's voice, low and steady, unlike the week before. The sky was dark and pregnant with silver storm clouds. Cassandra glanced up and readjusted the piece in her ear, simultaneously wiping at a damp bit of hair on her cheek. Her fin-gers fumbled for the denim of her jeans in a poor attempt at dry-ing. A particular footfall sounded behind her, and she slowed her pace.

"Good evening, Detective," Giovanni said. "Come to honor the dead?"

He held an umbrella in his left hand. His fingers tightened on the handle, and his shoulder tensed, as though he were about to fall forward and hold the umbrella above her head. With a slight laugh, he switched the umbrella to his further hand. His sharp profile glowed sallow in the fading light. He wore a deep red rain jacket and wide brown trousers, their hems dark with water stains.

"To honor the living," she amended, straightening her shoulders. Their steps were slow and steady, but her eyes pushed like fumbling hands through the crowd. There came a rustling of paper to her right, and Giovanni abruptly held a newspaper in his grasp. He shook it out like a father settling down to drink coffee before work.

"Recent murder victim found pregnant with twins. Stillborn Killer's latest crime?" he read. His eyes flicked over the newspaper to her.

"That true?"

"Why wouldn't it be?"

"Doesn't seem like something you'd want getting out. But if you wanted it to get out, that's a different story."

"There is no story, Singer."

"You know, that's a stupid name. Stillborn Killer. All names like that are stupid."

"I'm of a similar opinion." She lifted her head and glanced at the surging crowd. "However, it's–– I don't think the suspect would appreciate it. I think it shows them how much they've failed. I can accept that."

Giovanni Singer rolled his shoulders back and gave a thoughtful hum.

"Should I be looking out for anyone in particular?" he murmured.

"Yourself," she said, eyes flashing to him. She frowned before beginning again. "A man in his mid-to-late thirties. Nicer clothes. He'll be looking at the other mourners. Most likely asking about Una Boland's death–– especially her medical situation. He might have a–– a camera. With a Clemson strap."

Eyebrows raised, Giovanni turned and nodded in thought. Beneath the murmur of rain, she heard him give a noncommittal hum before he turned and slipped into the crowd. He moved with a quick surety through the trudging throng. After a moment, she noticed a small gathering to her left, and her earpiece came alive with noise.

"Suspect identified on Western rank. Repeatedly harassed Boland's mother about her disappearance. Claimed to be childhood friend, confirmed to be deceptive. Two officers on him. Transporting to nearest car. Continue march," came Crawford's voice. Cassandra peered through the wall of swinging arms and legs. A thin man sat on the curbside, his face scratched and raw. Crawford knelt beside him, speaking in a low voice, while Mills stood like a statue behind him.

Realizing that too much attention was being paid to her colleagues, she searched about for a manner of diverting their eyes. A deep rumble of thunder sounded overhead, and in the distant sky, she glimpsed a thin vein of lightning touching the horizon. With a low gasp, she pointed, garnering the interest of not a few onlookers. As they turned away, she noted a man, his gaze still directed at Mills and Crawford. The man was tall and thin, and his eyes darted about as though he were wary of being noticed. Clenched tightly in his hands was a small chrome camera.

In an impossibly slow moment, Cassandra gazed at the man, and he gazed back. An expression of intense fear came over his face, and he wrenched himself back, as though coming unstuck from a vicious grip. He fell back into the crowd like a fish slipping back into dark, treacherous waters. She cursed beneath her breath and began a brisk jog in the man's direction. Thunder sounded overhead once more, and a thicker downpour descended upon them all.

"Mills," she called into her earpiece, hearing only static in response. She gritted her teeth and moved into a sprint, barely catching the flash of the man's jacket disappearing between two houses. As she rounded the corner, she saw that neither house had fenced-in yards, the grass sloping down into thick, dim woods. She pulled her Maglite and service pistol. A high beam swiveled to the trees, and she caught a dark mass slipping into the shadows of the treeline.

"Hey!" she yelled. "Charleston PD. Stop!" Her orders were pointless–– one couldn't hear above the rolling thunder and rising cacophony of rain. She slid down the muddy end of the yard and sprinted into the trees. She could see the imprint of the man's shoes in the mud and slowed to a walk. She released a harsh breath, spinning in a slow circle with her pistol raised.

There was a queer placidity to the woods. She wasn't deep in the treeline, not yet. Rain trickled down the canopies overhead, and the gentle noise encased her like someone in an underground bunker with a tornado screaming overhead. She forced her breath down and listened to the silence of the woods. To her right, barely above a whisper, came strained breathing.

"I'm a detective with Charleston PD," she announced. "And I've got a gun aimed at your head. Step out now or I'll shoot you. Did you fucking hear me?"

The breathing ceased, and she realized how impossibly dark the woods had become. She adjusted her stance, and in the exact second her eyes flickered down, a mass flew from the trees. She shot once, the spark of gunpowder illuming the man's panicked face. There came a shout, a thud, and then he grabbed her legs, pulling her down.

In an instant, he was upon her, his thighs planted on either side of her torso. His hands, large and white, hovered above her face, as though he wasn't used to violence and was disturbed by the possibility of it occurring. She brought a fist back and smashed it into his cheek, sending him stumbling to the left. They had fallen into a mud pit. Any attempt at rising was met with squelching, yielding mud. Her gun had flown from her hand. Gasping, she turned over and searched for her pistol.

An arm looped about her neck and dragged her up. His forearm was a rope around her throat, and for an endless second, she felt the air steal from her lungs. Thrashing, she reared forward and leveled a kick into his groin with the heel of her boot. The man screamed, and she sank her teeth into the fleshy palm of his hand. She bit down until her teeth clicked together. Blood flowed from between her lips, and she threw her head back, spitting out the mouthful of flesh she had torn away.

He stumbled back, panting, his sleeve dark with blood. With poise she didn't feel, Cassandra haltingly backed away before collecting her pistol from the mud. She aimed it at the man, their heaving breaths rising like steam in the night. She moved to speak but paused. There came an intangible change in the air. She heard the cocking of a pistol hammer.

"I'm a detective with Charleston PD," came a low, creeping voice. "And I've got a gun aimed at your head."

There was silence.

"Isn't that how you put it?"

A chill of terror rose within Cassandra. The voice was nasally but smooth, shrill but placid. It was the calmness of it all. This individual was not unaccustomed to violence, as her first opponent had been. There would be no hesitation in shooting her dead.

"What do you want?" she asked, catching her breath. Her pistol remained steady in the air, like her arm had become immovable stone. Her eyes flashed in the direction of the voice, but they were met with dense, disgusting darkness. Moonlight fell in cautious, needle-like holes through the canopies. She examined the minute bits of light, terrified she would see them blink.

"Let him go. The easiest thing in the world."

"Did you kill those women?" Cassandra asked, the question harsh and ungainly in the silence. There came a gentle laugh.

"No," the voice answered. "You don't tell a judge he murdered someone when he sentences a man to death. It's his job. He's helping society for the better. It's his duty."

"What duty could justify the murder of innocent women?"

"It was their duty to die, and they undertook it willingly. I know what you're doing, Detective. Let him go, now. Or I'll shoot you."

Cassandra glanced down at the man. He was down on his knees, one hand cradling his injured palm. His face was dark with mud, and his shoulders heaved with heavy pants. She stepped back and released an aggravated breath.

"Leave," she ordered, her pistol still aimed at his head. The single word rang out, imperious in the silence. The man scrambled to his feet and fled into the nearby darkness. She remained standing for five minutes, her gun cocked in the direction of the voice. But both individuals were long gone. Her head like lead, she pulled her legs from their frozen position in the mud. An unprecedented exhaustion clung to her bones like the cold of a long, bleak winter. She stumbled to the ground, quiet and feverish against the forest floor. There came the noise of distant voices, and then darkness.

Cassandra awoke with her face pressed against the rough texture of her couch. Her eyes fluttered. The fake bleached wood of her coffee table, the scruffy red carpet. A large bowl filled with water sat on the table, and a dirty rag clung to the edge of the bowl. A bead of water hung from the tip of the rag. She watched the bead drip onto the table. Beside it, gleaming as though recently cleaned, sat her chrome lighter. The room was dark, a distant lamp illuming the edge of her vision. Muffled voices sounded from the next room.

They were not incredibly far away–– she lay in the living room, adjacent to the shoebox kitchen where the voices originated. Hissing under her breath, she sat up, got to her feet, and limped quietly to the doorway.

"You should have called an ambulance the minute you found her," came a woman's voice.

The woman's words were loud and shaken, and Cassandra was surprised to recognize Crawford's voice. Her fingers trembled against the doorframe. A weakness she had never felt before imbued her from head to toe.

"The roads are flooded, Virginia. There's a flash flood warning. I could barely make it to this motel. And who lives in a motel long term? It's not like she's making minimum wage."

Singer's attempt at flippancy burst with the anxiety he so often hid beneath academic jargon and awkward warmth. He offered Crawford a series of frantic, half-formed murmurs, giving up as his voice failed him.

"That's not the issue here, Giovanni. You're already far too involved in this investigation. I don't know what Chief Norton will think when he hears about this––"

"Norton knows everything. I called him before I called you."

"What?" Crawford said.

"FME's been contacted, too. It's just a matter of how they'll get here. You know what I think?"

"You always think I'm interested in what you have to say."

"What I have to say is usually super interesting. I think you need to question her as soon as she wakes up. She kept talking on the way here. There was a man with a camera. Said she shot him. Where's he at?"

"We have officers posted at most major intersections within a five-mile radius. Like you said, there's a flood. Comms are down. There are crashes all over I-26. We're doing what we can."

"Why does that never seem enough?" Giovanni said. Tense silence hung between them, and then Crawford's voice broke through.

"Why were you the one to find her?" she asked, voice gentle and low.

"I saw her sprinting between houses. I followed."

"Plenty of people noticed," Crawford said.

"Yeah, but did plenty of people care? Apparently not. Obviously not."

"Giovanni, she's not Beatrice."

An aggravated sigh.

"You haven't looked at me in three years, and this is the first conversation you really want to have?"

"I have reached out," Crawford said. "I have reached out, and you've ignored me every single time. I didn't stop caring about you. I haven't stopped. The love I have for you just can't overcome the hate you've leveled at me."

"You loved Beatrice," came a whisper. "I know you did. But you were so embarrassed about doing so. Why would I take kindly to someone who thinks the worst thing they ever did was love my sister?"

"You don't know what you're talking about," came Crawford's voice, imbued with stunning rage. "How dare you talk like--" Words drained into meaningless puddles down the pathways of Cassandra's mind. She crept back to the couch, every step seeming to take an hour. Blood rushed to her ears, and her hands shivered, clasping and unclasping at the air. Just as she sat down, there came a hard knock at the front door, and someone entered. She glanced up to find Mills in the front hall, his hesitant gaze focused on her face.

"What?" she murmured, straightening.

There came a thunder of footsteps as Crawford and Singer left the kitchen, spilling in behind Mills. Crawford crept forward, her palms facing her, and smiled.

"Wake. Do you know where you are?"

She flung her head up and glared at her, frustrated with the cautious question. There was no reason to handle the situation carefully. It was done and over with. Dedicated to furious silence, she reached down for her mud-caked boots and tried to pull one onto her foot. Neither the boot nor her foot cooperated, but she tried, nonetheless, refusing to acknowledge the worried looks thrown her way.

"Where's she going?" Mills asked, having moved before Crawford.

"An Olympus Trip 35. That's the camera he had. I recognized it. It was Una Boland's camera. For her eleventh birthday."

"It's flooded outside," Mills said exasperatedly. As though to emphasize his words, he gestured to his soaking uniform. His dark shirt and pants were stained black. Short, curly hair pressed in rainswept strands against his cheeks. With the gesture, a spray of water fell across the floor. He grimaced and muttered a quiet apology, looking to Crawford for help.

"Wake, you need to sit. We're waiting for the FME to arrive and evaluate you. We've done a quick medical exam, and nothing seems incredibly off. But we need to question you. Now."

At Cassandra's look of irritation, Crawford crossed the living room and gripped a kitchen chair. She positioned it at a careful distance from Cassandra and sat.

"Mills was actually just out there surveying the scene. Anything to report?"

The young officer glanced down at his hands, and Cassandra noticed for the first time the glint of plastic. He held a tangle of plastic baggies in his hands, and within them——

"What are those?" she asked, rising.

"Wake——"

She took them with a surprising gentleness, uncurling his fingers with her own. He cleared his throat as she turned the baggies over in her hands.

Two separate Polaroids gleamed within their plastic baggies. She pinched them like playing cards between numb, clumsy fingers. The first, the same man from earlier, the same man currently leaning against the entrance hallway of her motel room. Giovanni Singer. The second, a woman with curly brown hair and hard amber eyes. Cassandra Wake.

"The Olympus isn't a Polaroid camera," she said.

"Your outfits aren't the same, either," Mills noted, first pointing to Giovanni and then to Cassandra.

"They've been watching you for a while," Crawford said. Her words came slow and heavy, filled with a sense of chilling finality.

They delved into a tense, anticipatory silence.

Later that night, or early the next morning, Cassandra found herself on the sofa once more. However, this time, she had placed herself there–– a medical officer had finally arrived, conducting a more thorough examination. Immediately after, Crawford initiated a swift interrogation that had ended only twenty minutes prior. She had recounted the man with the camera, their fight, the faceless voice coming from the trees. Her cheeks burned with foreign shame, and she hid it in her pale, unshaking hands.

The man's bitten-off flesh had been collected and was being tested for DNA matches. Officers were pounding on every door nearby, asking business owners for access to security camera footage, homeowners for their doorbell recordings. It was still flooding outside, so results were disappointing and slow. People had hurried in and out of her rooms, checking and rechecking information, harried by the storm and the shock of the night.

From the kitchen, there came the gentle clatter of dishes being removed from the dishwasher and put into cabinets. She had lapsed in and out of ragged sleep, her heart rate skyrocketing and falling just as quickly. Her face grew unbearably hot, and she tore a blanket off, throwing it to the floor. She jumped up, crossed the living room, and shut herself in the bare motel bathroom.

Despite it being her own bathroom, she felt like an intruder, her frantic fumbling rushed for fear of being caught. She grabbed a washcloth from under the sink and shoved it under the tap. Cold water rushed over the washcloth and her fingers. She unfurled the washcloth and pressed it against her face. Cold droplets slithered down her neck and onto the collar of her shirt.

She had already been lightly cleaned, but streaks of mud still marked the corners of her temples, the insides of her wrists and ankles. Her skin felt raw and new. She released a long breath, the cold washcloth wetting her lips.

After a moment, she lifted her gaze and examined her reflection in the mirror. Sharp and pale. Blank amber eyes. Her hair was heavy and dark with rain. She flipped the tap, a torrent of scalding water rushing from the spigot. Fingertips played under the water, immediately flushing a harsh red.

Breaths came smooth and steady. She jerked her hand away and looked again in the mirror. Steam clung to its long surface. She glared into her face, now only an odd, dripping blur.

There came a gentle knock from the door.

"Detective? Do you need anything?"

"Why are you still here?" she asked, voice raised above the tap.

"The uh–– the department's having its busiest day of the year. Didn't want to leave you alone. Virginia made me stay."

"Please leave."

"Of course," he said. "Was just mopping. Muddy footprints everywhere, you know."

"Mopping?"

"It would be cruel to leave you with a messy apartment. I found the key in your wallet. It was closer than my place."

The door opened slowly, as though Giovanni were waiting for her to shove it closed in his face. He emerged from the thick steam. His sleeves were rolled up, and soapy water splattered the front of his shirt. Behind him was a bucket filled with murky water. A dried mop leaned against the wall. He noticed her gaze but remained silent.

He moved forward, reached across her, and turned the tap off. He eased the washcloth from her grip and wrung it out into the sink. Humming, he turned her wrist over and pressed the washcloth against her skin.

"And I will give a new heart to you, and a new spirit I will give into your inner parts. I will remove the heart of stone from your flesh. I will give to you a heart of flesh," he murmured. He lifted the washcloth to her hairline and dabbed at a streak of mud at her temple. The words registered dimly in her mind.

"You believe? After everything?" she asked.

He smiled, and a light giggle spilled from his lips.

"No. I can't bring myself to. But I am forever a preacher's son."

She grabbed his wrist and pulled his arm down. She strode out of the bathroom and sat again on the couch. He trailed behind her, disappearing into the kitchen. After a moment, he came back with a glass of water in his hand.

He crossed the living room, offered her the glass, and stepped back, hands folded behind him. His eyes swam about the room with strained intrigue, and he bounced on his toes with a restless jerk. She placed the untouched glass on the table.

"I no longer require your help. Thank you."

He had taken his glasses off and was wiping them on the hem of his shirt.

"Why do you live in a motel, Detective?"

"What?" she asked, her head aching.

"Why not an apartment?"

"Why does it matter?" she returned sharply. It had been an incredibly long day. Questions ground against her mind like mounds of hail on a collapsing roof. She reached for the glass but did not drink it, rather pressing the coolness to her forehead.

"It's convenient," she said, her words coming after a long minute of contemplation. "I can leave quickly if need be."

He had settled in a nearby chair, one knee crossed over the other. One of her magazines sat splayed open on his lap. She could tell he wasn't reading.

"You never want to own something? Not eventually?"

"Wanting to own things has ruined most good people."

"That's not necessarily true. There are as many ways to ruin a good person as there are stars in the sky."

She sat back, staring thoughtfully at the ceiling. Her headache had somewhat subsided, and she realized, abruptly, that she did not want to be alone.

"I was in a situation when I was younger. Got stuck in a place I didn't want to be in. This ensures I can leave whenever I want."

He nodded, his eyes like warm bits of glass in the lamplight. Cassandra held her breath for a moment and felt the cold weight of her body sink into the couch. Words fell like thick blood from her throat.

"Where I'm from–– it's a small place in Romania. Viscri. Too much snow, not enough money. It gets tiresome blaming the lack of money for everything that goes wrong. It becomes a witch hunt. Finding someone to blame. There was a homeless man." She faltered, frowning down at herself. "Who we chose to blame. See him in your yard, your water goes bad. Give him dinner, your daughter's engagement falls through. One day, out of the blue–– a horrible snowstorm comes in. The kind that freezes chickens where they stand. Everyone is safe inside except for the homeless man. He walks through the rising snow, but it only gets heavier, and the door to any nearby house remains shut. He falls to the ground and begins to freeze. Why would anyone help him? Why would anyone bring him in from the cold?"

She sounded delusional, on the edge of restless paranoia. Her face burned with something like shame, and she reached for her boots once more, intent upon escaping. Giovanni stretched his leg out from the seat, idly kicking his foot.

"Why would anyone help him?" he repeated under his breath. "Because he is alive and suffering. Because he is alive and can be helped."

"But he has only ever brought them suffering. He has never spoken a word that brought good things with it. His presence could have burned the town to the ground."

"A man's heart can survive the burning of a town. It cannot survive the deliberate avoidance of another man's suffering." He sucked in a deep breath and glanced into Cassandra's face. "We must do what we can to protect the human heart. That doesn't mean avoiding what can hurt it. It often means going straight toward those things."

Her hands fumbled with the laces of her boots, and with an irate sigh, she threw them down.

"What if no one helps the man?" she asked, her words like a breath.

He met her eyes from the darkness.

"The man must help himself. He must bring himself out of the cold."

Considering his answer, she sat back, the couch groaning beneath her. His gentle voice spurred a rage within her that desired nothing more than pain. Her lungs were iron, and her mind danced in a drunken stumble. She wanted him gone, wanted his warm shadow out. She wanted him to forget the words that had so suddenly spilled from some forgotten place within her.

"I listened to your conversation with Crawford."

"Oh," he said.

"I know she was engaged to your sister. That you've repeatedly ignored her."

"You don't know what you're talking about, Detective," he said, voice low. He had pulled himself up from his languid position, his back straight and palms flat on the cushion, placed on either side of his hips.

"I know you better than you think," she said. "How alone you are."

"Well," he said lightly, trying to ignore the caustic tone of her voice. "Someone murdered my best friend."

"What do you want? Really. Why aren't you leaving?"

"I don't––"

"Ask me. Ask me anything. I know you want to. I don't care anymore. Ask anything."

"Cassandra, please."

"Ask me, goddammit."

Giovanni crossed the room and knelt at her feet. A slow hand came and grasped her own.

"Are you all right?" he murmured.

She closed her eyes and released a strained breath through her nose. The floor creaked as he sat back on his heels.

"I know you, too," he said, voice deceptively gentle. "I know how that possibility makes you cringe."

"Get out of here."

"You don't want people to know you. And I guess that–– that storm is why. You think you're despicable. Unable to be loved. Undeserving of it. And you've justified a world in which you don't need it."

"That's what a doctoral candidacy in philosophy got you? A banal platitude that love is all that matters?"

"Love might be a banal platitude, but I will not suffer a life without it. And you're a fool if you think you can."

He rose, rain jacket under his arm. He paused and glanced at her. His face stretched in a hollow attempt at a smile, but he quickly gave it up. "Virginia just got a patrol car to sit outside for you."

He moved to leave but paused once more.

"Did you help him?"

She glanced over, a question in her eyes.

"The homeless man."

"Of course I did."

"And did something bad happen after?" he asked.

"Something bad always happens after."

The door clicked gently shut behind him, and she was left in the resounding silence. Overhead, someone flushed their toilet, and a thundering of water sounded through the walls. She released a breath and lay back on the couch.

14

Chapter Fourteen

A s soon as the roads cleared, Giovanni drove to Virginia Crawford's house. It sat in a nice, middle-income neighborhood with clean cars in the driveways and decorative garden gnomes dug gingerly into bright emerald grass. It was not bright at that moment, he admitted. The whole place reminded him of a cat coming out of the rain, sopping and filled with some vague hatred for the surrounding flood. He stood beside his car, breathing in the thick, heady air. He stepped forward and paused, a crunch sounding beneath his shoe. He glanced down to find the cracked wall of a hand-carved birdhouse strewn across the road.

He gave a breathy, desperate laugh and hurried across the street to the pale blue door. He briefly checked the numbers on the mailbox, having long memorized her address. After a stilted moment, he knocked.

"Who is it?" came a man's voice.

"Giovanni Singer."

The door swung open, revealing Richard Crawford. In his arms, wearing a pair of overalls and a brown sweater, was his son. The man offered him a slight grin but did not move from the doorway.

"I hope you've been safe in the storm," Richard said.

Giovanni rocked on his heels, hands shoved deep in his pockets. They had never met. It hadn't seemed necessary. His eyes remained fixed on the man's face, refusing to venture down to the child.

"Oh. Yes. So safe. I was wondering if Virginia was here."

Richard frowned before stepping back, gesturing for Giovanni to enter.

"She just got back. It's nonstop right now."

"Yes. Yeah. It won't be long, just wanted to check in," he said. His entire body burned as though on fire. He clenched his hands once, twice, stilling as he noted Richard's hesitant call for Virginia. They had a guest, he said. She should come down. He turned to leave but found Richard watching him, an honest warmth apparent in his face.

"I forgot something. In my car," he said.

"You'll be all right," Richard said. His voice was gentle, and Giovanni realized the man knew everything. Of course he did. Giovanni would not demand silence from Virginia, had no reason for it. Before he could form an answer, the stairs creaked to his right. He turned to find the tall, angular figure of Virginia Crawford frozen in the stairway. Her hair was dark and curled, still wet from a recent shower. He watched a droplet fall from her hair onto the wood of the stairs.

"Hello," she said.

"Could I talk to you?" he whispered.

Before he knew it, her hand was on his wrist, and they were sitting in a small office room. Reading glasses sat on the bridge of her nose. A stack of books balanced precariously on the edge of the table. Mindlessly, he read their titles, recognizing a few. They sat on a soft, low couch, pastel throw blankets tangled over its cushions. His eyes fell to her face. He let himself look.

"What's his name?" he said.

"Evan. After Richard's brother."

"He's beautiful." Giovanni hadn't looked at the boy, but his words still rang with startling sincerity. He believed it with the certainty that one believed in simple math, in the rise of the sun every morning and its fall every night. His face flushed, and he wiped his hands against the cotton of his trousers. A hand fell on his, stilling their motions.

"I'm sorry," she said.

"Don't say that, please. You don't have to be sorry."

"I thought everything would heal if I left you alone. But it didn't. Not at all."

"I shouldn't have accused you of not loving Beatrice," he said slowly. "That was cruel of me."

She nodded and sat back, her eyes remaining firmly fixed on his face. He felt something within him crack.

"I don't know what to do," he said, the rhythm of his words irregular and weighed down. "People have systems of valuation. What something means and why. And everything that meant anything to me was because of her. I think I've ruined everything. Not by doing anything, but by being the way I am. Being cowardly and full of hate."

"You find new things to value. Find people like Richard and Evan to care for."

"I won't replace Beatrice," he bit out. "I won't erase her from the life she deserved to have."

"It's not replacement, Giovanni. It's surviving."

One hand moved from his forearm and cradled his cheek. It burned like ice.

"It feels like she's gone from the world. Like everyone has moved on. But we haven't. We see her in the places she loved, in the songs she sang in the car. I see her all around me, but in nothing more than you. It's-- it's in the way you walk, the way you explain things. And I'm so sorry. I didn't realize-- I see her in you, and it's my greatest consolation. But you can't see yourself. You can't see how you're the greatest testament to Beatrice and the value of her life."

Her eyes were bright with tears, and she laughed.

"I know you don't believe. You never did. But to me-- God knows our faults. What we think our biggest failings are. And maybe God put you here-- put Wake here-- to show you how to be better. Maybe, if you can recognize that Wake is good, you'll recognize the goodness within yourself. Maybe there can finally be peace."

He leaned into her touch, his eyes closed. A board creaked on the stairs, and then Virginia's husband stood beside them, whispering quick words into her ear. After a moment, he felt her rise from the couch. One hand still clutched his.

"They want to meet you. Officially, this time. Dinner?"

A warm silence settled over them as he rose. Their hands remained clasped together, and as she led him down the stairs, a sharp thrill of fear ran through him. He drew a deep breath and straightened. He heard young, gentle laughter and the sound of small footsteps pattering over the wood floor. Cutting his rampant thoughts short, he plunged his left hand into his pocket and hurried down the remaining steps. Cool overhead light fell over them both, and when her hand tightened on his, he did not pull away.

Cassandra knocked twice on the broad wooden door of Cynthia Ellison's house. The sky sagged with rain despite it being the first dry day in a week. The air burst with humidity, and her clothes clung uncomfortably to her skin. It was a nice neighborhood–– children raced their bicycles in the street, and fathers pushed lawn mowers through their yards, their faces ruddy and gleaming with sweat. She straightened as she heard the door lock click.

"Hello?" came a frail, kindly voice. The door opened slowly but not hesitantly, as though that were merely as fast as it could open. Behind the door, bundled in countless woven, multi-colored shawls, peered a small woman. Her pale blue eyes swam behind thick glasses, and her thin, veiny hands grasped the door frame.

"Hi," Cassandra began, clearing her throat. "I'm Detective Wake with the Charleston Police Department. I was wondering if I could ask you some questions about your son Fred."

Rather than wilt in sorrow as many mourning relatives did, Cynthia Ellison beamed up at Cassandra. She shuffled aside and gestured for her to come in. As Cassandra stepped into the home, she cut her eyes swiftly to the walls and doorways, her heart quickening in her chest. Flushing, she tightened her hands into fists and planted her feet on the dark wood of Cynthia Ellison's home.

It was a quaint, older home, the sort that lingers on the border between obsolete creepiness and nostalgic warmth. The walls were a soft pink, contrasting nicely with the deep wooden accents of the furniture and wall trimmings. Pictures of smiling loved ones were organized neatly across most surfaces, angled in a way that one could view every image should they be interested. She turned, realizing Cynthia had been watching her, a slight smile on her lips.

"I keep it clean," she said, her voice swelling with knowing pride. "I can give you a tour if you'd like."

Cassandra politely declined, instead sitting where Cynthia directed. A round tin of cookies already decorated the vinyl coffee table. Before she could decline once more, Cynthia had gotten a napkin for her and divided four cookies between the both of them. She was agile for her age, agile and perceptive. Images flashed across her mind of the obese, roach-like figure of William Serk, and she fought down a bitter smirk.

"You want to talk about Fred?" Cynthia began.

"Yes, ma'am. A woman went missing in June of 2022 in your son's apartment complex, Cooper's Dell. I know he lived there around that time. Did he ever mention anything about a woman named Clara Thompson?"

Cynthia's hands crept to an unfinished knitting project previously discarded on the edge of the couch. Her fingers played with the frayed ends of thread, twirling them between idle fingertips. She stared down at her hands in thoughtful silence.

"He was a talker. Always spoke more than any of my other children. Just a big nose for other people's business. I can't remember anything specific, but if she lived in the same place, he certainly knew about her."

Cassandra frowned and sat back. According to William Serk, Ellison had been an opportunistic creep much too interested in the lives of two women. Even then, should she discard the words of William Serk, Alex Wendel herself had alluded to Ellison's participation in crude catcalls and harassment. Perhaps he had been led on like a child in a group of larger, more malicious friends. She sat back and smiled at the older woman.

"How many children do you have, ma'am?"

"Five," she answered. "Fred was the third eldest."

"A true middle child," Cassandra said. "I never had any siblings, unfortunately."

"He got along better with his younger siblings, my two daughters. There were a few years between him and my other sons."

"How would you describe him?" Cassandra asked.

Cynthia blinked, fiddling with the knitting material once more.

"My answer would be a little biased, I think."

"Give me your biased answer, then."

A moment of silence. Cynthia Ellison reached up and began to mindlessly play with her gray hair.

"Nosy, like I said. Always wanted to be involved in something. He wasn't a bad person, not at all. But if it meant he wouldn't be left behind, I wouldn't put it past him–– he was kind. Kind and thoughtful. More emotional than my other two boys."

"Any romantic partners?"

"A few." Cynthia shrugged and put the material down. She reached for her napkin and took one of the cookies. Cassandra paused at the woman's reticence, crossing her legs as though to seem more approachable.

"Anything of note there, ma'am?"

"No," Cynthia said. "All the others are married. Nothing ever seemed to work out. I remember, now. Something about that Thompson girl."

"He mentioned her?"

"He was making a table. Said someone had stolen their table, and he thought it was a shame. It was the last thing he made. That's why I remember."

Cassandra tilted her head, and information settled slowly in her mind. Verified certificates of death, both from the hospital and morgue, were in Fred Ellison's file. He had died of terminal pancreatic cancer, had been receiving treatment for a mere two months prior to death. He had most likely been feeling the effects of said illness when Clara Thompson disappeared. Perhaps his unexpected turn in fate had resulted in a change of heart and attitude.

"Mrs. Ellison, we have witnesses stating it was Fred himself who stole their table. It went missing in December of 2021."

Cynthia Ellison glanced up, smiling slightly. "That's simply not possible. We fly to London every year for Christmas. My late husband's parents are there. And they certainly can't come to us."

"He couldn't have stolen their table," Cassandra repeated.

"I have pictures," Cynthia said. "We take the same picture every year. But then Fred passed, and so did my husband. But we had pictures that year."

She rose, and Cassandra followed her with her eyes. After a moment of fumbling, the woman returned with a picture frame in her hand. And there he stood. Fred Ellison grinned out from a myriad of similar faces. His reddish hair had blown up from his forehead in the wind, and one hand was on his mother's shoulder.

"Thank you for your time," Cassandra said, rising. In an instant, she was on the porch, fingers dancing quickly over her phone screen. She stood, restless amid the stuffy warmth about her, and listened to the persistent, unanswered ring of her phone. She tried again, and again the phone remained unanswered. William Serk had proven a liar, had quite thoroughly thrust any suspicion onto his dead neighbor. She imagined Serk had been there in Fred Ellison's last months, had watched the man grow thinner and weaker. And as his final consolation, Serk had labeled him a malignant stalker.

She slipped into the driver's seat and pulled swiftly out of the driveway. Sun pooled across the hoods of parked cars, and as she blinked, the world seemed engulfed in a bright, unnatural light. Her hands tightened on the leather of the steering wheel. Breathing deeply, she fumbled with a switch in the door, waiting as the window slid down amid a stream of thick, warm air.

Later that afternoon, Cassandra found herself once more submerged in the records room. She did not yet know what she searched for, had only longed for some semblance of familiarity with the names that swirled in her mind. Her coworkers would not talk, barring her from some clandestine truth. Even Crawford and Heyward stood at a distance from her. Alongside the current investigation, half of her job was bridging the vacuous gap between that which her coworkers would acknowledge and the rest that remained unsaid. But the documents had no such hang-ups.

Her fingers and eyes ran lightly along the crisp files. She sought out case files and reports completed by Beatrice Singer herself. Countless noise complaints. Even more minor traffic violations. Her official career had been blaringly uneventful. She blinked and tore her gaze away from the papers that seemed to glow in the darkened room.

Cassandra wondered if they did not prefer their worlds this way. Disconnected from the horrors of the past. As though it could be avoided if one stayed quiet long enough. As though it did not exist if one did not look at it. Virginia Crawford had married and raised a son. Would she wish, even now, that Beatrice Singer had not died that night? Could one be grateful for the events that ruined their first life, so as to start anew?

How many unfathomable steps had been taken to reach the acceptable *now*? Heavy footsteps passed the closed doorway to her left, and she shook these thoughts from her mind. She rose and began a wandering path through the dark records. Something glittered in the edge of her vision, and she paused, allowing her eyes to adjust. Tucked between two brimming cardboard boxes was a cheap black picture frame. She pulled it from the shelf. A battalion of young, uniformed officers greeted her. As Beatrice Singer's lively face peered out from the left corner of the photo, Cassandra figured the staff photograph had been taken sometime around early 2017.

The glass of the cheap frame had long ago been removed. She fiddled with it for a moment, attempting to straighten the photo within, and watched as it slipped from the frame, fluttering to the floor. She knelt, placed the frame on the ground, and pinched the photo between two fingers. Mindlessly, she turned it over and read the description on the back.

Department Staff – February 2017

Her fingers shuffled on the edge of the photo, and as they moved, she noted a scribble on the bottom right corner. She narrowed her eyes against the thick darkness and parsed through the words.

Right after father's death. Happy work anniversary to me.

She pulled the phone from her pocket and dialed a number. Giovanni Singer picked up after two rings.

"Yes, Detective?"

She began to speak but paused. His voice beamed with an uncharacteristic lightness. It lacked the sharp wit so effusive in his regular conversations. For an instant, she felt as though she were talking with a stranger. The silence ticked on, and she heard him shuffle on the other line.

"Are you all right?" he asked.

"Your father," she said, then stopped. "Did your father pass in February of 2017?"

"I'm open to talking anytime, Detective, but this topic seems a little gloomy."

"Did he?"

"He passed in January of that year. It was a month before Beatrice hit her first year at the department. We had a party planned. And then. You know. Seemed silly to celebrate after that."

"Could I ask how he passed?" she murmured.

"Brain aneurysm in his sleep. They took him straight to the coroner."

"No hospital visits?"

"No need. We found him cold as ice."

Cassandra hummed, fingers light on the edge of the photograph.

"Do you need anything else?"

She fiddled with the photograph until it sat neatly in the middle of the frame. She closed her eyes and listened to his faint breath across the line.

"No," she said. "Have a good day, Giovanni. Please."

"Well. Since you asked so nicely, I'll try my best."

15

Chapter Fifteen

It had not started as one suspected. Had not been as he knew. Some tenuously hung thing within him came undone, whipping about like a beheaded snake. There was no putting anything back together, as the old arrangement hadn't been any good, hadn't been helpful to anyone at all. It had started with Virginia's strained face in the lamplight.

It was not dark outside, but the broad blinds of his office cast an artificial gloom about them. His eyes strained to read in the darkness. A battered copy of The Consolation of Philosophy held tenderly with two hands. His scuffed dress shoes crossed on the edge of his desk. He blinked and tore the glasses from his nose.

His phone sat beside his laptop, warm from his recent call. Cassandra Wake's voice sounded through his mind, and he wished to remain quiet for an instant longer, remembering it.

"Any news on Ronald White?" Virginia asked, situated in a straight-backed wooden chair closer to the door. He placed a finger between the pages and glanced up.

"He brushes his teeth with Crest. You can smell it from a mile away."

"About any domestic issues with him and Kira. Particularly close to her abduction."

Giovanni did not want to talk about Ronald White. An odd feeling arose within him that he was betraying the man, a sentiment he knew to be irrational. He felt Virginia's eyes on him, and he sat straight in his chair, his legs falling to the floor.

"They seemed, actually–– pretty healthy. For them being alcoholics and drug addicts. But he was on the road a lot. Which makes it a miracle he never got charged with a DUI, if you think about it."

"What about any medical stays?"

"I'm not his therapist, Virginia," he said.

"It's important. I wouldn't be asking otherwise. Any stops at the major hospitals around here? A clinic? Anything."

"He overdosed the same night Beatrice went missing, you know that."

"Anything." Her voice sank into the silence, heavy with hope and desperation.

"What's so special about hospital stays? You think–– you think something happened at a hospital? That Kira Rushton met someone at a hospital, or what? I don't know what you're looking for."

"Clara Thompson was an artificial insemination. We're trying to track the sample, but the procedure requires medical knowledge. We're looking into medical professionals."

Giovanni put the book down.

"And domestic issues?"

"Wake noticed a pattern with the victims and their families. They weren't doing well, with public confrontations very close to their disappearances."

He frowned at the wall, unwilling to meet her eyes.

"Do you remember–– after our father passed. I was in the hospital for a week. Do you remember?"

Virginia's eyes flicked up, bright with something like nerves. She gave a gentle laugh, attempting to dispel the dark atmosphere.

"I do. You beat me at thirty-nine consecutive games of chess."

"Did you and Beatrice ever fight? Did you ever fight when I was in the hospital?"

Virginia's fingers tightened in her lap.

"Maybe. Beatrice was so worried about you. We both were. It was difficult thinking about anything besides how you were doing."

"I need more than a 'maybe,' Virginia."

"For that whole month–– between your father's death and your breakdown, I don't remember a time we weren't fighting. She was just so angry."

He gave a low, thoughtful hum, whipping his gaze away from her in an abrupt termination of the conversation. He picked up the book and began to read.

"Giovanni, please––"

"Though thunderous winds resound and churn the seething sea, hidden away in peace––"

"What are you doing?"

"And sure of your strong-built walls, you will lead a life serene and smile at the raging storm," he read, a tone of finality in his voice. In the midst of his reading, he had stood. His head spun in the gloom.

"What's going on?"

"Each victim had public domestic problems? And they might have been exposed to their murderer through a hospital stay? Is that what you're saying?"

"They're patterns based on grounded inferences," Virginia said, hesitant. "Can you sit back down?"

"I'm sorry," he said, falling back in his seat. He pressed his palms into his eyes. Bursts of light played across his eyelids. A shuddering breath shot through his nostrils. Sharp elbows dug into his shaking knees. A cold sweat gathered on his forehead, and he gave a panicked laugh.

"Calm down before you get hurt," Virginia said, rising. He felt her hand on his wrist, attempting to pull it away from his face.

"How are you sure Kira Rushton was the intended victim?" he breathed out.

"What?"

"None of the patterns you've noticed fit with her. But they sure fit with-- with--"

"And the child was naturally conceived," Virginia said, frozen in place.

"She was a druggie, a criminal. But Beatrice wasn't. Beatrice ran every morning."

"We'll talk about this later," she said, hands on his shoulders, keeping him in place. "We'll crosscheck NICU workers around that time--"

He rose abruptly, giving a dreadful groan. His skin burned. A constant tremor ran through his legs, his lungs, his reddened fingers. All the air in the room turned to water, clinging to his clothes, clothes clinging to his skin. He could feel the years like chains hanging from him, him, the ghost of whatever past threatened to spill onto *now,* onto the insurmountable future.

There came a light, muffled music, as though his head were submerged under water. The sweet, smoky taste of burning leaves on his tongue. He was impossibly small, had been a sickly, furious child intent upon showing the world he was worthwhile. His navy-blue Converse scraped the mossy brick step of his childhood home. The air bit at his skin, and he shoved his hands under him. From the edge of his consciousness, a gate swung open.

"Why are you still awake?" came a hushed question.

He grinned, and the air suddenly did not seem all that cold.

"I wanted you to get home safe," he said. Rather than hurry past him–– for they were both up long past their curfews–– Beatrice slumped down on the step beside him. She drew him close against her. He smelled the floral scent of her shampoo and basked in the warmth of her arm around his shoulder.

"It's my special skill," she said into his hair. "Getting home safe. I think you just wanted an excuse to stay up." In an instant, she was up, her tight grip on his arm demanding he rise, as well. Her eyes flickered to the neighboring fence, behind which filtered soft, rolling music. One of her sneakers began a rhythmic beat on the grass, and she lifted an arm over their heads, forcing him into an awkward twirl.

"What are you doing?" he whispered.

"It's a free concert, Giovanni. You've got to dance."

"You just came back from a concert. Aren't you tired of dancing?"

"My favorite partner wasn't there. Now dance with me, loser."

Their laughter faded into the night like vapor dissipating in the sky. There was no light, as their father was a rather judicious enforcer of rules and curfews. Discovery would strip them of time with friends, of favored television programs after dinner. Beatrice's face glowed in the moonlight, and he closed his eyes as she led him in a stumbling dance around the backyard.

"Giovanni?" Virginia murmured.

He turned and, with a great clatter, tore the window blinds up from the glass.

Sun spilled in, stinging his eyes and curling like a flashbang through his mind. His hands returned to his face, and his arms would not budge despite Virginia's gentle attempts to bring them down to his side.

"I can feel all the years," he said. "Every year we lived and every year before us. Like they're walking beside us. It's all happening now. I can feel it. All the sadness. All the loss. All the good things that could have happened, and all the horrible things that did. Can't you feel that? Can't you?"

"Giovanni, please calm down. Please."

"Can't you feel it? Why is no one screaming? Everything—— everything's falling down, Virginia. Everything's coming down on top of us."

Hurried, hushed words flushed over his consciousness and then were gone. Someone had pushed him to sit on the ground. He felt the cold wood beneath him and the hair in his hands. Somewhere in a corner of his mind, he despised his seat on the ground, despised his outburst of irrationality and senseless proclamations. But there seemed a time for irrationality. This was the time, this very moment. He would climb on the table, would trumpet some declaration like a herald shouting—— he ground out a heavy breath, and his hands dug into his face.

A searing pain shot through his stomach, and he awkwardly bent over, vomiting onto the floor. He clambered up from his seat and coughed again, his throat burning. Voices sounded from the doorway of his office, different voices and different people.

"Stop it," he said, clenching his eyes shut against the world. And for a moment, drenched in the abrupt light streaming through the window, he sat suspended like a mite of dust, shivering and shaking as he hissed to himself. "Stop it."

He closed his eyes even tighter and let the world settle somewhere unheeded in the background. His ears rang, and his heart scrambled in his chest. He whimpered as his mind drifted. As though toppled with a sudden breeze, his thoughts stumbled, stopped, and fizzled out into oblivion.

They stood in a bleak MUSC hallway, neither speaking. Crawford sat hunched in an ugly, sterile seat pushed up against the wall. Her foot bounced incessantly, betraying the furious race of her thoughts. Directly across from her, Cassandra leaned with one boot against the wall, arms crossed over her chest. She did not move, hardly breathing. There came a rush of footsteps down the hall.

"Are you–– are you here with Giovanni?" a young man asked breathlessly.

Crawford did not look up and did not speak.

"Who the hell are you?" Cassandra bit out.

"His roommate. Cellmate. I mean–– that's what he calls me. Sorry. It's not the time. We live together. Cody Lenniker." The man offered her a hand, smiling sheepishly but with determination. After a moment, she took his hand and nodded.

"We've been working with him on a recent case. You're his emergency contact?"

"Yeah," he said. "I just found that out thirty minutes ago, actually. Yeah."

She glanced past him as a nurse emerged from the closest room. The woman appeared relatively unharried, her pale blue scrubs unstained and bright in the sallow overhead lights. She noted the congregation of people in the hall and offered them a gentle smile.

"Mr. Singer's doing well. He's cleared a Virginia Crawford to receive any medical information. Is that any of you?"

Crawford slowly raised her hand and stood, her face drawn. She and the nurse began a quiet conversation that led them on a slow walk down the hall. Both Cassandra and Lenniker followed the pair with their eyes.

"Do you know what's going on?" Lenniker asked.

"Do you?" She returned, an inexplicable restlessness overtaking her limbs. She released a breath through her nose, rocking on the balls of her feet. "Sounds like a drug overdose kick-started a nervous episode."

"That's just a guess?" Lenniker asked, giving a rough laugh. After a moment, he shook his head. "He's clean. The cleanest person I know. It's 'cause he's so nervous all the time. Didn't want to mess with his head."

"His eyes were red, and he couldn't stop shaking. Threw up all over his office."

"You were there?"

"I cleaned it up. Crawford called me while he was freaking out," she said.

"Food poisoning, then."

She watched him, an odd seriousness settling in her stomach. She moved closer to Lenniker and grabbed his shoulder, forcing him to face her.

"He hasn't been acting erratic? Nothing unusual?"

"I bake bread from dawn to dusk. I'm not paid to be observant." He paused, a look of thoughtfulness overtaking his features. His voice came low and resigned. "He's always erratic."

Giovanni Singer lay in the slim hospital bed, pallid and still like a monument cut from white stone. A thin IV line stuck to the crook of his left elbow. His dark brown hair stuck up in odd directions, stiff with sweat and grease. His face seemed disarmingly blank without his glasses. A narrow stretch of pale skin interrupted by chapped lips and furious brown eyes.

Cassandra stood equally motionless, poised like a gargoyle at the edge of his bed. She tightened her shoulders before letting her arms fall uselessly to her sides.

"Your office is cleaned," she said. "None of your coworkers saw anything."

"I'm sorry," he whispered.

"For what?"

"I got nervous."

"I did, too," she whispered back. "Did you know your mercury blood levels were 48 nanograms per milliliter?"

"They told me. Don't know how that happened."

"Have you eaten anything out of the ordinary? Anything at all?"

"No, Detective, I haven't. I don't know what happened."

She hummed, watching him. Her hand came to rest on the plastic rail at the edge of the bed. Slowly, her steps light and measured, she rounded the bed to stand at Giovanni's side. She dropped to her knees and examined his face.

"Why did you get so nervous?"

His eyes tightened, and his head swung away as though he had smelled something too pungent. Her fingers brushed the coarse cloth of the hospital blanket. She felt his warmth like that of a flickering fire. She stood before almost immediately falling into a seat shoved in the room's corner.

"Virginia told me about the profile you made. About hospital visits and family problems. I'd had something like this," he gestured to the hospital room. "Something like this when Beatrice was alive. It was after our father died. I'd freaked out and–– and ended up here. And–– and that was a few months before Beatrice went... went missing."

"You're assuming your sister was the intended target?" Cassandra murmured.

"You're not an idiot," he said, sneering. "Don't tell me you hadn't thought of that."

"I hadn't known about your medical issues. Or Beatrice's marital conflicts."

"Me neither." His voice was low with grief. "But if the suspect is a medical professional, then I–– then her visiting me here. That's where this guy saw her. Where he decided that she would die."

"If you hadn't gone to the hospital," she said. "If Beatrice hadn't pulled Kira Rushton over. If some man hadn't woken up one day and decided he'd take a life and enjoy doing so. It's happened, Giovanni. It's over. You can blame yourself or the wind or God. But that doesn't make it right. And that doesn't make anything easier."

Giovanni stared at the far wall, his head leaned back against the board behind him.

"Some things are by their nature temporary. That doesn't make them less valuable," he said. "If love lasts only a day, that's the nature of love. You can't have it any other way. Then it would be something else. If someone dies at twenty-five, then it's their nature to do so. There never was going to be a seventy-year-old Beatrice Singer because she died decades before. Some things are by their nature temporary," he repeated. His voice was light but firm, imbued with uncharacteristic certainty.

Sun fell across his face, giving his pale cheeks some color. Her hands tightened on her knees. He glanced over, and they sat for a moment in silence.

"I just wish your sister wasn't," she said.

"Some boys, being who they were, died young. Some men became lawyers. Others became deadbeat fathers. Some girls ventured out in the snow to help an ailing man."

"And some men, because of who they were, killed others?" she asked, voice tinged with disbelief.

"The future is not inevitable, but the past is," he said. He turned, and she winced as the IV line in his arm pulled taut.

"There are men who, because of their natures, kill others. But there are others who will stop them. And that is simply who they are. There is no Cassandra Wake who did not go out into the cold. Because that girl who stayed inside–– that couldn't have been you. Another Cassandra Wake, another girl, but not you."

"And a Giovanni Singer whose sister lived to seventy-five?" she murmured.

"Not me," he said. "There might be a world where Beatrice and I live together for the rest of our lives. But it's–– that's not this world. And that Giovanni Singer isn't me."

She watched him, and a light heat, like a breeze, rolled over her skin.

"I have to go," she said.

Like dark marbles, his eyes rolled and followed her as she crossed the room. Not another word was said. The click of the door settled into silence. Cassandra glanced to the colorful signs overhead that indicated hallways and room numbers. Her steps were quick and determined on the tile floor.

She did not acknowledge Cody Lenniker when she burst from the room and hurried down the hallway. The walls were a sour yellow, the shade of yellow characteristic of bloodless cheeks and dry-rotted papers. A distant murmuring sounded to her right, and following a series of sharp turns, she came upon a wide, open-walled office filled with bustling nurses and hospital officials.

After a quick conversation with a stern-faced woman, she found herself ensconced in a cramped office with walls lined with rusted green filing cabinets. The switch for the overhead light had been flipped, but the bulb was long dead. She sat in darkness, her heartbeat loud but steady in her ears. She examined the far wall, bent halfway out of her chair as though desperate to see but cautious of being caught. Her fingers caught the edge of a scratched, pale wooden desk, and with a quiet decision, she jumped up and turned to the nearest filing cabinet.

A brief investigation confirmed that each filing cabinet was locked. A clerk was supposed to arrive any moment with the correct keys. She examined the bleak walls, pushing her mind into action. They were filled with papers pinned to bits of cork or kept up with wadded scraps of tape. Her phone flashlight caught the imprint of ancient fingerprints left on tape. With a low hum, she moved on, tracing the walls with her fingers and eyes. As she made her way around the desk, the door opened. Pale, sterile light fell in like a burst of water through a cracked dam, and she straightened, awaiting the clerk.

"I see you've already begun looking around," the clerk noted. She was a slight woman with reddish hair and mint green scrubs. She supported a plastic clipboard between her side and elbow, the sort that opened and closed. She sat it on the desk and opened it. Cassandra raised a hand and touched the side of the filing cabinet to her right.

"What are these?" she asked.

The orderly frowned at her question and came over. On the side of the cabinet were odd pieces of film pasted with bits of painter's tape. They depicted a handful of smiling, exhausted mothers. Their faces gleamed with sweat, and she could very nearly hear the shriek of the infants held close to their chests.

"Mementos," the orderly said. "We take Polaroids for some mothers if they want something to remember the day by."

"These are film, not Polaroids."

"Yeah. Those are older. Polaroids made more sense. Someone would have to go and develop these films, and sometimes the mothers didn't stay in the hospital long enough for results."

"When did this practice start?" Cassandra's voice was insistent.

"A few years ago. Is something wrong?"

"Do you know who started it? Please."

"I'm not–– I'm not sure. You requested employment records? I have the key right here."

Cassandra closed her eyes and drew in a sharp breath. A smell had lingered on the edge of her consciousness, strange and inde-cipherable against the haze of chemical solutions that had seeped indelibly into the hospital walls. She surged forward, around the orderly, and pressed her face close to the cracks between filing cab-inet drawers. After a cursory investigation, she passed on, pressed close to each metal face.

"Ma'am?" the orderly murmured.

"This one," she said. "This one. Open this one, please."

"Those aren't the employment records."

"Open it, or I will."

The clerk fumbled with a ring of keys, the quiet jingle of metal on metal filling the silence. After a moment, she pushed forward and, slipping a key into the lock, slid the drawer open. In an in-stant, Cassandra was upon the files. She dug through them with an almost studious intensity, her phone's flashlight peering alongside her. With a triumphant hiss, she pulled her jacket sleeve over her hand and reached in. The orderly watched as she retrieved two brittle, yellowed bits of film and dropped them on the desk.

"Those are mementos, too," she said. "Some of them went bad. We're not sure why."

"Vinegar Syndrome. If they're exposed to too much heat or poor weather, they can become brittle. It occurs with cellulose acetate film."

After an extended period of silence, the clerk retrieved the initially requested employment records. Cassandra sat at the desk, finger tracing the pages, face pressed close to each line of names. She had demanded the orderly find someone who knew the developer of each memento. So far, there had been no progress. She sat back and dug a hand into her pocket, taking out her phone. Her fingers numbly dialed a number, and she pressed it to her ear.

It rang once, twice, three times. Her face tightened as the silence continued. There came a click and a rasping breath.

"This is William Serk."

"This is Detective Wake," she returned. "I was going over some notes. I'm not sure if I spelled some of the surnames correctly. Could you go over them for me?"

There came the shuddering artificial wheeze of a ventilator.

"I don't think I'd be helpful," he said.

"Fred Ellison. Is that two L's?"

"I can't help."

"You won't help," she corrected. Her voice shot like a bullet over the line. "You won't help, William." She settled in her seat and tightened her shoulders against the back of the chair. "I'm going to charge you with obstruction of justice. Is this truly worth it? How long do you think you'll last in prison?"

"Are you allowed to say that?"

"I'm allowed to speculate how long you'll survive as some murderer's bitch."

There came a distant shuffling across the line.

"Two L's, then."

"Tony Weaver? Is that right?'

A sound of affirmation.

"And the other one? I can't read my notes. There might have
been a D somewhere in there."

"Danny Litch," he murmured.

"And you said he was married?"

"No, I didn't."

"Was he married?"

"Yes."

"To whom?"

"I didn't catch her name."

"You lived in the same apartment complex for years," Cassandra said, then paused. Whirling thoughts coalesced in her mind,
and she drew in a quick breath. "That watch."

"What watch?"

"Yours. That lovely gold watch. I looked it up. It's an old Rolex
Explorer. They sell those on eBay for thousands. Usually around
ten thousand."

"So?" he said, irritation creeping into his voice.

"You're on social security, and your child bride takes care of you
all day. Where'd you get the money for that watch?"

Cassandra cleared her throat as the man remained silent.

"Has someone been paying you off, William?"

"No," he said breathlessly.

"Who broke that table? The table on Clara Thompson's balcony. I know it wasn't Fred Ellison."

"I don't know who."

"Yes, you do, William. Just tell me. Tell me and it'll be easier for you in whatever hell the judge decides you'll rot in."

"You bitch. You don't know what you're talking about," Serk said, seething. When he spoke next, it was not as though he were confessing, but bragging about something hitherto unspoken. "Yeah, I broke the table. But that's it. Then I went back. Tried to apologize, okay? She wouldn't let me talk. We had a fight, but the girl wasn't dead. Litch said he'd get rid of her. Then the cash came every month. But I-- I don't know the wife's name."

A great surge of static came over the line. She heard the sharp murmur of words obscured by static, and then the line fell dead. She jerked up as the orderly opened the door once more.

"An old pediatric nurse," she said. "She's moved to Trident. But she's the one who developed everything for us. Her name was Missy Litch."

She put the phone back in her pocket and glanced down at the papers on the desk. Her left pointer finger lingered on a line, as though it were accusing the paper of something heinous. At the end of her finger, marking the paper like a dark scar, sat that very name.

Cassandra jumped up and took the woman's hand, squeezing desperately. In an instant, she was out the door, flying back in the vague direction where Giovanni Singer and, she hoped, Lieutenant Crawford remained. Sallow walls and sterile clouds of chemicals sailed by, unnoticed. In the distance, she saw Crawford rise, intrigued by the concentration on Cassandra's face.

"You took your patrol car here?"

Crawford nodded.

"Where'd the kid go?"

"He had to leave," Crawford said. "Ronald White's in there with him."

"Excuse me?"

"He seemed genuinely concerned. And staff comes in and out every hour or so."

Cassandra glanced at the shut door and nodded, hurrying toward the exit. Words spilled from her mouth, and they engaged in hushed, fervent conversation all the way to the car.

16

Chapter Sixteen

There came the muffled suck of water being flushed down a toilet. He had awoken with Ronald White perched at his bedside. Whatever sleep he had gotten after his conversation with Detective Wake had worked only to convolute his already meandering thoughts. A vague frustration grew within him. He could not think, not very well–– like a man intent upon running but able only to stumble. A hand came to his forehead and wiped at the cold sweat gathered at his temples.

A crumpled brown paper bag. What had been inside? Half a sandwich lingered still on the cramped desk in his bakery flat. He watched the door, eyes intense but mind wandering. After a moment, his gaze fell away, and he shivered as he pulled against the IV line in his elbow. Nurses rotated in-and-out every hour, with the last nurse having just cleaned up his bedside and checked on his vitals. He strained to push his hearing outside the room but was met with nothing louder than the feeble beat of his heart.

He glanced up to find Ronald White standing in the bathroom doorway. His stoic face twisted in an odd expression of concern. With a gentle click, he shut the door behind him and crossed to the chair beside the bed.

"How are you doing?" Ronald asked.

"Do you have my clothes? The ones I came here in."

"They were folded up in the bathroom," he answered. "Do you want them?"

Giovanni nodded and waited as the older man retrieved them and put them at the foot of his hospital bed.

"I was wondering," Giovanni said slowly. "How you knew I was here."

Ronald twisted his hands in his lap and looked to the gentle light falling through the window.

"I wanted to go to Hampton Park like usual. Kept calling. That officer answered."

"Who?"

"Her uniform said Crawford."

"My, uh–– my phone doesn't have any recent missed calls from you."

"The storm probably messed with some reception. I know my phone's been acting strange."

Giovanni nodded, muttering something about technology. He fingered the call button under the blanket, nodding still. A flush rose in his face as he narrowed his eyes, forcing his attention into a pinhole.

"Did you hear about my blood mercury levels? I mean, that's a lot of–– a lot of fish. Swordfish and shark. Tilefish, too."

"What?"

"I keep thinking about that thing you said. When we first met. If I didn't have the pills, someone else brought them. If I didn't take them, someone else made me. Like that."

"You shouldn't put that much thought into things I say," Ronald murmured.

"And I keep thinking, too, about you. About your face and your daughter."

Ronald did not answer, his feet shifting on the tile floor. An AC unit kicked on overhead. They both jumped. A slight breeze fluttered the hair hanging over Ronald's forehead.

"And all the food you've given me. When you found out I had no money. I thought you were being nice. Making up for something."

"I was being nice. Trying to be," he said, straightening.

"No," Giovanni said, face red. "I was being nice. I didn't want to hate you. It's so tiresome. So I tried to understand you. And I did. I thought you were worth it."

"Worth what?" came his quiet words.

"The pain of caring about someone again. And then you go and do this."

"This? I don't know what the hell you're talking about."

Giovanni's eyes were bloodshot amid a flushed, furious face.

"It's like talking with a goddamn child."

Ronald stood with a groan, plastic cane clutched in his white-fingered hand.

"Where's that button? I'm calling a nurse."

"What you're gonna do–– you're gonna go into the bathroom. I'm gonna change. And then you're giving me your keys. No–– wrong order. You're gonna––"

"You can't drive in this condition. And I don't know what you're saying, but––"

"You put me in this condition, you jerk. You goddamn idiot. Can't even muster up the courage to admit what you did. What'd you use, huh? Break some thermometers?"

Ronald stood in the corner, poised awkwardly as though preparing for escape. He frowned as Giovanni tore the IV line from his elbow and reached for his discarded socks, attempting to stifle the blood flow that already dripped sluggishly down the inside of his forearm.

"Mercurochrome," he whispered, stepping back.

"If this gets out, you're never seeing your daughter again. I won't tell if you get in that bathroom. And give me your keys." He held out a trembling hand.

"They–– they said they'd free Kira if I incapacitated you. Just put you out of the situation for a minute."

The question of "they" fluttered through Giovanni's mind, and he jerked his head, denying the thought any further progress. He released a sharp breath and ignored the rising myriad of doubts within himself. His fingers closed around the keys in his hand, and he gestured for Ronald to leave.

"Bathroom," he said.

"You truly shouldn't drive. If not for yourself, then for other people on the road."

"Shut the hell up and leave me be. I don't take advice from people who try to kill me."

Ronald gave a heavy sigh and began toward the bathroom.

"It doesn't matter anymore, I guess. But I–– I wasn't trying to kill you. Really."

He watched as the older man shut himself in the bathroom. With heavy hands, he pulled his clothes on and attempted to neaten his hair. He reached for his folded glasses and shoved them onto his nose. Blinking away a headache, he crossed the room and slipped into the hospital hall. His steps remained steady while his mind faltered. He had not thought this far ahead, had simply wanted to leave and the freedom to do so. There came a gentle buzz from his pocket, and he answered the phone without any further thought.

"Who's that?" he murmured.

"Mr. Giovanni?"

"Henry? How'd you get my number?"

"Mr. Giovanni, please. My parents–– they're not acting right."

Giovanni surged forward as the exit doors wheezed open.

"What do you mean? Scaring you?"

"They've taken Beatrice. It's not the right time."

"They have every right to take Beatrice. She lives with them," he said. "But I can–– I'll head to Hampton Park now. Isn't that near where you live?"

"No," Henry said, hushed. "Beatrice doesn't live with us. She's not–– she lives with that foster family. But I don't. She's not supposed to be here."

"You're her foster brother," Giovanni said, stopping on the sidewalk. He heard wet breaths on the other line. "That's your foster family, too. Right?"

"I'm not," Henry said, strained and quiet. "Her foster mom. That's my aunt. My mom told her to do it."

Tires crunched wetly over the long gravel driveway as Cassandra and Lieutenant Crawford approached the old farmhouse purportedly owned by Danny and Missy Litch. It sat in an empty field on the edge of Goose Creek. Thick, gnarled trees groaned overhead as though pressed down by some ancient weight, and their gray beards of Spanish moss glittered with the remnants of rain. It was not yet dark, but the trees and their hunched bodies cast a strange gloom over the driveway. The lieutenant guided her car slowly, hesitantly, both women restless and observant of every stray flutter of leaves, every wayward needle of light peering through the foliage.

She had explained everything to the lieutenant, in the way she knew how. They delved into anticipatory silence. She acknowledged the tightening of her lungs and the quick patter of her heart, but with a stern thought, these sensations slipped from her mind. Through the trees rose a pale white house, its walls like expanses of bleached bone. She glimpsed peeling red window shutters and the flimsy light of hanging oil lamps. A shrill ring sounded from the lieutenant's pocket, and both women flinched.

Lieutenant Crawford answered it then slipped the phone back into her pocket. Her hands tightened on the steering wheel before she reached over and put the car in park.

"Little Beatrice has gone missing," she said.

"What do you mean?" Cassandra murmured.

"She and her foster brother were playing in the front yard. Foster mother went outside, and they were gone."

"Beatrice Singer doesn't have a foster brother," Cassandra said, frowning. "Her foster family was new to the process."

With a stern reminder to get back to this matter, Cassandra undid her seat belt and slipped out into the warm air. The lawn had been recently cut, most likely right before the disastrous flooding. There still came a slight squelching beneath her boots as she stepped. Two cars, a Mazda and a Toyota, slumbered like metallic beasts in a slim concrete expanse before the garage. Crawford crept out of the car and crossed to stand beside her. They watched the house, both caught too much in their own thoughts to talk.

After a moment, she began across the lawn, trotted up the front brick steps, and pounded on the door. Crawford stood on a lower step, attempting to conjure a sense of normalcy. They did not have enough for a warrant, had only enough to ground a handful of suspicions. They would find something and confirm the location with Heyward, who had been briefed on everything. From inside came the groan of old wood flooring, and then the door swung open.

A woman stood in the darkened doorway. Her skin was pale, nearly white as the house's wooden walls. She stood taller than either of them, certainly over six feet. Cassandra cleared her throat and bounced back on her heels. She offered a hand, which the woman easily took.

"I'm Detective Wake from the Charleston Police Department. This is Lieutenant Crawford. Are you Missy Litch?"

The woman nodded, a curious look in her eyes.

"We wanted to ask you a few questions about some neighbors you had in Cooper's Dell."

"Oh," Missy Litch said. "Of course. Come in."

She did not recognize the woman's voice. No shiver of fright ran across her spine at the flowing syllables. Her heart didn't stutter, and her soul didn't freeze. Then again, she could not trust every remembrance of that night. Of the frigid voice that crept like mustard gas from the trees. She drew in a deep breath and followed Missy Litch inside. She fell onto a pouchy leather couch situated against the far wall of the living room. Crawford chose to remain standing.

"So. An old neighbor in Cooper's Dell?"

Litch settled in a floral chair on the other side of the coffee table. A random smattering of magazines sat neatly on the table, and Cassandra leaned forward, leafing through them. She spoke without raising her eyes.

"Are you aware of the recent homicides in Charleston County? Namely, the woman found in Drayton Swamp."

"As aware as anyone else. I'm lucky to live further away from Charleston nightlife."

Cassandra smiled, nodding in agreement. "That you are. Can't say it's easy sleeping with all that noise around you. Anyway. We have reason to believe William Serk and Fred Ellison worked together to kill these women. As Ellison is dead, we have only Serk in custody. He won't speak. But I know you and your husband lived in the same apartment complex for a few months."

Missy Litch reached for a glass of lemonade on the table. It had been sitting there already, and Cassandra could see a sweat ring on the table. She reached over and placed a coaster before Litch could set her glass down again. She nodded as though in thanks, clearing her throat.

"Yes, we did live there. It was before Daniel's parents passed and we inherited the house. But–– you truly think they were involved?"

"I have witnesses claiming they catcalled and threatened women on multiple occasions. Including a known homicide victim. Did you experience any of this?"

The tall woman snorted. The ice in her glass clinked as she replaced the glass on the table.

"No. They were both cowards who wouldn't go after a married woman. Couldn't defend themselves against someone their own size. Or someone bigger," she mused. "And Fred had something for that victim. Clara."

"He did?"

"He climbed up to their balcony one day. Broke a table and everything. Or that's what Daniel told me. He spent some time with them. But I assure you–– he was not doing any catcalling. Nothing like that. We wouldn't be married now if he had done anything like that."

Her words were issued in a conspiratorial tone, as though they were schoolgirls gossiping over the latest adolescent romance. Litch's eyes flicked over Cassandra's shoulder, and she turned to see Crawford waving an apologetic hand.

"I hate to ask, but could I use your bathroom?"

Litch gave her a brief series of instructions, and then they were alone. For the first time, Cassandra glanced about, noting the neat, warm decorations placed smartly around the room. Two filled bookshelves stood like broad-shouldered guards on either side of a large television. The walls were a deep green, the sort that painted rich jewels beset in gilded chains. A crackling fire, just lit, cast a frail but determined heat over the room. The windowsills brimmed with potted plants, and the pots themselves had intricate patterns.

"I don't want to say it was a blessing when Daniel's parents passed, but it got us out of there. Gave us a bigger space to work and live. Helped us raise our son."

"Son?" Cassandra murmured. She blinked and tightened her shoulders, attempting to hide the brief shock displayed on her face.

"Yes," Litch said. "He's turning thirteen this November. Do you have any family, Detective?"

"No."

"You must have come from somewhere."

"My parents died several years apart. I was raised by an uncle here in the States."

"It's not all blood," Litch said. "Some friends can become family. Coworkers, maybe."

"Have you or your husband kept up with William Serk? He's recently married again."

"To a child," Litch said sharply. "She was legal for a day when he proposed."

"Do you think he's the sort of person capable of killing women?"

"And what sort is that?"

"Desperate. Desperate to be special, unable to convince himself and others of it. And the only form of superiority he could get was the violation of younger, weaker women."

"Violation?" Litch murmured.

"It's violation when a thief steals someone's belongings. We own nothing if not our physical body."

"Is it violation when a thief enters someone's house and gifts them a thousand dollars?"

"Yeah," Cassandra said. "It is."

Litch waved a hand in the air, as though dissipating the sour mood around them. She tilted her drink over, taking a small sip. Breath clouded the edge of the glass.

"I didn't know him well enough to say anything like that. But he's not a good man. And Ellison wasn't either."

"Did you attend his funeral? Saw a newspaper clipping about it."

"I did," Litch said. "Was down there at Saint Lawrence's. The priest gave a lovely sermon. About those who die young. About God, of course." She crossed her legs and leaned back. A fan shuddered on in a distant part of the house, and Cassandra was struck by the gentle tranquility of Litch's home. The taller woman picked up her glass and swirled it, listening to the ice clink. When she spoke, her voice was thoughtful and low.

"My husband has killed your partner by now."

The words curled around Cassandra's throat like a gnarled claw, and her mind flashed to the dark night of Una Boland's vigil. Her face flushed, and every muscle in her body tensed to an iron band. As though reassuring Cassandra, Missy Litch nodded and glanced over at the ornate clock hung from the wall.

"It's been ten minutes. That's more than enough time."

Cassandra's tongue grew coarse and unmanageable in her mouth.

"You forget I've fought him before. He's too much of a bitch to kill anyone."

Litch gave a noncommittal hum, her eyes pinned to Cassandra's face like two violent, clasping hands. She turned and cleared her throat.

"Kira, come here."

Cassandra, against her will, turned her gaze to the adjacent hallway. There came the light pad of footsteps, and then a pale, gaunt woman stood like a ghost in the dark. Hair like long strands of fire hung over her shoulders. Cassandra blinked and could not move.

"This is the detective who's been following your case. Trying to see where you were," Litch said, tone light and conversational.

"Oh," Kira Rushton said.

In an instant, Cassandra had her pistol leveled at Missy Litch's head. There came a shuddering, shrieking gasp, and Kira Rushton stood splayed wide before Cassandra. Her eyes caught the warm overhead lights, like a skull with eyes of flame, and she waved her hands frantically as though discouraging an angry opponent.

"She didn't mean it," she said thickly, stumbling over her words like an overwhelmed child.

"I just wanted to show you," Litch said. "They don't do it against their wills. They want it. They ask for it. They'll die for me because they know that's what matters. That I matter."

"What the hell are you doing?"

"I want you to listen. Listen to Kira. Haven't you wanted answers? Haven't you been denied the truth by everyone? And I'm here, staring right back at you, and you're about to miss it."

Cassandra's mouth creaked open as a gunshot, sharp and singular, sounded from outside. Litch moved forward and grabbed Cassandra's left wrist. She felt carved from ice, as though her muscles and mind were out of her control. With a gentle hand, Litch guided her to the couch once more.

"That wasn't a service pistol. More like my husband's rifle. Your partner is dead. Now listen."

17

Chapter Seventeen

Giovanni Singer parked the borrowed car along the mile-long driveway leading up to Henry Litch's house. They had shared a clipped, breathless conversation in which the boy had dithered about any personal information regarding himself or his foster sister. Giovanni ran a cold hand over his forehead as he stepped out onto the shoulder of the gravel road. Non-foster sister. Just a girl, he remembered. That's what Henry had said.

Henry had called, and Giovanni, like a hapless fool, had answered. Had driven down the mossy annals of unlit backroads until he stood a mile outside Henry Litch's house. It presumably sat beyond the thick stretches of oaks and poplars that twisted up through the black soil beneath his shoes. His eyes strained in the darkness.

His grandmother had lived out in the country, somewhere like this. Her driveway had taken thirteen minutes to walk at a reasonable pace–– five minutes to sprint in a race. There had been a camera leveraged half-a-mile down the driveway, meant to give his grandmother some time to prepare for visitors. Mindful of the noise his steps made in the grass, he slipped into the treeline to his left and moved forward.

A hissed breath came through his teeth. He could think more clearly than an hour before, but nothing yet was comprehensible. He recognized rather than understood the thoughts that swarmed his mind. Unbearable surges of emotion flashed like a dying light through his consciousness. His hands trembled, and his breath came out in stertorous haste. He moved between trees like an undead beast filled with inexplicable direction. The boy. Henry. He had called. And what was Giovanni to do but answer?

His eyes stung with the abrupt introduction of light, albeit flimsy and inconsistent. Through the trees rose a low wooden shack. Gaping holes pocked the shack, as though its molded skin had been eaten through by insects or harsh rain. He came to the edge of the trees and crouched. A shining field of mud stretched out from the shack. Collapsed lines of wire fence demarcated the field of mud. He breathed in the thick stench of rain and shit. An abandoned pigpen.

The light came from a bobbing lantern leveled somewhere in the air around the shack. A faint whistle drifted over the wind. Giovanni realized a man, tall and solid, was holding the lantern. A wide stained bandage encompassed his left palm. The man's face glowed red in the lantern light, most likely from the exertion of whatever chore brought him out to the edge of the woods. Giovanni glanced around, shifting on his heels. The land proved barren and flat. There was no house to be found, at least not from where Giovanni crouched amid the trees.

He would follow the man. Find the house he inevitably retreated to. The man grunted and dropped the lantern. Giovanni glimpsed the harsh outline of steel-toed boots caked in black mud. The lantern soared up once more, bobbing as the man hissed and examined the bandage on his hand. A chill passed over Giovanni's skin, but his mind had not yet recognized what his body understood to be true. The man pulled a phone from his pocket and read a message. Clearing his throat, the man glanced up and gestured to something behind the small shack.

"Get away from them," he said.

There came a stilted silence, then a young voice.

"But they're young. And no one else can take care of them."

Giovanni froze, barely breathing. He recognized Henry's light voice. Usually bright with enthusiasm and curiosity, Henry's voice crept forth as though scared of being beaten. He edged slowly along the treeline, hands trembling but steps light and controlled. He rounded the shack and found Henry kneeling beside a writhing bundle of fur. The boy plunged a hand into the bundle and lifted out an orange kitten.

"No one will take care of them. Go. Get cleaned up," the man said.

"But I can," Henry said. "I can, and I want to. Why shouldn't I?"

"Excuse me?"

"I didn't mean it like that––"

"What did you mean it like, then? How am I supposed to take that?"

Henry carefully knelt and put the kitten back with its siblings.

"I'm sorry."

"Go. Your mother has some company over. Go in through the backdoor. I'll come and get you for dinner."

Giovanni watched as Henry walked toward a distant line of trees, presumably one that sheltered a house. He intermittently looked back, steps dragging as he chased fleeting glances of the kittens pressed against the rotted shack wall. The boy disappeared, as though he had never graced the night, had never played with the kittens wriggling ten yards away. Silence settled around Giovanni like dark, stagnant water, and a cold sweat began on his forehead.

He examined the man, and after a moment, he crept forward, away from the edge of the forest and to the far wall of the shack that Henry had just stood behind. The kittens' eyes glowed in the moonlight. One released a hoarse *meow.* Above the small, lively noises, Giovanni heard the crack of a twig. Without thinking, he turned to the shack, eased open its backdoor, and slipped inside.

It was dark within, and he didn't dare flip on any lights that could be seen by the man outside. Immediately, he noted the shocking cleanliness of such a haggard shack. Cool linoleum tile stretched out beneath high rows of stainless-steel cabinets. Gleaming glass jars filled with syringes and flat wooden sticks crowded the counters. It looked as though someone had stolen a single examination room from the local doctor's office.

He stepped forward, and his right hip bumped into something heavy and hard. A hand reached forward and brushed a long expanse of leather. His fingers moved, traced up the armrest of the exam chair, and came to a stop on a thick ring of metal. There were manacles on the armrest. He wrenched his hand away, unnerved by the furious beat of his heart.

He moved around the seat and spread his hands on the cold stainless-steel counter that wrapped each wall. A small stretch of sterile wall parted the upper and lower rows of cabinets. He leaned forward, noting the gentle reflection of moonlight on something pinned to the wall. He blinked, adjusting his eyes. On the wall, small and neat, hung a collage of images. A few, those pinned on the furthest left, seemed to be yellowed and curled at the edges. The furthest right images were brighter, less crinkled. This was the type of Polaroid he had been sent. The contents of the images were dim, nearly too dark to see. He feared he would recognize the deceased women within them.

"What the fuck?" he whispered.

A kitten yowled outside, and in an instant, the door flew back, crashing against the nearest row of cabinets. The man stood frozen in the doorway, his chest heaving. His face was slick and ruddy, as though he had been running, and his eyes were black as tar. His haggard breath filled the air between them. Giovanni shifted his weight, intent upon escaping the shack through the other door. As he moved, the man mirrored him. In his hand hung a thick white rope.

"You're not supposed to be here. Not yet," the man said.

"What?"

"You heard me. You're lucky there was no one in here. There would have been no explaining that."

"Someone in here?" Giovanni repeated, dazed.

The man nodded, and as he took a step forward, Giovanni whipped about and lunged at the opposite door. His fingers grazed the chilled metal of the doorknob just as a rope, hard as a cord of steel, wrapped about his neck. Breath stumbled in his throat. A large hand reached past his head and wrenched the door open. Suddenly he was flat on the ground, having been thrown out of the shack and into the pit of mud. The rope wrapped once more around his throat, and with a grunt, the man lifted him into a kneeling position.

"Just sleep," the man said. His fists tightened on the rope, pulling it in a harsh burn against the soft skin of Giovanni's throat. His breath was hot and sour against Giovanni's ear.

"You'll wake up again. I promise. Just sleep for now." It was unnervingly quiet, the moment in which Giovanni confronted the possibility of his death. He had not acknowledged the discontent within himself, had not acknowledged the possibility of its end, convinced that no matter his stance on life, it would go on. Spit slipped out from between his teeth, wetting his lips. He threw his head back and groaned as a burst of static curled through his frenzied mind.

He saw his life stretched out before him like a desolate wasteland. He stood, a weary traveler, against the vast, empty expanse, devoid of direction and purpose, frozen beneath the impossibly heavy sky. The years behind him flashed colorless and lifeless. He remembered the trudging of the years, the noiseless, ineffectual rage of someone neither dragged nor hindered by the demands of time. He stumbled, sat still, went backward. It didn't matter. Any action of his changed the course of time not an inch, not a step disturbed in the insurmountable march that was this wretched life. The knowledge that he was empty, desolate, not resigned to his hollow existence but to hatred itself. The pointless fury instigated by the continuation of an unnecessary, unwanted life.

Frigid wind flew against his face, and he spluttered. Eyes rolled to the back of his head. Memories like warm spots of light flashed through his mind, and he gave a weak cry. The knowledge that anything that mattered was now gone, would never return, and with it any beauty or purpose had dissolved like tears in an ocean. The inevitability of his deep, lifelong sadness burned within him. He felt as though everyone could see it hanging from him, like some form of leprosy or a bum leg he dragged ever behind him in the dust. A sharp certainty that life itself was not the gift, but Beatrice, his Beatrice, and life without her was akin to a clock in a world without time.

His hands faltered from their place on the rope caught about his neck. His fingers scrabbled fruitlessly in the mud, and the heels of his shoes scratched jagged lines into the sparse grass. The sharp tang of rain slid over his tongue. The gentle sounds of the night fell upon his ears, and if it were another day, another life, he would have relished this earthly beauty. Now, after the past five years, it made his skin crawl, made electricity course through his insides. He had ignored the world long enough. It would force its way in. His eyes fluttered shut.

Cicadas whirred from the hunched trees, and the heat of a quiet southern night encompassed the back porch. His fingers tightened against the mossy, wet brick. It was him *now*, the doctoral candidate, the roommate to four bakers, tall and solid compared to the child in his mind. To his left, muffled by a line of bushes, came the sound of a gate opening.

"Beatrice?" he murmured.

The gate clicked shut, and he expectantly raised his eyes. A light breeze rolled over the backyard. The night pulsed around him. There came no footsteps.

"Beatrice?" he repeated, voice high and panicked. "Beatrice, I'm here. I've been here."

He shot up from the steps and rounded the bushes. The gate, squat and white, came up to his waist. He fumbled with the lock and threw it open. His eyes darted through the darkness. There stood no girl. There was no sister. There was no home for her to return to, not anymore. He groaned and grabbed at his hair, hands trembling.

"I'm still here," he said. "I've always been here. Please. Please come back. I'm still here."

His eyes flew open, and his words caught on the rope wrapped around his throat. His entire body quivered, as though every taut muscle were straining for breath. Blood rushed thick over his lips, spilling from his bitten tongue. An odd chill rose within him, clashing violently against the febrile heat of his skin. He went to cough, his esophagus filling with blood, but he could only open and close his mouth, air whistling through his stained teeth. His teeth clicked shut, and he swallowed, heart pounding as his lungs shuddered. A pained sob began in his throat. He wanted to be good. He wanted to try. Even if it was for nothing. He wanted to try.

With a choked grunt, he scooped up squelching handfuls of mud and ran them over the rope. His fingers scrabbled like claws over the man's own clenching hands, coating everything in slick, black mud. His lungs shivering, he dashed forward, jerking violently against the rope about his neck. He jerked again, and the rope snapped free, having come loose from a frantically grabbing hand. A hoarse breath filled his lungs, quickly forgotten as the man grabbed his shoulder and shoved him facedown into the mud. The heavy weight of the man's knee pressed down onto his back. Desperately, he bucked, torqued, twisted like a worm beneath the creeping shadow of a raised boot. Feeling the man tense and rise, he brought a sharp elbow back into the man's neck.

He shot up, heavy but trembling with primal fear.

"Where did Henry go?" he said. His voice was like that of an animal slowly learning to speak. The man lowered a hand from his neck and glared across the mud.

"Home."

"Take me there."

The man snorted, and in the lantern light, his eyes sparkled with amusement. Giovanni examined the dim horizon. A small barn made of thin, ugly bits of dry-rotted plywood sat sullenly in the distance. He'd go in the direction that Henry went. Yes. No one lived in the shack. That was clear. Not at the moment. His mind raged. Abruptly, he realized the man was talking.

"I know he called you," the man said. "He thought you would keep him safe. He doesn't realize—— that's all I want. It's all I ever wanted."

Their heavy breaths mingled in the air.

"Who are you?" Giovanni asked.

The man turned and reached for something strewn on the ground. Recognizing the flash of metal in the man's hand, Giovanni pulled his shoes from the mud and burst into a ragged sprint. Blood pounded thick in his ears, nearly drowning out the sound of equally furious footsteps sounding in his wake. There came the crack of a rifle bolt shooting back into place.

"I don't want to shoot you," came a hoarse shout from behind him. "My wife wants you alive. That's what we told White. But there are other things I can do."

His limbs seemed filled with tungsten, and each breath tore from his lungs like it didn't want to leave. He stumbled in crooked zags, aiming for the distant treeline. Part of him wanted the man to pull the trigger, to notify someone in the area that he was being hunted like prey. He had been stupid, unbelievably so. No one knew where he was. The closest bet was Ronald White. Thoughts of the man raced through his mind, and he blinked back tears. He reached a knobbed tree and slid behind it, its coarse bark slick with rain.

His hands clenched into white fists. Cold sweat tickled his temples, but he would not move to wipe it off. The man's steps came impossibly close, and Giovanni dropped, bracing himself in the underbrush. The man toppled over Giovanni and fell heavily, a shoulder slamming into the ground. The gleaming line of his hunting rifle fell away. Giovanni brought a shoe down on the man's head. Panting, he dropped to the ground once more and brought a fist crashing into the man's gut.

"You motherfucker," he said. His words came out hoarse and stumbling, thick with saliva and blood. Another fist struck the man's cheek. Warm blood rushed across his knuckles, and the man's cheekbone sliced through the stubbly skin of his face. Sweat dripped into his eyes as he gripped both sides of the man's skull and slammed it into the ground.

"Wait—" the man whispered, crying as another blow struck his temple.

Giovanni sank back on his heels, cracked knuckles resting on his dirt-stained knees. His eyes flickered to the man's left hand. The bandage had fallen away to reveal a freshly healed wound on the edge of his palm. A deep tract of flesh was missing, torn away by the clenching of vicious teeth. He glanced back to the man's chest, watching it quickly rise and fall.

Giovanni's mind settled for the first time in years. With a fortifying breath, he stood, walked around the man, and retrieved the discarded rifle. His hands shook as he examined the safety and chamber. After a quiet moment, he brought the rifle up and aimed it at the man's face.

"I'm a father. You saw that," the man said.

There was silence.

"Please. I'm not the best father, but I–– I love Henry. If you kill me, do you really think he'll give you a chance? You think he'll love you after you kill his dad?"

"You didn't care about that," Giovanni said. "All the people you killed. People loved them. And you still killed them."

"I loved them. We gave them another chance. You don't understand. They were useless until we helped them. They had no purpose until we gave them one."

Giovanni jerked the gun forward as though to shoot. Something inside him tightened as the man flinched. He longed to see the man suffer as he had. To confront the empty life he had grown accustomed to. A strange, wailing voice poured into the silence. His head pounded, and his words became strangled, animalistic curses.

"You shut up. Shut the hell up. My sister wasn't useless. She—-she was a person. She was a person. And now she's dead. She's dead because of you."

"Then let me learn," the man said, shifting in the mud. "You study philosophy. Teach me. Teach me how to change. We want to learn from you, from Henry and Beatrice. Would you deny us that?"

His arm became a steel beam. The decision began somewhere south of his heart, slinking up through his arteries into the curve of his bicep, the twist of his forearm. A breath puffed through his lips. From the corner of his gaze came a flash of color, and a hand stretched out to the rifle barrel. His finger pulled the trigger as the hand, shooting from the darkness, wrenched it to the side. The bark of a darkened poplar exploded in a smattering of sawdust and smoke. The shot crackled through the night. His skin tingled. He glanced over to find Virginia Crawford nursing a burned palm, her eyes on him.

"Why are you here?" she whispered, breaths staggering her words.

They regarded each other for a moment, and then he surged forward, wrapping his arms around her. He breathed in her familiar scent. Unnoticed, the rifle dropped to the ground. His fingers tightened into the cloth of her uniform. His eyes burned, but he would not cry, merely tightening his grip on her. She whispered vague, soothing words in his ear, her hands warm on his back. Remembering the man behind him, he pulled away and retrieved the discarded rifle.

Wordlessly, he offered it to her, his fingers burning as though he were the one who had grasped the barrel. He reached for the handcuffs on her hip and unclipped them. Then he knelt beside the man and clicked them around his wrists. His movements were imbued with a gentle fragility, only lightly adjusting the man's position on the ground. Standing up, he tore a strip from his shirt and gestured for Virginia's hand.

"I'm sorry," he said. His voice was soft, but it trembled as he wrapped the cloth around her palm. "I wouldn't have tried anything if I knew you'd get hurt."

"My hand doesn't matter." She pulled it gently from his grasp and nodded over her shoulder. "Wake's in there with the wife."

Immediately, Giovanni wrenched the man to his feet. They began in a grim half-run past the shack, where Virginia said a large house awaited. Giovanni paused halfway through the pigpen. With a quick wheeze, he retrieved the bit of rope only recently wrapped around his neck. Wiping it on his pants proved a fruitless task, and his hands wavered ineffectually as he tied the rope around the man's face like a gag.

"Hurry up," Virginia said, pulling the man along. He could do nothing but follow.

18

Chapter Eighteen

They sat together in a pale mockery of familial discussion. Kira stood by Missy Litch's side like a nervous servant. Cassandra noted the sickly sheen of her face, the flexing of her fingers at her sides. She wore a long-sleeved sweater, the sort unusual in such humid weather. Cassandra knew the sleeves concealed tracks of bruises made from needle marks. Some sort of sedative or date rape drug. As though noting Cassandra's thoughts, Missy Litch gestured for Kira to sit on the ground between them.

"Sometimes she needs it," she said. "It gets stressful–– all these things they say about her in the papers. We try to stop her from reading them. She thinks you're here to arrest her."

"She thinks that, does she?"

"Ask her if you don't believe me. It was a difficult time after the shooting. She was lucky I was there. I whisked her away. Sobered her up. Got rid of the car."

"You were following Beatrice Singer. That's why you were there in the first place."

Cassandra turned to the thin, waif-like woman and examined her face. Her eyes gleamed like those of pain-crazed cattle. Cassandra's gaze flashed to the woman's hands, and she noted the chipped nails and reddened nail beds of her fingers. Clearing her throat, she sat back and smiled at Kira.

"Why did you jump in front of Mrs. Litch just now?"

The answer came quickly, without reflection or hesitation.

"She keeps me safe," Kira said. "She saved me that night."

"That night?"

"When I–– When I disappeared."

"When you shot a police officer. When you shot Beatrice Singer."

Kira grimaced and swiped a hand through her thin hair.

"I'm making up for it. You would arrest me before I could."

Across the coffee table, Missy Litch uncrossed her legs and nodded, as though encouraging a young child.

"We have roles in life," Missy said. "It's the hardest thing to figure out what yours is. That's why we turn to drugs. To alcohol. We feel as though we are meaningless. But that night." She laughed, a gentle, frigid sound. "That night gave Kira meaning. She was nobody before then. Killing Beatrice Singer was wrong. It was horrible. But horrible things must be done, sometimes, to find who you're supposed to be."

"I'm somebody," Kira reiterated. "And you would have just kept me in prison. I couldn't fix what I did wrong. But I can fix it. I have. I've fixed everything."

Her words rang with a startling sense of clarity, of confidence in their content and sentiment. Cassandra's right hand flexed on the handle of her pistol. It lay on her thigh, aimed still at Missy Litch's chest. Neither woman acknowledged it, enraptured in their own conversation.

"How have you fixed it?" Cassandra murmured.

"I'm giving you meaning. I'm telling you what you were born to do. I'm somebody, and you are too, because we're doing what we're meant to."

"You were somebody before," she said.

"Not like this."

"Yes, like this. You were somebody before. I was, too. And any association with this psychopath will not change that."

"It already has," Kira said, irritation in her tone. She did not like being interrupted.

Cassandra adjusted her position on the couch, the pistol moving on her thigh.

"There's a cruel and irrational habit people have of attempting to justify their being born. As though they have to make up for it. But you don't. You just have to exist. You're alive, and you don't have to explain that. Don't you see that?"

"Do you really believe that, Detective?" Missy said.

Cassandra met her eyes across the room and nodded once, her throat closing as she choked on a response. Missy released a thoughtful hum.

"You were wondering what sedative Kira uses. We're fond of diazepam. It's not usually lethal, no matter how much you take. Of course, there are exceptions for everything. You know that."

After a moment of silence, Cassandra shifted and moved as though to grab Kira's hand. The smaller woman froze, and Cassandra fought back a frustrated sigh.

"Kira, I've–– I've become friends with those who loved Beatrice Singer. They're not mad at you. She was engaged, you know. To a friend of mine. That friend now has a husband and child. And–– Beatrice's brother. Giovanni. He's doing fine. He's not mad at you."

The glass previously grasped in Missy Litch's hand shattered on the wooden floor. Missy stood and towered above both seated women.

"We don't lie here," she said, voice hard and unyielding. She trembled with sudden intensity, and Cassandra realized how the woman could have killed so many people. A long, accusatory finger pointed at Cassandra's chest. "He's in the hospital for a nervous episode. Another one. We take responsibility here."

"I did that," Kira said, nodding. "I hurt him. But now everything will be better."

"Tell her, Kira. Tell her what she said," Missy Litch murmured.

"She needed to get back home," Kira said. "She had to get home safe."

Cassandra's tongue was thick in her throat.

"Who?" she whispered.

"She had people waiting for her. She needed to get home."

"Who the hell are you talking about?"

Missy Litch cleared her throat and regained her seat.

"Why did you leave Romania?"

Rather than answer, Cassandra turned to Kira, her eyes placating.

"You can't save someone by killing them. You can't fix a problem by destroying those it affects. Then there's just no one there. Don't you understand that? All she's done is murder people. You can't make that better. You can't attach some higher meaning to things that don't make sense."

"I'm meant to do this," Kira said. She coughed, a harsh, cracking sound. "It's what I was born for."

"What is this? What is this?"

"Why did you leave Romania, Detective?"

Cassandra's eyes flashed between the two women. Kira had gradually flushed a deep red, as though she were not pulling in enough air when she breathed. Pained wheezes started from her mouth, and her eyes bulged like balloons in a tight fist.

"What's happening to her?" Cassandra asked, rushing forward to look into Kira's face. Kira's eyelids flickered. Spit gathered in thick strings along her lips. She tipped Kira's head to the side and watched bile fall to the couch. Thoughts of diazepam flew through her mind. She wasn't officially on duty. Any overdose reversals were with Crawford. Flumazenil for diazepam, naloxone for opioids. Her hands trembled at her sides. There was no hydrogen peroxide to dump down her throat. Her teeth were clenched too tightly for any finger to get through.

"Why did you leave Romania, Detective?" Missy Litch had risen, standing beside them like a deathly specter. In her hand, gleaming in the firelight, were a syringe and a small glass bottle. Cassandra could only hope it would save Kira Rushton.

"Family problems," she said. She turned and grasped the pistol before leveling it once more at Missy Litch. "I left Romania because my mother died. I had nowhere to go."

Ignoring the pistol, Missy Litch moved forward and showed Cassandra the bottle. *Flumazenil* stretched across the label in cramped script. The woman paused as Cassandra delved into anticipatory silence. Her grip tightened on the pistol, and she gestured for Missy to continue.

"I don't care if she dies," Missy said. "Tell me about your mother. How you found her."

A particularly violent shudder surged through Kira's body. The sharp scent of bile burned Cassandra's nose, and she noted the growing stain of spit and sweat on the couch. An aggravated breath tore through her lungs.

"She was in bed. I thought she was sleeping. She'd overdosed. Like this. She couldn't move or breathe. But she kept trying. I heard the air in her lungs. It couldn't get out."

"How long was she trying to breathe?" Missy murmured.

"Ten seconds. Forever. They found us two days later."

"Why two days?"

"There was so much snow. There was a–– a homeless man in the shed. He heard my screams. He tried getting people to help, but they couldn't get in the door. I dug my way out to get away from the smell."

Missy knelt and flicked the edge of the syringe. She slipped its cap off and plunged the needle into the muscle of Kira's shoulder.

"Why did she do it?" Her words came quietly, nearly drowned beneath her dutiful ministrations.

"I don't know."

"You don't?"

"I don't know. Only she knew."

Missy released an intrigued noise, her hands gentle on Kira's face and neck.

"Do you ever wonder? What drove her to leave you."

"No," Cassandra said.

"Maybe it was you."

"What?"

"Maybe she killed herself to get away from you."

Cassandra froze, breath pooling in her lungs like frigid water. Her eyes fixed to the slowly rising swell of Kira's chest. Her eyelids no longer fluttered. She seemed asleep.

"I always wondered," Missy continued. "Why my mother didn't do that. She was so unhappy. It would have been better for everyone."

"I don't understand."

"My birth was rough. Mother, she died for thirty seconds. The moment I was born, she was dead on the table. Born to a corpse. And every brother or sister I had–– they arrived dead. She died six times. Like a light. On and off. An addict who never learns."

She turned to Cassandra, and her eyes gleamed with startling sincerity.

"I wanted to make something good. So many people waste their lives. Ruin their families and make everything harder. So I give them the chance to start anew. To give a child to the world. Make a family. When I realized Kira was pregnant, it was like divine intervention. The perfect child. The perfect Beatrice."

"You killed them," Cassandra said.

"They killed themselves. They were useless until I gave them a chance. They chose this path. If it kills them, that's nothing to do with me."

She rose. In her hand, collected from somewhere behind the couch, was a canister of lighter fluid. Cassandra stumbled back, the pistol slipping in her sweaty grasp.

"You came here looking for meaning. And I'm giving it to you. All those people who denied you answers. All those people who looked at you like you were someone else. I know who you are. And this is the only chance you'll get."

Staring into Cassandra's face, Missy raised the canister in the air and tipped it over her head. The clear fluid splattered over her hair, turning it a pitch black. It trembled down the pale planes of her face. Wordlessly, she turned and threw fluid over Kira's prone body.

"Like a forest. Burn it so the soil has more nutrients. My husband knows what he's supposed to do. It'll be Henry and Beatrice left. Then Giovanni Singer will love them. That's all I ever wanted, Detective. A family that thrives. It was never going to be me. I was born to a corpse. What can you do? What can you do?"

Missy Litch took the canister in both hands and flung the rest of its contents over Cassandra. The liquid was cold and thin, burning her skin where it clung. Imbued with startling speed, Missy groped in her pocket and retrieved a small matchbook. Her fingers were wet and slippery, unable to flick the box open.

"Please don't," Cassandra said, blinking as the fluid stung her eyes. "The photos. The film you used. It's–– it's ruined. It's got something called Vinegar Syndrome. They won't last. Don't you see that? You've done your best to make something new, something that will last for years. But it won't. Because you ruin things. You make things fall apart."

"I can acknowledge that truth about myself. What about you, Detective?"

"They call you the–– the fucking Stillborn Killer. Does that sound like someone who makes something new? Who saves lives? Anything you try to save or rebuild died a long time ago."

Their heavy breaths mingled in the resulting silence.

"How many lives have you ruined?" Missy Litch wondered aloud. Cassandra rolled her shoulders back and swallowed down a shuddering sigh.

"I won't do calculus with lives. I mourn every person I've hurt, and I work so it never happens again. That's all I can do," she said.

Missy paused and glanced to Cassandra, her face stern as though giving a lecture to a disruptive student.

"You love Giovanni Singer. That's what White said. He cannot start anew if you are there beside him."

"Ronald White's an idiot," she said. "He's wrong."

"I don't think he is, Detective." Her fingers latched onto a match as Cassandra lunged forward, knocking the book from her hand.

She fell to the ground, the book already grasped between white fingers. Strong hands clasped onto her shoulders, wrenching her back. Her hand tightened on a jagged shard from Missy Litch's broken glass and, as she was dragged up, she turned and brought the shard in a wide slash across Litch's face.

The gaunt woman screamed, a hand coming to press at the deep slit across her cheek and nose. The other reached for Cassandra. Stumbling away, Cassandra drew an arm back and threw the matchbook down the dim hallway from which Kira Rushton had emerged. There came the hollow *thwack* of matchbook against wall, and then the piteous wail of a voice.

"If you stop now, they'll never get better. You haunt people. They can't get rid of you. If you live, you'll see. They'll leave. He'll be gone. And you'll remember this minute. When I gave you everything. And you wanted none of it."

A gentle, hissing click caught her attention. It came like a knock, like a sliding rhythm barely louder than a breath. Cassandra's hands swept desperately over the bulk of her pockets. They were all empty. An electric fear coursed through her body, and she bit out a strangled shout. *Sic. Slide. Sic. Slide.* The fumble of finger over spark wheel.

Just as Cassandra fell back, the women before her burst into vivid, roaring flame. Kira Rushton, strewn across the couch, lit like the end of a torch. The flames crawled up the pant legs of Missy Litch, caught the edge of her sweater, and engulfed her head. Cassandra turned and stumbled to the floor, her back pressed against the firm edge of the chair behind which she hid.

The thick, rank stench of burnt flesh filled the air, and she shoved a sleeve against her face. A figure emerged from the gloom.

Stamping feet, pumping arms, the rocking of a massive head. Spit lathered its gaping maw. Deadened eyes glared through the smoke. The dark outline of a bear jerked and swayed, devoid of the frantic energy she remembered from her childhood. It rocked as though directed by some parasite, as though held up with invisible strings threaded through muscle. Behind the bear dancer came a flood of color as drummers dashed about in a mad circle. Their bellows sounded beneath the hiss of flame. Her eyes clenched against the smoky air. Tears streaked down her cheeks. Her biceps clamped like bands on either side of her head, and she imagined she was elsewhere.

As Giovanni crossed the starlit yard, he picked his head up and noted a thin line of clouds floating across the moon. His fingers tightened on their prisoner's shoulder, and the man, catching his glance, also looked up. A muffled jumble of words rushed against the rope in his mouth.

"They're not clouds," Virginia said.

"What?"

"That's smoke."

His thighs ached as they trudged up the crumbly side of a hill, and his mind stumbled alongside him, nearly unable to process her words. He found himself watching the man's face. Tears streaked down his cheeks, gathering in unsightly smears upon meeting the rope. His face glowed a pale orange, and the tears were like drops of fire against his skin. Something shuddered to a halt in Giovanni's mind, and he swung his head about. A thousand meters away, outlined like a beast from hell, sat a white-slatted house on fire.

In an instant, he was down the hill and sprinting across the remaining field. Ash and smoke bit at his eyes and lungs as he surged forward. The house's door swung open, and soot spilled out in heavy waves, as though the house were coughing something out. A small figure emerged from the doorway. Henry was black with ash. In his arms, equally disheveled, clung Beatrice. Recognizing Giovanni in the darkness, Henry threw his head up and released a hoarse sob.

"My mom," he said. "My mom."

"Where is she?"

"Inside. She's inside. I couldn't carry her."

Giovanni pushed past them and burst into the house. His eyes lighted upon an earthly hell. Thick wooden rafters hung from above like dislodged ribs. Sparks flitted and slurried through the dense black air. He brought a sleeve to his nose and mouth, his heart pounding thunderous in his ears. His eyes stung like an open wound exposed to salt. As he drew a deep breath, ash crackled in his lungs, and he coughed out a weak call.

"Cassandra! Detective! Where are you?"

A harsh black trail of burned wood marked the floor, centered on a dark pit near the coffee table. His eyes fell upon the blackened shape of a body, sprawled as though in slumber across the couch. A similar pile of flesh and hissing flame sat on the floor, directly amid the pitch pit of scorched wood. He stood for a moment, electric in the burning dark.

"Cassandra?" he whispered. Gleaming amid the smoking remains sat a lighter. A pained noise welled within Giovanni, smothered by the roar of cracking wood and whistling air.

He turned away from the burning mass, knocking into a melted recliner. He rounded the recliner and tripped, tumbling to the ground. He came face-to-face with Cassandra, her eyes bright in the darkness. For an impossibly long moment, he watched her, his heart fast but weak like a skipping record. Wordlessly, he took her hand and pulled her up.

"You're all right," he said. "You're okay."

He moved with a clarifying swiftness, almost knowing where he needed to step, where he needed to hold his breath. He pulled Cassandra behind him, and when she stumbled, he hooked his arm through her elbow, his hand braced on her back.

"You're all right," he repeated, lost beneath the deafening hiss of fire. The entire house seemed about to collapse, its main support beams and rafters cracked and wrapped in vines of flame. His lungs quivered as smoke stung his eyes and throat. There rose a distant square of natural light. Moonlight fell across smoke, turning it a queer silver. He pulled Cassandra behind him, and in an instant, they spilled out into the clear night.

Fresh air flooded about him, and his skin tingled, like when a child thrusts their frozen fingers beneath scalding water. His knees hit the grass as he pulled in a deep gulp of air. Cassandra stood beside him, and he listened to the rattling rhythm of her breaths. She turned and looked up.

"She's alive," Cassandra said.

"Who?"

Rather than answer, Cassandra strode forward, meeting Crawford halfway. She put an ash-stained hand on the older woman's shoulder, as though confirming she were really there. Her gaze turned to the man beside Crawford.

"This is the husband. Where's the kid?"

Giovanni rose and pulled in a deep, cracking breath.

"He was just here. I just saw him."

There was the dull whistle of wind and fire. Then came the click of a gun safety.

Henry stood, his arms extended awkwardly before him like a young knight unaccustomed to a sword. Beside him, a small hand wrapped in the edge of his shirt, stood little Beatrice. Henry's eyes flashed from father to stranger. His face gleamed a febrile white. Giovanni noted the tremble of his fingers. The tremble meant death.

"Put the gun down," Cassandra said, quivering lungs squeezing out tight words. "Put it down."

"You're going to kill my dad."

"No," she said. "I won't. Never." She took a step forward, freezing as his face twisted. "If you shoot me, you're going to get hurt, too. I don't want that."

The boy's eyes flickered behind her, where Giovanni stood in the darkness. There came the gentle crinkle of grass under feet. A hand brushed against her shoulder, and then Giovanni Singer stood beside her.

"Henry," he said, voice soft and fragile. "Henry. Please. Why are you pointing a gun at us?"

"You're going to take my dad away," he replied, tears bright in his eyes. "I'm going to be alone. Beatrice will be gone. He'll be gone. I'll be here."

"Your parents are bad people. You know that. You're smart. I've seen you thinking. They hurt others. They don't care how much. We're not—we're not gonna hurt your dad. He's gonna go away. You're right. But I'd rather he were in jail than taking care of you."

"But I wouldn't be alone." The reply was petulant, frenzied, lingering like a shot in the silence.

"You don't know what to do," Giovanni said, and his words wavered as he drew in a breath. "You don't know where to go. Or who'll take care of you. Let me take care of you. I lost my sister. And nothing made sense until I met you. So let me–– let me pick you up from school. Let me buy you sweaters when it's cold. Let me–– let me pack you lunch."

A minute lapse overcame Henry, his grip loosening ever slightly. His eyes no longer flickered to his cornered father. They were pinned desperately to Giovanni's face, unwilling to acknowledge anything else in the yard.

"I love you, Henry. I love you. I won't let you down. Please don't shoot her. She means the world to me."

The gun fell to the grass. Henry bolted across the yard and was ensconced securely in Giovanni's arms. Their embrace was fierce, unyielding. Henry was soon lifted entirely off the ground, the toes of his sneakers an inch from the mud and grass. A large hand cradled the back of his head, and Giovanni murmured in his ear, his face white, breath strained.

Cassandra rushed to collect the discarded pistol. She returned it to her holster and picked up the little girl in the mud. There came the distant sound of sirens, still too far to clearly be heard above the roar of the burning house. She felt incredibly small beneath the whirl of wind that swept unceasing over the bare acres around her. They stood in silence and waited for the sirens to draw nearer.

They sat together under the cool moonlight. She had refused the shock blanket clutched in Mills's hands, squeezed into the open backseat of Heyward's patrol car. After numerous refused offers, he had hurried away, content to leave only after wrapping her in a suffocating embrace. Crawford stood across the yard, engaged in hurried, hushed discussion with Chief Norton. Officers flooded the clearing, dashing about in a senseless frenzy as though there were still someone to chase.

Giovanni leaned against the tire of the car beside her. Little Beatrice was fast asleep in his arms, and Henry sat, thinking, at his feet. She watched as Giovanni shifted, his eyes dancing over the smoke that lingered in the moonlight.

"I thought you were dead," he said.

"Not yet."

"It was horrible, you know. Thinking you were dead."

"I thought I was dead, too."

"I'd given up on life. That guy–– Danny Litch, or something. He beat the shit out of me. I thought he was gonna kill me. And I thought I was ready. Ready to see Beatrice again. I thought I'd be okay with that. But I wasn't. Because I thought of you. Do you understand?"

"Yeah," she said, words no louder than a breath. "I think I do."

He watched her across the darkness. He went to speak once more, but a small hand tugged at his sleeve. He glanced down as Henry struggled to his feet, sleepy but determined. The boy whispered to Giovanni, the words impossible for Cassandra to hear. Henry grabbed his hand and began toward a nearby treeline, only thirty-or-so yards from the edge of the house. Cassandra followed.

Their steps slowed as the trees loomed above them. Wind bit at her face and swept her hair in gnarled tangles over her shoulders. Henry slipped between two trees, stepping into the gentle darkness. She heard their steps continue a ways into the trees and then stop. After a moment, she found them standing before a low, gleaming stone.

Giovanni lowered himself to the forest floor. His fingers ghosted over the stone, on which two neat lines of script were carved:

Beatrice Singer, 1992 – 2017.
Remembered forever in everlasting love.

A trembling hand came to cover his eyes. A stifled groan began under his palm, and tears crept from under his fingers down his chin. Reaching up, Henry took his hand and pulled it to his chest. His face was solemn in the moonlight.

"I'm sorry," he said. "I don't remember much. We went out here sometimes."

Giovanni nodded, and for the first time, his eyes left the stone. He looked down to the little girl in his arms and drew in a deep breath. Behind them, Cassandra remained standing, her gaze fixed on their bowed heads. A curious heat had begun in her chest, curling through her extremities like a burst of morphine. Slowly, not wanting to disrupt the placid scene, she knelt and examined the stone from behind them.

Henry extended another hand and pulled her closer. Her eyes ached as though she had been staring long at the sun, and she was embarrassed to note the film of sweat on her palm. She breathed in the fresh air and examined the stone, unwilling to look elsewhere.

Giovanni and the children burned like a fire beside her, bright and new with something she was scared to name. A gentle warmth enveloped the small clearing. Lulled by the queer tranquility, she sat in silence. It was a privilege to be there, now, at that instant, a witness to such profound grief. For if someone were to choose their own destruction—what sweeter Armageddon than the devastation that love left behind?

She glanced up from the stone and found Giovanni's eyes on her. They watched each other. After a moment, her eyelids fluttered shut, and the warmth of the night fell down upon them all.